GOAL CHASER

LAS VEGAS VIPERS BOOK FIVE

STACEY LYNN

Goal Chaser

Las Vegas Vipers Series

Book Five

Stacey Lynn

Content Editing: My Brother's Editor

Proofreading: Virginia Tesi Carey

Cover Design: Shanoff Designs

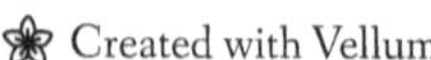 Created with Vellum

ONE

KANE

I stepped off the ice and tapped Ryder Bromann's stick as he passed me. "You looked good out there today."

Our new defenseman, traded from Florida to take Max Mikolajczyk's spot on the team when he retired last month, was a good guy. An even better player. He played hard and clean but wasn't afraid to throw his body around to protect his teammates when needed.

But he wasn't Max, and we all felt that loss like a limb. Particularly the first line. Most especially, me, since I was named captain after he retired. We all liked Ryder, but there was still something missing. A flash of excitement, an expediency Max always brought to the game and forced us to rise up to meet. He'd been one hell of a captain and now that burden to lead, encourage, and excite fell on me.

And I wasn't getting the job done.

"Thanks. Let's hope I look as good when games start."

I stopped him outside the locker room. Most of the guys were already in, but I pulled us to the side as Alix stomped up to us on his skates.

"Hey, Halvrick." I shoved my hand to his chest, stopping him. "You know what we need?"

He took off his helmet and wiped sweat off his forehead. "Someone to kick our asses into high-speed gear?"

Definitely that. We were playing well. But not fast enough. Not good enough. We'd gone out last season in the playoffs earlier than we wanted, but as the previous season's champions, we all wanted that cup in our arena long-term. The addition of Bromann, and the loss of Max, had stalled us.

"Clubbing night. Not a chill night at Joey's bar, but a good night."

Alix's eyes gleamed. The man could party. Typically, not my gig, but hell. For the team, as their captain, I'd do it.

"Nine o'clock at Piazza Romana. I'll let the team know."

Leave it to him to know exactly where to go.

I faced Bromann. He'd been a loved player in Florida, and there were already several memes online with him wearing his new Vipers jersey and BRO-MAN stamped across it while he skated across the ice, on one knee, fist-pumping during one of our practices. The man could play to the crowd.

We needed him to play with the team. Accepted by everyone. End all chatter of his former *bromance* with fellow Florida player, Rudy Petrov, and hell, maybe solidify a new one here. We needed it to happen fast.

"You need to come," I told him.

He looked warily at the open locker room door as Alix walked in, already shouting out the details of the required team event. Cheers echoed as the door closed behind him.

Yeah. Leave it to Alix. He'd make sure everyone was there.

"This shit takes time. I know that."

"Yeah, but we're also a family and the sooner we groove off the ice—"

"The sooner we find it on the ice. I got it." He tapped his stick to mine. "Thanks, Andrews."

"Doing my job." But in truth, I needed this as much as the rest of them.

I'd always been a quieter guy, but life had thrown me a handful of curveballs over the last couple of years. If I was a baseball player, my batting average at those curves would be less than five hundred. I was also older now. Wiser. More serious. Perhaps, I'd also lost a bit of the fun edge I used to have.

I stayed in the hall for a minute after Bromann went inside and rested against the wall.

Max retired. Two years younger than me, and he was out of the league. Yeah, he'd gotten injured, had some concerns about the number of concussions he had. But we were both getting old.

I had five years max left in the league, and as a center, chasing after guys twenty to twenty-five, five years was a long shot.

What did I have to show for myself?

A failed marriage. A townhome in a luxury community.

Millions in the bank I'd never be able to spend at this rate, a few investment properties, and no family to leave it to.

Fuck.

I was getting old. And grumpy.

Already my head was hurting at the thought of all the noise to follow later tonight.

If it hadn't been my idea, I'd bail.

But our team needed this. The guys did.

And they were all I had left.

As much as I'd already failed at so much in life, I wouldn't let them down.

By the time I got to the locker room and stripped out of my gear, my phone was buzzing like a beehive.

I grabbed it.

Four missed calls from Heather.

Six texts.

My little sister was five years younger than me, living the high life with her job as a personal chef for the uppity, richest people I could ever imagine.

Yeah, I had millions, but there was a difference between having money and being rich.

Those who hired live-in personal chefs topped the list.

Fortunately, Heather loved her job immensely.

I went to call her when I was jolted from behind, and my phone fell to the floor.

"What the hell?"

"You coming out tonight?" It was Joey, our assistant captain and one of the best guys I'd ever met. Hell, his whole family was.

"I'll be there."

"Good. Good. It'll be good to see you let loose a little bit."

"I let loose frequently."

"Sipping one drink when you show up at my house isn't letting loose."

He had a point. But the guy was smart.

"Gabby coming out with us?"

"Nah. She said she'd get the girls together, watch the kids so we could enjoy it."

He scanned the locker room, eyes stalling on Bromann. "Team is different this year. I mean, we always have new guys. They come and go, but..."

"Max is gone."

"Yeah. For such a loud asshole, he was the glue."

I couldn't argue. Max was the life of the party. The guy was always ready to pump someone up and cheer them on. Until his most recent injury, I'd never seen the guy not smiling. Life moved on though, and we had to adjust without him. Hell, based on his most recent text, he was loving his life out in California with his new girlfriend, Kimmy.

We'd still see him. Just because he wasn't on the team didn't mean he wasn't still part of the team.

"Bromann will click soon."

"He better." Joey sighed, ran a hand through his already showered dark hair, and shrugged. "We'll figure it out later. Who knows, maybe all we need is a night to act like idiots together to bond."

I'd prefer a round of golf or a boating day. My ass was too old for clubs with the constant flashing lights and ear-piercing music.

"Maybe," I agreed. Because hell, we'd already tried everything else.

I picked up my phone and headed for the showers. Heather was known to have a crisis a day, and god love her for it, but she could wait.

My team, on the other hand, could not.

***

"THIS ROUND'S ON ME!"

Arlo had to lean in and shout over the massive table Alix had somehow secured in the VIP section of Piazza. An Italian-style dance club sat atop one of the casinos on the Strip, I couldn't remember the last time I'd been here. Yeah, when I'd first been traded, the Strip was cool to visit. Back then, I'd had Ava with me, though, and at twenty-five, we were growing out of the constant clubbing scene. We'd been talking about having kids, starting a family once I got settled in Vegas and with the team.

Then she left. I couldn't blame her for it, not now, not when I took the time to look back, but God.

I fucking missed her.

I grabbed one of the shots one of our newer players, Calix Weekes, bought. Recently turned twenty-one and excited as hell to finally be able to buy his team a round, he couldn't wipe the smile off his face all night long. Bromann threw his arm over his shoulders, and they took a shot together.

Apparently, *Operation: Bond Bromann to the Team* required tequila.

The entire team was out, including Dominick Masters, who'd

only really started opening up to our team last season. Seth McCabe and Braxton were there, taking a rare night out from their wives. Didn't blame them though. They both had young babies at home.

The only guy missing was Garrett, but he'd called and said one of his twins was throwing up and he didn't want to leave his wife, Lizzie, to deal with it alone. Even if I heard her screaming in the background that she'd be fine.

Understandable. Fortunately, the rest of the team was here, tossing back drinks and trading battle stories of our time in the junior and minor leagues. The mood was light, and I was probably the only person sitting there with regret lining my stomach.

Fuck it.

Three shots and two drinks in, I was ready to forget Ava for a night. Hell, maybe I'd find someone else. Life had been too busy to date much in the years since she'd left, and it took me a full year to even consider it, but I'd never met a woman who measured up.

Doubtful anyone would. Ava had been made for me—and I'd screwed that up nice and well.

Fuck. A night of drinks and friends was what I needed. Not a night thinking about my ex-wife, who was getting married over Thanksgiving weekend. Some asshole with three first names or something or other she'd met shortly after moving back to her family's house on Long Island.

Whatever.

"Dance!" Alix cried and jostled my arm.

My head spun, and yeah... I was good and drunk. Maybe I could grab a woman for a night of barely-satisfying sex for the first time since my wife left me. Maybe that was what I needed.

A jolt to get back into the game.

Better than going home alone.

"All right, all right." I shoved off the chair and waited a minute to make sure I was steady.

Goddamn. Thirty and too old for this shit. My body was probably as sore as my dad's after a day of working the cattle. Except he was fifty-five and had been hauling hay and cattle and horses and hogs since before I was born. He had an excuse.

But damn, I felt old as I followed Alix and Ryder down to the dance floor. I squinted to block out the glare of the lights and almost stumbled on one of the steps on the way down.

Shit. I was drunk. Alix turned back, smiling like a jackass, clearly catching my near fall. My cheeks were numb. Must have been smiling.

Yeah... good and drunk.

Now to find a barely dressed chick on the floor, perhaps one from the trio of blondes Alix was leading us to. Two of them had been smiling up at the second floor where we were perched all night. Neon-colored, skintight dresses, with slashes of fabric missing at their sides, above their hips, the necklines dipped low, showed off ample cleavage.

All blonde. All wavy, curled hair. Barbie triplets. All grinning at Alix as he made his approach.

The fucker was never turned down.

Could be the Swiss-French accent he had. Probably the tousled blond hair and cut jaw with a scar. More than one random he met brushed their finger against it. How in the hell women found facial scars attractive was something I never figured out, but hell if they did. I'd had the same questions asked.

"How'd you get that scar by your eye?" "And your nose? It looks like it's been broken?"

Puck Bunnies-R-Us were a dime a dozen once you hit the pros, and their lines were as manufactured as their tits.

But they were tits up for the offering tonight. A vile taste rose in my throat and I fought it back.

I wasn't this guy. Not anymore. Hell, I didn't want to be this guy ever again.

My phone buzzed in my pocket again.

Shit. I'd never called Heather back. I declined the call. No way

I could talk to her now, but as I did, I noticed missed calls from my neighborhood's security office.

What in the hell?

"Hey, there," one of the blondes practically screamed in my ear.

Her hand slid up my arm, and an icy, sick feeling spread all over me.

Yeah.

I was out.

"Sorry," I shouted back and turned.

Left the dance floor.

Left the bar.

The younger guys could entertain Bromann. As soon as fresh air assaulted me, I stumbled back on the sidewalk. Throngs of people lined the area, screaming and shouting as a few people followed me out.

Damn it. It was midnight my time.

If Heather was still calling...

I grabbed my phone and called her back, barely got out a "Hey," before my sister blurted out her own response.

"Thank God you finally called me back."

"What's wrong?"

"Oh. Nothing. Well, not with me, anyway."

"So help me God, Heather. If you called me in the middle of the damn night to talk about some vegetable or herb plant of yours that is dying—"

She laughed. Had to be, what? Three, four o'clock in the morning, her time? She needed to be working in a couple of hours, for fuck's sake.

"No. It's not that. Remember my friend Emmersyn?"

Heather had dozens of friends. Was always bringing them out to catch a game or taking me out to meet someone when I was in the New England area. Girl was the reigning social butterfly and had been ever since elementary school when she proudly came home carrying a "Talks too much" warning note from her teacher.

"What about her?" It was late, and I didn't have the mental bandwidth to start a guessing game of who was who. A taxi pulled up, and I flagged it down.

I slid into the back seat as she said, "Well, the thing is, she's in trouble. So I sent her to your place. She should be there..."

"You did what?!"

TWO
EMMERSYN

"Please. Is there any way you can call Mr. Andrews? He has to be in."

He was expecting me. Had to be. There was no way Heather would let me down. She'd promised me her older brother would take me in.

I had nowhere else to go.

"I'm sorry, Miss..." The security guard, Kevin, glanced down at the note he'd written and back to me. "Miss Houghton. Mr. Andrews is not in, and I'm unable to reach him on his personal line as of yet. If you can pull off to the side for a few moments, perhaps he'll respond to either mine or the calls you claim his sister made."

Right. Because I was making all of this up. I'd known Heather since we lived across the hall from each other in college, but that wasn't how we met.

She'd almost punched a guy in a bar when he hadn't been willing to accept the fact I didn't want a drink from him. I was with friends, but they'd all paired up with other guys. Seeing I was alone and ready to bail after that encounter, Heather invited me to join her friends, at least until the guy left. I bought her a drink as a thank you, and the rest was history. We bonded immediately, and while I'd only met her brother once, it was easy to say Heather was his biggest fan.

"She made the calls." She had to have. Heather was my best friend, and she and her brother were closer than close.

In front of me, my taxi driver sighed. "Miss, I do have other runs to make."

Great. "I know. Please, just a few minutes."

It was late. Maybe Kane was sleeping. "Five more minutes, please."

"Five," my taxi driver said.

I leaned back out the window through the driver's side rear door. "Please. Can you please try Kane again?"

He sighed but reached for the phone, but as he did, it rang in his palm. I waited while he announced himself, and then his eyes widened and slid slowly toward me. "Yes, sir, Mr. Andrews. There is a friend of Heather's here... okay... yes, of course, sir." He hung up the phone and looked almost bummed Kane had called him. He reached for a button on a panel. "You may continue to his house, Miss Houghton. He told me to tell you he'll be home in twenty minutes. You may wait outside for him."

Relief washed through me like a wave. "Thank you." Finally, something in this horrific day had gone right.

The driver made his way through the neighborhood. It was dark, but there was no mistaking the elaborate homes of cement and stucco and brick and rock that were hidden behind gates and elegant landscaping.

The mansions faded as we drove through the neighborhood, a wealthy area of Las Vegas, but I'd been born to wealth, even if I chose not to live like it, mostly due to circumstances I wasn't willing to currently consider.

Figuring out my next step would happen tomorrow. Or the day after. Once my bruises healed and the stitches were removed, but damn, I desperately wish I still had my phone.

Townhomes appeared, large and vast and as rich as the

homes, if only smaller in size, until my taxi stopped in front of a building, two townhomes next to each other, both with three-car garages attached. Both homes were completely dark, not an outdoor light on at all, but I figured safety wasn't much of an issue in this neighborhood. Not with Officer Kevin at the gate and his weathered, aged, but irritated face and muscled body to protect them.

I almost snickered at the thought, but the taxi slowed and pulled to the curb of one of the homes.

"This is it." He glanced around, probably noticed the lack of lighting like I had, and met my gaze in the rearview mirror. "I can wait. To ensure you are safe."

His gaze dipped to the gash near my left eye. It still throbbed with pain, but less than earlier. "Thank you, but I'll be okay."

I used the credit card Heather gave me earlier for "incidentals" as she called them, seeing as I shared an account with my ex-fiancé and I didn't want him knowing where I was. At least, not yet.

I stepped out after I paid and hitched the small overnight bag I'd bought at Target filled with a couple of days' worth of clothes and makeup and hair products. Basics, until I could get a new bank account and transfer money.

I closed the door, and the taxi waited until I was on the dark front porch and the bag dropped to my side.

Twenty minutes. I had nothing to do, nothing to keep me occupied. So I turned, plopped my ass down on the top step, and rested my head against the wall as the taxi slowly pulled away, seeming hesitant to leave me there alone.

A stranger had been more kind to me than a man I was supposed to marry.

The thought made my nose and throat burn, and as I sniffed, the very painful and vivid reminder of what Lincoln did earlier pulsed at my cheek. Above my hip.

It was nearing midnight, but that meant it was three o'clock in the morning my time, and I'd been up for almost thirty-six hours.

I hadn't even been able to sleep on the plane. Every time I closed my eyes, I saw Lincoln.

His fist.

I shook my head and tried to brush the images out of my mind.

One fight. Hours in the emergency room. Three hours later, Heather was there, rushing to me after hopping a ferry from Martha's Vineyard, where she was working for the summer, to be at my side.

"That's what best friends do," she'd said, hugging me tightly.

One hour later, I was discharged, and I turned down the offer to press charges.

I doubted anyone would believe me. Not in Boston.

Not in the entire state of Massachusetts. Or hell, all of New England, most likely.

Heather, smart as a whip and more protective than a lioness with new cubs, had formulated a plan before she ever arrived and saw my face.

My voice had said it all. *He hit me.*

We went straight from the hospital to Target to grab necessities, and she dropped me off at Boston's Logan Int'l Airport with a flight for three hours later to Las Vegas.

How in the hell she managed to do all of it was anyone's guess, but I'd long since stopped underestimating Heather.

She would do *anything* for the people she loved.

Lucky for me, she loved me.

Now, I was sitting on the front stoop of a practical stranger's house in the middle of the night, my head aching, my side bruised to hell and back, five stitches on my upper cheekbone outside my eye, my palms and knees still scratched up, and the pain pills wearing off trying to stay awake for a man I'd met once.

Kane Andrews.

Heather's older brother.

My best friend's incredibly sexy, professional hockey playing and super kind, older brother.

Who wasn't here like Heather promised he would be.

Hell, what if he said no?

There were a million reasons why he wouldn't want my current drama dropped on his doorstep.

"Crap," I whispered and propped my elbow on my knee, my chin into my palm, careful of my stitches.

I probably looked like a victim straight out of a teen horror film, despite Heather's attempts to clean me up with Target makeup and clothing.

I needed sleep.

Tomorrow, I'd figure things out.

You can return home when you're ready to apologize.

Home.

Bullshit.

I was never going home again.

Lincoln Powers, future heir to the Regal Hospitality and Travel mogul, could fuck. Right. Off.

"HEY." A gentle poke pushed at my shoulder. "Hey. Emmersyn?"

I must have been dreaming. The man's voice was quiet. Deep. A rumble that reminded me of distant ocean waves. "Emmersyn. Wake up."

He jostled me more, the voice became louder as he prodded my shoulder again and I opened my eyes.

My head jerked up, shooting pain through my side and the stitches on my cheekbone.

"Oh." I blinked. "Did I... Kane Andrews?"

I recognized him immediately. Hard not to with the pictures Heather always showed, bragging about her awesome older brother. I'd met him once when Heather had taken us all out when he'd been visiting Boston. We'd gone to his hockey game and met him and some of his teammates for dinner after. He'd been loud then. Easy smiles and love for his sister, constantly jostling her and calling her a brat. He had a thick beard then.

Not now. No...

Now he was scowling at me like he wanted to rip my head off.

"Who in the fuck hurt you?"

"Oh." Right. Heather promised he was a good guy. The best. That he was almost a full country away from my current problem was a bonus. "Um. Hi?"

Two thick black brows rose on his forehead. Almost to his hairline. The move only set off the tightness of his jaw, the arch of his cheekbones. He had a scar on his jaw from a hockey stick smacking him in the face when he was in college.

"Hi?" He stood and stepped back.

I took a minute to scan myself. I'd fallen asleep on the cement porch. My leggings cut into a bruise at my waist but was still hidden by the oversized, long sleeve shirt Heather bought. The sandals were cheap foam flip-flops. My bag was still next to me, though, and held the only thing I owned before today: my driver's license.

"My sister calls me, tells me a woman I've never met before is in trouble and is probably at my home, and I show up, and you look like someone beat the shit out of you, and all you say is 'hi'?"

As he ranted, he shoved his hands through thick black hair and tugged. A waft of his breath hit me, and I caught the faint scent of alcohol.

"Are you drunk?" I asked.

"No, I'm not drunk." He squeezed his eyes closed, scraped a hand over his jaw, and dropped it to his side. Grumbling, he said, "Fucking Heather. The shit she gets me involved in." He stepped back and swept his hand toward the door. "Come on. I bet you're tired. Maybe tomorrow we can figure this shit out."

I gaped up at him. "You're okay with me staying?"

Delirium. Had to be the lack of sleep making me not understand what was happening.

"Yeah," he huffed and bent toward me. His hand came out so fast I flinched back.

Kane cursed. "Not going to hurt you, just helping you with your bag. Do you need help getting to your feet?"

Pain pulsed in multiple areas in my body, but it was the shame that had my head ducking. He'd gone to *help* me, and I'd flinched.

When has that ever happened to me? I wasn't immune to men's attention. I might not have been the prettiest or slimmest woman in the world, but I received enough attention to know I looked good to others.

Until last night...

I shook my head and braced a hand on the wall to stand. It took a second, and I cringed from the pain at my knees and hip as I stood.

"Thank you," I whispered. Shame and embarrassment rattled me, made my skin hot and my throat burn.

Great.

He gestured for me to walk with him and started talking. That quiet voice I'd heard the first time he said my name, but this time he drew the words out.

Cautious-like. Like I was an imbecile.

Or a frightened, beaten woman.

I preferred when men thought me crazy, which ironically, only occurred in Heather's presence.

"Heather's a pain in the ass and one of the best people I've known my whole life. If she needs help, I'm there. If her friends need help, she knows who to call. I'd like to know what I'm getting myself into, but we can talk about that at your pace, okay?"

I licked my dry lips. "Thank you."

"Come on." As he keyed in the code to his door, he nodded toward the home next door. "Just so you know, the guy who lives next door is also my teammate. His name's Alix, and he stops by. I'm sure you'll meet him. Blond hair, French accent... he's hard to miss. But he's a good friend and an even better guy. Has a younger sister back home in Switzerland he wishes he could move out here."

"Okay..."

The door beeped, the lock unclicked, and he pushed open the heavy, black wood door.

"What I'm trying to tell you, Emmersyn, is that you're safe here, yeah?"

I was a woman who'd lived her life in Boston. Grew up on the streets of a major city and was taking the subway by myself at the age of twelve but was as equally used to being driven around in a limo or town car. Safety had never been my concern or my fear. I carried mace and always wore a bracelet with an emergency alert. Perhaps I'd always considered myself invincible.

I wasn't though. I had just never imagined that the worst possible danger to me was a man I thought I'd spend forever with.

I swallowed the thick rise of emotion threatening to release from my throat and nodded.

"Thank you," I whispered, right as a yawn hit. I covered my mouth and stepped in as Kane held the door for me.

Once it was shut, he locked it, hit a bunch of numbers on a blinking pad by the door, and another series of beeps on the security system followed. "I'll give you the code tomorrow. Let's get you to bed, okay?"

"Thank you," I said, hand still covering my mouth. "It's been a long day."

"You want a tour now or a room?"

Everything was modern from the little I could see. Black metal railings and dark, shining wood floors. Straight in front of us, past a living area, was a wall of floor-to-ceiling windows, and as he flipped on lights in the small hall, our reflection appeared, along with a mirror image of his modern, masculine, and black metal loft-style home with an exposed ceiling.

I wanted a tour of this place, but my knees wobbled.

A bed had never sounded so good.

"Room, please."

"All right." He walked around a pool table beyond the kitchen bar where three black metal stools with dark wood seats were on the way to the stairs.

At the top of the stairs, he pointed out his room at the opposite end of the hall, closed off with French doors. A hall bathroom. Two more closed doors, and at the opposite end of the landing we stood on, one more door.

"You can have this one. It has an attached bathroom. I usually let my family and Heather stay in this one when they visit. That okay?"

"Wonderful." My eyes closed slowly, and I forced them open.

Darn. I could fall asleep standing up.

Kane must have noticed because he chuckled and opened the bedroom door. He flipped on the lights, and I followed him. The room looked like a hotel. All white, fluffy linens and pillows. Speckles of eggshell blue in a couple decorative pillows and a corner chair.

"Your mom decorated this," I said, knowing Tracy. The woman decorated everything with a beach theme.

"Nailed it." Kane set my small, lone bag on the bed and stared at it, hands on his hips.

Working something out.

Probably who in the hell I was. What was going on. What in the hell was wrong with me.

Slowly, his head turned until our eyes met. His jaw worked back and forth, and finally, he pressed his lips together and sighed, shaking his head.

"We'll talk tomorrow. For tonight, you're safe here. If you need me…"

He pointed down the hall.

"I'll be fine. Thank you. Again." I tried to smile, but I was so tired my muscles wouldn't cooperate.

Probably came off more like one of the horror victims I currently felt like.

Kane's eyes drifted over my face, pausing on the stitched up gash from Lincoln's fist before dropping to my side.

My hand was there at my waist. I hadn't realized I was putting pressure on it until he looked at me. I dropped my hand.

Kane yanked his gaze back to my face, looking me directly in the eye. "Good night, Emmersyn."

He left and closed the door behind him.

I summoned the energy to use the bathroom, brush my teeth, and minutes later, I was in a bed, in a strange new state, in a stranger's townhome, feeling so damn grateful for a comfortable bed that even smelled like Heather's mom, I closed my eyes.

Where sleep could find me.

Until that is... I woke up screaming.

THREE
KANE

"Get off me!"

A violent scream ripped through my townhome and I was up and out of bed before I processed what the hell was going on.

Another scream. "Stop! I'm sorry!"

Who in the hell?

"Oh, shit." I hurried to my feet.

Emmersyn was screaming like she was being tortured in my own damn home.

I threw open my bedroom door and sprinted to hers as she cried out again and I flung open her door.

She was tossing and turning in the bed, covers and sheets twisted around her. The room was dark, but she'd left the curtain and blinds wide open, so I caught a flash of her chocolate-colored hair when she screamed and thrashed again.

"What the fuck?" I rasped, voice thick with sleep and adrenaline racing through my limbs.

I rushed to the bed and pressed a hand to her shoulder to still her. "Emmersyn. Wake up."

She swiped at my hand, and I pulled back. I knew better than to wake people in the throes of a nightmare, and I didn't need her nails scraping my skin.

"Emmersyn!" I barked out her name, hands at my hips. And only then did I realize I hadn't thrown anything on over my boxer briefs. Fuck. Too late to change now. I called her name again, followed by a harsh, "Wake up!"

She thrashed again, moaned, and I imagined it was the painful sound she'd made when whoever the hell beat the shit out of her did it. Her hand went to her side, but she calmed, applying pressure and grimacing in her sleep.

No longer thrashing and screaming, I moved closer again and settled my hand on her shoulder to give her a gentle shake. "Come on, Emmersyn, wake up." Her skin was lined with sweat, her shoulder clammy from it. "Come on. It's a nightmare. You're safe."

Emmersyn's breathing slowed, and then her eyes jerked open. Dark pools of fear slammed into me, and I stepped back, lifting my hands.

"It's me, Kane. Kane Andrews? Heather's brother," I stammered it out fast so I didn't scare her more.

"What?" She looked around. "Where?... oh God... was I?"

"Screaming? Yeah."

She took in the room, eyes sliding every which way, and once she blew out a breath and scrubbed her eyes, I was finally able to relax.

"You okay?"

"Shit." She pushed herself to sit. The move shoved the blankets down farther, exposing the spaghetti strap cotton top she wore with a deep V-neck. I yanked my gaze off her ample cleavage. "I was..."

"Having a nightmare. You okay now, though?"

Her eyes were glassy. She shook her head and looked out the window before a tremble coursed through her shoulders. Her breasts shook, and I tore my gaze off her body.

I didn't know her. And I didn't need to be staring at her like that, not after she'd clearly been beaten. What I needed was to have a serious conversation with my sister as soon as I knew she'd be awake.

"I'm so sorry," she rasped, and her voice was dry. Probably from all the screaming. How long had she been doing it before I heard? "I woke you up."

"It's all right."

"It's six in the morning. You need your sleep and shit... I'm so sorry."

"Emmersyn." Her name was more of a command, one she heeded. Once her still hazy gaze met mine, I held out my palms. "It's fine. We're good. All good. I get up soon anyway."

Total lie. I didn't have practice until three, which meant normally I wouldn't wake up until ten. Considering last night's late night, I was exhausted.

I also knew I wouldn't fall back asleep, considering the way I'd been woken.

She didn't need to carry more guilt.

"Do you need anything? Water?"

She swallowed and cringed, and as she did, her chin dipped down. Eyes widened before she yanked her head back up, eyes meeting mine again.

Shit. My boxers.

"Fuck. I'm sorry," I started to say and stepped back.

"You're apologizing for me waking you up?"

I had no idea what happened to her. How badly she'd been hurt. A half-naked man, especially a guy my size in general, could do more harm than good, I figured.

Still there was humor in her tone, better than the fear, and if I wasn't mistaken, a slight flush to her cheeks.

Shit on a cracker. I did not need this.

I took another step back. "I'm headed to the kitchen. I'll make some coffee. I can bring you water."

"No. It's okay." That lost look returned, still better than fear.

Or the screams. Damn, she had a set of pipes on her. "I'll, well, I might as well get up, too."

I didn't move right away. Her eyes had fallen to my chest. My abs. Something stirred in my dick and that woke me up.

Her body was the kind men like me dreamed of. Thick thighs, tits bigger than a handful. There'd be softness in her stomach and her hips. Plenty to grab on to, and maybe that wasn't some men's type, but I'd always loved a woman with size to her. Not so... breakable.

Except she'd been broken recently, and I was being a fucking asshole.

"Right." I cleared my throat and turned, grabbed her door handle. "I'll be downstairs, then. Come down when you're ready and once you wake up, I can give you a tour. Of the house and the neighborhood, if you'd like."

"Thanks, Kane."

I shook my head and tried to clear my brain. Images of her body were the last thing I needed on my mind.

This woman needed my help.

My sister needed her head examined.

And me?

I didn't need to be fucking ogling a woman in my house.

No matter how damn sexy she looked barely dressed in one of my beds.

I closed her door behind me harsher than I should have and hurried to my bedroom, where I threw on shorts and a Vipers T-shirt.

By the time I was downstairs, water was running in the guest bathroom, clueing me in that Emmersyn was out of bed and getting ready.

What the fuck was happening? I hadn't reacted to a woman like that in three years. More than, really. But the last woman I needed to be reacting to was this one.

I had minutes to get my dick calmed down and my head in the right frame of space.

Good thing I excelled under pressure.

BY THE TIME SOFT, hesitant footsteps echoed along my wood floor, I had my protein smoothie prepped and ready for the blender, eggs scrambled in a bowl, and spinach and mushrooms chopped to add to them. My blender was insanely loud, so I waited until Emmersyn came down so I didn't frighten her with the noise.

Given how hesitant she looked, hands at the hem of an oversized T-shirt with Rolling Stones stamped on the front and wearing a pair of black leggings, I was glad I waited.

"Hey. You hungry at all? I was getting breakfast ready."

She scanned the vegetables and eggs and turned up her nose. "I'll have coffee. Thanks."

"Not a fan of eggs?"

"Vegetables," she replied, and her lips pushed into a quick smile. "Where's your coffee maker? I can get it started?"

I pointed to the far edge of my kitchen. "Keurig is in the corner back there. Coffee pods and mugs are above it."

"Thank you."

A large kitchen with a bar that could seat up to six. My kitchen rivaled my living room for size and could easily fit five or six adults working at the same time. The best part of it was the view of the backyard through my all-glass and steel door that lifted like a garage door. Beyond my hot tub and pool and cement fence was the golf course. Red Rock State Park viewable in the far distance. Off the second-story balcony of my bedroom, the view was breathtaking. One of my favorite places to hang out.

Sharing my space never felt strange, but today it was different. That unease palpitated every atom in the air and I cursed Heather in my mind for putting me in this position.

Especially with a woman who had an ass that filled out her leggings and couldn't be hidden by that T-shirt so damn perfectly my mouth watered to take a bite of it.

Too bad I didn't stay in the bar last night, find one of the puck bunnies for a quick stop in the bathroom before leaving. Maybe now I wouldn't be acting like such a perverted asshole.

Facing the stove, I gave Emmersyn more space and time to grab her coffee and poured the eggs into my heating pan. I had questions. Bucket loads of them for her and Heather, but they could wait.

A barstool scraped across the floor, telling me Emmersyn had taken a seat, and I grabbed an avocado from a bowl on the counter and turned to start slicing it up.

I caught sight of her looking at it before glancing away and bringing her coffee mug to her mouth.

Don't stare at her lips.

Right. I was working on not being an under-sexed, overly needy teenage prick.

At the first slice into the avocado, Emmersyn looked at me. "Do you have more of those?"

"I thought you didn't like vegetables."

"Avocado grows on trees. So it's a fruit."

I glanced up, took in her smile, the sparkle in her green eyes, and almost sliced off a finger. She was so damn pretty.

"With toast?" I asked and grabbed another one.

"Please. And thank you." She took another sip of coffee while I cleaned out the pit and started peeling the outside. Yeah, you could scoop it, but I preferred slicing. "You're being very nice to someone you don't know."

I shrugged. "Not going to lie, I want to wring my sister's neck and I have a gazillion questions for you, but I figured you wouldn't want to share those answers with a stranger."

My eggs were sizzling, so I slid the spinach and mushrooms

into the pan, popped some bread into the toaster, and turned back to Emmersyn.

As I did, my phone rang on the counter, and I grinned at Emmersyn. "Heather must have known we were talking about her."

Her name was on the screen, and this time I didn't let it go to voice mail. Two quick presses and I said, "Hey, brat. Aren't you supposed to be working?"

Her easy laugh echoed through the kitchen, and Emmersyn leaned in closer. "Yeah, yeah. Let's clock our hours and see who works harder, you, skating around for funsies, or me, working my ass off in a garden sweating my tits off."

"First... funsies? And second..." I pointed my knife at the phone even though she couldn't see. "Never talk to me about your tits again."

"Sure, sure." She was still laughing. My sister was a pain in the ass of the best kind. "So, you found Emmersyn I take it since I didn't hear from you."

"Yeah, and—"

I went to tell her we were on speaker, but she didn't give me a chance because my sister, being the bulldozer she was, kept talking. "I know I'm asking a lot, but it was an emergency. Her fiancé's a royal complete pain in the ass. I have her phone. He's been calling my phone and hers since she didn't come home yesterday."

Fiancé?

Phone?

My gaze met Emmersyn's, and that worry was back, turning her green eyes to forest green. She bit down on her bottom lip and her eyes came to mine.

"You're on speakerphone, dumbass, and Emmersyn is right here. How about you let her tell me all the ugly shit going on in her life, would you?"

I could feel Heather's flinch from a country away. "Sorry, Emmersyn. I thought you'd still be sleeping, and I needed to vent."

"It's okay." Her smile returned, barely there, but better. "Your brother is making me breakfast. I uh... woke him up..."

"It's fine," I reiterated because Jesus. I was not the guy to be apologizing to.

"Kane doesn't mind. He's practically still on vacation."

"First game is in two weeks," I reminded her, although she knew. She always did. She had my games on her calendar the day the schedule came out.

"Pre-season," she huffed. "Like it means anything. And you could sleep through your games and still kick ass."

I shook my head, turned back to flip my eggs, and grabbed the toast from the toaster.

"Keep talking shit, and I'm hanging up and changing my number."

"Liar," she teased right back.

My sister kicked total ass, even if she was a pain in mine most of the time.

Her tone softened then as she asked, "How are you, honey?"

Clearly meant for Emmersyn, my part of the conversation most likely done, I slid the phone closer to her. "You can take that if you need it."

"I'm okay," she said, and her hands stayed cupped around her coffee mug. Eyes came to me before flicking back to the phone. "Sore. Tired. Is Lincoln really that mad?"

"Oh... he's *big* mad. But I'm screenshotting everything and voice recording his voice mails to my phone."

"What's he saying?" Emmersyn's voice trembled.

I bit my lip and gave her my back. If she didn't want full privacy, I could at least give her the illusion of it.

Heather's tinny voice through the phone sounded like she was trying not to rage out. "I'm not telling you. Not now, but I promise it's for your own good, and I'm glad you got out of town."

"He'll trace my phone to you."

"Fucking let him," Heather said. "I'd like to leave an imprint of *my* shoe on his ribs, too. And then his dick. Maybe his skull."

Holy shit. I whipped around and braced my hands on the counter. "A *shoe print?*" I seethed.

This fucking asshole. Yeah, I knew she was holding her side. The slashes on her face were obvious due to the stitches. "He fucking kicked you?"

"Settle down, tiger," Heather said, but her voice wasn't teasing. "You'll scare the girl."

"I'm fine," Emmersyn said. And looked at the phone then me. "I'm fine. Or I will be. I just... need to figure some things out. Lincoln has a long reach."

"True. And thanks, brother, for all your help. We appreciate it."

"No problem."

Technically I hadn't really had a choice, considering how it'd been handled. Hell, by the time Heather called me the first time, she already had Emmersyn on a plane headed my way.

What kind of asshole would say no then?

Although, based on what I was hearing, *Lincoln* might.

I plated up Emmersyn's avocado toast, slid my pepper and salt-shaker in front of her.

Done with that, and then mine, I grabbed my eggs and held both of my plates up. "I'm going to eat outside. Give you a minute," I said quietly to her.

She nodded and turned back to the phone. "Thank you, Heather, for everything. I know I asked a lot of you yesterday—"

"Shut up, brat. You didn't ask anything more than what you'd do for me."

I shut the sliding door, drowned out their voices, and another rush of anger pummeled me.

The very idea of a man treating Heather like what'd been done to Emmersyn was enough to make me want to murder anyone who so much as looked at her.

FOUR

EMMERSYN

After the night I met Heather and she threatened to rip off the balls of a man she didn't know who was also three times her size, we'd quickly learned we just moved in across the hall from each other in the dorms. The first day I went to her room, she told me all about her awesome, professional hockey-playing brother. She never hid the fact of who her brother was, how successful he was, or how proud she was of him. Heather loved her family so deeply and in such a healthy way it always made me admire her and a little jealous of all the goodness she'd had in her life.

Her brother, on the other hand, dear sweet baby Jesus in a manger... he became fodder for *all* the girls in our dorm. So damn hot.

Is he single?

Do you have another brother?

I'd ride him.

How big is his other stick?

How flexible is he?

Can he work his hips like that off the ice?

We didn't even care he was married, but then it was all in good fun for us.

Heather heard it and laughed her ass off. To her, Kane was her awesome big brother.

To us? He was the man who, over the years, we'd all spent time thinking about—mostly, his personal stick and those hip swivel videos she'd show us just to laugh her ass off at our sexual comments.

I know I thought of him at least a time or twelve.

Seeing him in person again?

Holy hot shit. The man was hot enough to melt all the common sense from my brain. Even beaten, abused, cheated on, I could take a quick second and enjoy the tightness of his ass as he walked away.

"So tell me," Heather said as if she heard the door close as Kane left. It wouldn't be a surprise. "Be honest. How are you?"

"Lost. Scared." I pushed away my toast, losing my appetite despite how delicious it looked. "I don't have anything, and I know Lincoln isn't going to back down. He'll find me, Heather. Force me back to Boston, or..."

Worse... bury me in the desert and tell everyone I left him and then mourn when my body was found, becoming even more rich and famous.

Until two nights ago, I couldn't have fathomed Lincoln was that kind of guy.

But now?

I doubted I knew him at all.

"Bullshit. You'll be fine. Kane will take care of you, and I've already Venmo'd him money for anything you need."

Ridiculous. She'd already given me her credit card. "I can't—"

"You can and you will. You'll pay me back. Or make it up to me in a thousand other ways. I'm not doing this just for you, either. I need to, okay? I forced you out there. Between Kane and I, let us take care of you. It's about time someone does."

I flinched. Thank God she didn't see. So I didn't come from a family of caretakers like she did. She'd known that for years.

"Trust me, my plan is perfect."

At the mention of her ridiculous plan, my stomach dropped. I was still uncertain. And how in the hell would I bring it up to Kane in the first place.

Hey, I know Heather says you were devastated after your divorce, but hey... want to help me out? I need to get married to access my trust fund... and since my fiancé turned out to be a raging asshole... what do you say?

No way in hell was I ready to broach that subject.

"Give me a day, okay? I need to think some more about this."

"Fine. Take some time, I get it. Go play a round of golf. Do all the things rich ass stuck-up snobs do. Plan your next steps and do it all without looking over your shoulder or having to deal with soon-to-be eunuch Lincoln. Because trust me, you get me around him, I will be thrilled to make it happen. But while you're thinking, think about this. The faster you get married, the quicker Lincoln will move on."

I snorted. Wouldn't put it past Heather to do that either. She was very good with a knife.

"Golf course?" I ignored the rich ass snob comments.

"You haven't seen it yet? I thought it'd call to you as soon as you woke up."

Unfortunately, I woke up drenched in sweat with a behemoth of a man standing over me in nothing but his underwear. Looking outside hadn't occurred to me. "No... I'm in the kitchen."

"So turn your ass around. It's right there. Good grief, I can't believe you didn't notice it first."

"Shut up," I said, spinning on my stool, and "Holy freaking shit. There's a pool... and a golf course."

I didn't know what to focus on first. The pool was small but filled the yard perfectly, and behind the privacy fence, up on a slope, were bright green fairways, even brighter white sand traps. They rolled out across the enormous, flat view from the floor-to-ceiling windows with red, flat-topped rocks in the distance.

My breath whooshed from me and thank goodness I was already sitting. It was gorgeous. I caught sight of Kane out there, legs kicked up on a lounge chair in the shade, one of his plates in his lap before Heather distracted me.

"Yeah, wait until you see the view from upstairs. It's incredible. Whatever, take whatever time you need to relax. Hit the greens or whatever you golf people say and have some fun."

My excitement, the first real burst of it I'd had since Lincoln's fist smashed into my cheek, vanished. "I don't have my clothes. Or clubs." Oh God, my heart was racing. "Or anything else I own or the cash for fees, or..."

Nothing. I had nothing. I'd let Heather put me on a plane with an airline ticket, a bag of items from Target, and my driver's license. Other than that, I'd fled like some kind of freak in the middle of the night from everything I knew. Everyone I knew. My life. My belongings. My savings and credit cards...

"Oh holy crap, Emmersyn, *breathe.* We'll *handle* it."

She shouldn't have to.

"Listen." And it was a rare moment when Heather turned serious. Voice lowered, she quietly continued. "None of us could have predicted Lincoln would be this much of a monster. He fooled us all. This is *not* your fault. It's his. All of it. Now, will you please let me be one of your best friends in the universe and spoil you for a little bit, so *I* feel better I fell for all of his bullshit?"

Tears rose then and before I knew it, before I could stop them, fell down my cheeks. "I thought he was perfect." My finger touched the cut at the edge of my eye. Five stitches. "How could I be so stupid?"

"You're not stupid. You're the smartest woman I know."

"Liar," I snorted, because even crying, we could call each other on our bullshit. "I'm not."

"Well, you're the most beautiful. The sexiest, and soon you'll learn you're the strongest, too, okay? Take some time for yourself.

Figure out what you want before dealing with Lincoln. I'll deal with him here."

His name sent a shiver down my spine, straight to the bruise he'd left at my side. No broken ribs, thankfully, but every step took effort.

I'd heal though. Physically.

"Thank you," I whispered and wiped more tears away. "Thank you for always being there."

"It's what friends are for, dumbass, and now that the serious shit is out of the way, what do you think of my brother's place?"

"I'm eating avocado toast he made me."

"Damn straight you are. You hit the jackpot. He's almost as good of a cook as I am. You hang out there and you'll be fat and happy in no time."

"I'm already fat," I retorted. I wasn't. I had curves and hips and a stomach that rolled over my waistbands. I worked out. I was strong, and I knew I looked good despite always being the heaviest in my friend group. I'd worked hard to be confident in my body since there was no way I'd ever be a size two or four.

"Fuck off. I could use some of your curves."

"Stop living on kale and herbs. It's all those vegetables you eat," I teased her right back.

We were laughing. Which I figured was her intent, and as we volleyed back and forth over whose ass was better, I tugged my plate closer and munched on my avocado toast, took a deep breath, and tried to do what Heather said.

I could do anything I wanted.

Everything would be fine.

I would be fine. Especially if Kane agreed to Heather's idea.

BY THE TIME I finished my avocado toast and a second cup of coffee, Kane came back inside, made his protein smoothie, and after we cleaned up the dishes, me insisting since he cooked, he gave me a tour of his townhome.

The house was gorgeous, modern with black metal railings, exposed ceilings, pipes painted black, and fixtures that were all oversized, bare light bulbs. His furniture was dark gray, soft and his sectional couch in the living room was made for lounging and binge-watching your favorite television shows or movies. His house was pristine, and whether that was because he hired someone to clean it or because he lived alone and was adult enough to pick up after himself was anyone's guess. The glass door leading to the pool opened like a garage door and stole my breath once he opened it. I could imagine his team there, in his space, guys partying and drinking and women in tiny bikinis lounging in the hot tub.

Then I kicked that out of my brain because I didn't need to be thinking about Kane in that way.

I didn't ask Kane to show me his bedroom—I'd seen enough of him this morning when he woke me out of my nightmare. A vision I'd spent the first fifteen minutes trying to block from my brain's recall. There was some generic artwork on the walls, a few of his jerseys hung in his guest bedroom slash office, and the last room, which was next to his and connected to it via his outdoor, second-floor balcony, he'd set up as a weight room.

His home screamed all male and muscle and athlete, and yet was still somewhere you wanted to spend time and relax.

"You ready to roll?" Keys jangled in Kane's hand as he spun the keyring on his thumb before clamping them in his fist.

"Sure." I hitched up my new purse onto my shoulder. "I don't mind wandering around later, though, if there's something else you need to be doing."

The last thing I needed to be was a pest.

He dropped his hand to his side and took a step toward me. There was something in his eyes. A flash of darkness that made my breath catch.

"Let's get one thing clear, right now, since I already got the notice from Heather about the money she sent me. I'm here to help. I want you comfortable, acting like this house is yours for as long as you're here and not some guest. You don't need to act like you're bothering me, because trust me, if you do, I'll let you know. And I don't offer to do anything I don't want to do. So if I offer to take you to show you the neighborhood so you know where shit is, it's not a hassle. Got it?"

His throat worked, bobbed as he spoke. Pretty sure I only caught every third word I was so mesmerized by him.

And damn... he smelled good. Spicy and masculine with a hint of something minty.

I still caught enough to get his point. I was apologizing too much, and he was done hearing it.

"Right. I get it."

"Good. Then let's go."

He guided me around the back of the staircase, through the laundry room that had a drop zone and was filled with sports gear, cleats, and piles of dirty laundry on the floor.

"I hate laundry," he admitted when my eyes widened at the sight.

Maybe... if it wouldn't piss him off, that was something I could do for him.

I didn't ask, and he didn't give me a chance either before he opened the door to the garage. Three cars filled the otherwise empty garage. No tools. Nothing stored. Just a golf cart with a bag of clubs strapped into the back area, a large black SUV, and a sleek black sports car.

"Feel free while you're here to take out either of the cars. I'll show you where I keep the keys when we get back."

Was he serious? "You're giving me access to your cars?"

He dipped his chin, peered at me over the brim of his sunglasses. "Can you drive?"

"Of course I can." Learned in Boston, and if you could learn there, my grandfather always said I could drive anywhere.

"Then, yeah. Unless you have a habit of crashing them. It's fine. I usually take the Land Rover when I go to games, but I can take the Aston if you'd be more comfortable driving the SUV."

"Maybe I'll just stick to the golf cart," I muttered. Because seriously?

Yeah, we had money. Bucket loads of it. At least, my parents probably still had buckets of it unless they'd both wasted it all. I hadn't talked to either of them in any real way since I turned eighteen.

"Your choice," he finally said and slid into the cart's driver's seat. "But they're yours. Just sitting here otherwise since I can only drive one at a time."

He had a point.

"Thanks. That's really nice of you." I'd have the freedom to run to the store or window shop through a mall. Hell, maybe I'd walk the Strip at some point, or slip into a casino and see if I could get lucky.

Until I could figure out how to get my money out of my joint account without Lincoln knowing where I was, a little bit of luck at the tables could help.

Alternatively, if Kane agreed to his sister's plan, that would become a whole lot easier.

"Not a problem." He hit a button on the cart, and the garage door behind us opened. The golf cart beeped that annoying tone when he put it in reverse and then we were off.

I hadn't thought to grab sunglasses in my mad dash through Target, so I squinted once the sun hit my eyes. It was already hot, but there was a breeze that kept the heat from being unbearable.

"I overlook the fourth fairway," Kane said, clearly in tour mode.

"I saw that. Course looks beautiful."

"It's not bad. I like getting out every once in a while and play-ing, mostly during the off-season but the great thing about living here is being able to play all year round."

My fingertips buzzed with the desire to rip his driver out of his bag and take a swing. The course was luscious. So at odds with the desert sand and rocks surrounding everything. "I'm a bit jealous."

He turned to me and grinned. "You play?"

"Yeah." I swiped my hands down my thighs. I'd never lived *on* a golf course, but I grew up a member of a country club. And I didn't usually brag, but I was sitting next to a professional athlete who I figured would appreciate my competitive spirit. "I grew up playing. Won State a few times back in high school, had a few full rides for college but turned them down."

"A few times? How many is that exactly?"

"All four years." I grinned.

He grinned back, and it was filled with approval. Probably shouldn't have made my chest swell with pride.

"That's awesome. I'm not good. Just like to have fun and I like doing some of the charity events with other players. Maybe I'll have you give me some tips, so I stop getting my ass beat so badly."

I laughed and grinned up at him. I couldn't see Kane Andrews getting his ass kicked in anything.

"I'd take you up on it if I had clubs."

"Right." His own smile vanished, and he turned back to the path. "We'll see if the pro shop has any to borrow or rent or anything. They might for visitors."

"That'd be awesome."

It'd at least give me something to do with my time once my side healed, even if I only went to the driving range.

We toured, kept driving along. He showed me the pool, the tennis courts—asked me if I kicked ass on those two to which I had to reply not in the least.

"Good," he'd said. "Maybe there's something I can beat you at then."

Like we'd be friends who hung out.

It must have been that, that made me feel so welcome, maybe the quiet teasing and the kindness all around, or maybe that he was Heather's brother and they shared so many similar mannerisms that allowed me to drop my defenses, forget about why I was there, and enjoy the hour we spent tooling around on the golf cart.

Because for some reason, as we were headed back, my face full of sunshine and my chest swarming with excitement to get some golfing in, I leaned back and closed my eyes and found myself saying, "I found out my fiancé was cheating on me, and when I confronted him, he beat the shit out of me."

I'd tried to keep my mouth shut. Tried so damn hard I almost broke one of my crowns. But damn, I couldn't imagine. This sexy as hell woman who smelled like springtime. Whose laugh forced me to think of hockey stats so I didn't sport a hard-on as I showed her around the neighborhood so she'd know where to go.

Every time I caught sight of the scrapes on her face, the stitches done so perfectly she hopefully wouldn't scar, I wanted to beat the shit out of someone.

Anyone.

Too bad we weren't playing Colorado for a couple of weeks. There was a giant asshole on that team I'd love to greet with my fists as I thought about the cuts on Emmersyn's face.

I forced myself not to slam on the brakes once she spoke.

She reached up and rubbed at her stitches and grimaced.

"What in the hell?"

"You ever use a dating app?" she asked, so quietly, so brokenly, I almost cracked the steering wheel.

"No. They don't go well for guys like me."

"Right. Well Lincoln did. Lots of them. Apparently ever since we moved in together last year he's been using them. Who knows how long he was on them before then."

"You're shitting me."

"Nope." She popped the p and looked off in the distance. The views were gorgeous, Red Rock Canyon far beyond the golf course with nothing stopping the view from being perfect.

Like hell she was seeing it though.

"And I did the dumbest thing when I caught him."

"How did you?"

"Walked behind the couch where he was watching TV and on his phone, happened to glance down at the wrong time." She shrugged and trailed off.

"Sounds like the right time to me." I hadn't been a great husband. Hell, I was up there on the scale of shitty meter, but no good man cheated on a good woman.

If Heather loved Emmersyn this much to help her out and knew I would, Emmersyn was one of those good women.

"Yeah. Maybe."

"So you confronted him and he lost his shit?" Or fuck, could I shove my foot into my mouth anymore?

Another rub of that cut. "He's never done that before. Ever. Never could have imagined he had that in him."

I turned a corner on the cart and headed toward my garage.

"That's why Heather is so mad. She's pissed he fooled us, you know? Because we thought he was so nice. So sweet. He always took such good care of me, helped with the house, made me feel special. I thought I was the luckiest girl in the world."

I pulled up to the garage and waited for the door to open. The third one of Alix's sports cars, this one bright orange and obnoxious as fuck, was sitting in his driveway. Guess he finally came home from last night's party.

"I'm sorry, for all of it."

"Yeah. Me too. But to answer your question, I didn't confront him about the cheating that night."

"You didn't?"

"No." There was a tiny smile before she wiped it away.

I parked the cart, and we stepped out. Once we were inside, she continued. "I needed to make sure, you know? I wanted to be able to talk to him about it and *know*, so he couldn't lie and leave me guessing."

Not what I would have done, but I didn't fault her logic. "That was a good idea."

"At the time, I was wondering if he was getting cold feet about the wedding or something. Having a freak-out or whatever and wanted to double check we were doing the right thing? It sounds stupid, and I'm trying to justify it, I know now, but that's what I was thinking. Maybe it was harmless flirting."

I wasn't sure harmless flirting existed when you were about ready to commit to marriage, but I let it slide. "All right."

She rolled her eyes. "I know I sound dumb. I had a plan."

Not dumb. Naive maybe. Or in denial. "So what was your plan?"

"Well, at first, I waited until he'd gone to bed and got into his phone. That's when I learned he'd had the account for so long. He wasn't freaking out over a wedding, he was... God... the number of women on there... the pics he sent to them." She made a face as her chin shook.

Shit. I could handle the crying, but I didn't know her well enough to comfort her if she needed it.

"You don't have to keep going."

Emmersyn ran her fingers through her hair and blinked away the tears. "No. If you don't mind... but do you have something to drink?"

Now she was speaking my language. "Follow me."

I led her to the kitchen, where I had two cupboards stocked with every liquor imaginable. Beneath the bar, I pointed to the wine fridge. "Pick your poison."

"Gin?" she asked.

"Yeah, but no limes or tonic, if that's what you're looking for." I made a quick mental note to get some for her, though.

"Oh. Well then maybe a white wine?"

I opened the door and pulled out the four I had. "Sweet or dry?"

"Sauvignon Blanc if you have it."

It struck me then that she wasn't ending every sentence with please, or I can do it, or you don't have to.

Maybe what I'd told her sunk in earlier.

Maybe she was getting more comfortable. After only a few hours, I liked the idea of that. Emmersyn padding around my home, comfortable in the space.

I shook my head as I pulled out a bottle and grabbed the wine opener. She was my sister's friend. Not to mention she had her own shit to deal with.

She was a guest.

Not a new roommate... or anything else, despite my attraction to her.

"So, you found out he'd been cheating for a while," I said while I opened the wine to get her back to talking.

"Yeah. I made a fake account. Downloaded a picture of a woman—"

"You catfished him?" I didn't think she'd have it in her. That'd be something Heather would do for sure, but my chest swelled with pride all the same. Good for her, for not just catching him and walking away.

I handed her the wine and after she took a sip, she nodded. Pointed to her cheek. "Didn't go so well."

"What happened?"

I braced my hands on the counter to stop her from seeing my fisted hands. Might need to leave for practice an hour early to give me time with a punching bag at this rate.

She slid onto a barstool and took another sip. I grabbed a glass and filled it with water. "I made sure we matched. Waited for him to make the first move. It took him three days to ask me out."

My brows rose on my forehead. Clear signs of a guy just wanting a hook-up.

"And you went."

"Yeah." She gulped her wine and then set it down, fingering the base of the glass with fingers that were long, thin, and manicured a perfectly pale pink. "Want to know the funny thing?"

"There's something funny about any of this?"

Her lips twitched. "I showed up, told him who I was—the name of the girl on the app—and I tossed my engagement ring onto the table. Told him we were done."

Damn. The balls on this chick.

I crossed my arms over my chest. Things were starting to make sense. No guy, even the ones who cheat would want to be caught so blatantly or publicly. "So you ended it and he got pissed."

"No. I don't think he would have gotten pissed about that. Not really. I think he was more embarrassed."

"Embarrassed?"

"Yeah. I embarrassed him in public. The second I threw the ring down and showed him the picture on the dating app, the waiter came up. Heard everything. I think *that's* what made him mad."

Jesus. Who was this fucking guy? Royalty? Who gave a shit if a waiter saw you get your ass handed to you?

I sure as hell wouldn't, but then again, this guy and I clearly had nothing in common.

"Probably because he's an entitled piece of shit."

She frowned, drained her glass, and reached for the bottle. Let her have it all. What else was she going to do today? Hell, if I didn't have practice to get to, I wouldn't mind day drinking right along with her.

Be there for her.

Soothe her soul.

Make her laugh.

I took a large cooling chug of my own water. Did nothing to help the heat quickly building. Yeah, maybe I was an ass for thinking she was hot while talking about her ex.

But it couldn't be denied.

Emmersyn was gorgeous.

Every decent man's wet dream.

Too damn bad I had to keep my hands off her.

"Anyway." She shrugged and bit her bottom lip. "He dragged me out behind the restaurant and did *this…*" She circled her face with a finger. "And then after, he told me I could come home when I was ready to apologize for my behavior."

She had to be joking. Except she wasn't, which was all the more shocking. "The fuck?"

"Yeah."

"All right." I lifted a hand. "I've heard enough and don't get all scared if I sound pissed right now, because I'm fucking pissed off as hell. But you need to hear a couple things and hear me well, okay?"

"Oh. um. All right."

The glass trembled in her hand as she brought it to her mouth. Great. I was making her shake.

"One, Lincoln, whoever the fuck he is, is a fucking loser and a giant piece of shit. You deserve better, you'll find better. Any man who puts his hands on a woman is scum. Got it so far?"

I waited until she nodded.

"And second, I don't know why you and Heather thought the only safe place you could come is here, but you're here now. And you're staying for as long as you goddamn want, okay? My season starts soon. I'm going to be on the road a shit ton. Frankly, I don't mind the idea Alix and I's places won't be empty all the time. You want to be here, lick your wounds, get over the fucking punk, you can do it here. And anything you need, just ask, or take. My cars, my food, my wine," I threw in as she took another healthy gulp.

Her answer was a timid smile. One that looked way too good on her, given the shit I was saying.

Focus. Right.

"It's all yours. For as long as you need it. Okay?"

"Have you ever heard of Regal Hospitality and Travel?"

"Excuse me?"

"Lincoln. He's set to become the next president and CEO of the corporation. Regal Hotels? Cruise lines? Restaurants all over the globe. It's his family's company, started by his great-grandfather, then his grandfather, and now his father, Elias Powers, owns and runs it. That's why Heather sent me here without my credit cards or phone. He has the means to find me and drag me back home if he wanted to, so she wanted me somewhere safe where he couldn't get to me."

Well. Fuck. "I've heard of them." Who hadn't?

They owned the most exclusive resorts in every luxurious vacation destination. I'd stayed in them when Ava and I used to take a two-week vacation every summer to the Caribbean. Pretty sure we stayed in one of their private resorts in Fiji, too.

"Yeah, great mom, well, stepmom. Dad's not bad, just a bit absent, but he liked me. I think, looking back, it was because Lincoln was always kind of a black sheep. Partied his way through college, typical trust fund kid, you know? He'd gotten into some trouble for gambling and drugs and that kind of thing that was making it harder for Elias to bail him out of, but once we met, he settled down. Started working at the family company. Proved himself. For the first time, his dad was proud of him. Wanted us together."

"And if you break up with him, he's going to be embarrassed in front of his dad. If he did that to you over a waiter seeing him being rejected..." I let that trail off. Her fear was valid. What would he do to her if she embarrassed him in front of the one man he most wanted to impress?

"Yeah."

She closed her eyes and her head tipped down.

What a fucking mess.

I gave her a minute. Hell, I needed five of my own because this was some messed up shit she was dealing with. Some pretty powerful people included.

"I have one more question and then we're changing the topic before I start breaking shit with how pissed I am."

That earned me a soft, quiet laugh, but she raised her head. "What is it?"

"How are you doing? Truly, with all of this?"

"I don't know," she sighed and sipped her wine. "I think, well, I think I'd already started emotionally leaving him once I found him cheating, if that makes sense."

It did. Completely. Lord knows Ava emotionally detached from me months before she walked out the door. Couldn't blame her for that one, considering I was the dick who hadn't noticed until it was too late, though.

"So, I mean, I'm pissed. I'm mad that he cheated, that he fooled me for so long. I'm mostly pissed the asshole beat me, and I *never* would have imagined he'd have that kind of monster in him. And I'm sad, because we were supposed to be planning our wedding. I'd planned my life with this guy, saw forever, a family... and now, shit... everything I know has changed."

She brushed her fingertip over the gash at her eye and flinched as she cringed.

"Your body will heal," I said quietly. "And so will your heart. Even if it takes time, but no one gets to tell you how you heal or move on, you know? So do what you need to do and if that means healing here, like I said before, my house is yours."

"Thanks, Kane. You're much sweeter than Heather said you were."

I huffed, finished my water, and refilled my stainless-steel bottle. "You're full of shit. Heather thinks I'm awesome."

"Yeah," she said. "But she's wrong a lot, too."

Chuckling, I turned back to her. Color rose on her cheeks, and she quickly yanked her eyes up to meet mine.

From where they'd been on my ass.

She cleared her throat, sipped her wine while staring at my stove on the other side of the kitchen.

I gave her that play.

And then I turned away from her and readjusted my dick before she realized knowing she was checking me out was making me hard.

Shit.

SIX

KANE

"You're joking." Emmersyn gaped at me and then the card I was holding out in my hand. "I am not using that. And besides, Heather gave me hers, too."

"Yeah, but then she sent me cash for you, too. Buy whatever you want. Tomorrow, or whenever we can work it out, we'll go get you a phone, put you on my plan for as long as you need it."

I was certain there was more to the story she shared earlier. But I'd had hours to think about what she had said while I got ready to go to practice.

I meant every word I said to her. She was safe here. And she'd stay that way for as long as she wanted.

Which was why I'd already placed a massive order she'd probably kill me for, and that was before I tried to give her the card she was still staring at.

"You've lost your mind."

It was possible. I hadn't been this twisted up over anything in years. Not even when we lost in the playoffs last season.

"What did I say about offering shit if I didn't want to?"

"I am not going on a shopping spree and going on your phone plan, Kane. That's insane."

"Heather said you'd easily be able to pay her back for that money once she can get some cash out of your account for you. Until then, get what you need or want. You'll pay me back. And for the phone, it'd be the easiest way, wouldn't it?"

I was right. The way her lips pressed together and her nose scrunched proved she knew it, too.

My guess, she didn't want to rely on another man after one she trusted hurt her so badly.

But fuck it.

I tossed the credit card to the counter next to the laptop I brought out earlier for her to use.

"I need to leave for practice. Might as well find something to do with your time. Order some clothes, Emmersyn. Anything to help make you feel normal. FaceTime Heather from the app on the computer. If she has your wallet, she can pull out cash and mail it. Lincoln will probably assume you're there anyway, and you can pay me back then."

"That's a good idea," she finally said and slid the card closer to the computer. "All right. Thank you."

"You're welcome. And while you're shopping, buy some things to go out, not just lounge around here. My teammates like to get together quite a bit at the beginning of the season. I'll take you with if you want to go. Maybe you can meet some women to hang with while I'm on the road."

What the hell was I saying?

I couldn't take it back now. The very picture of Emmersyn in a summer dress, showing off her curves, made the suggestion ridiculous. Same with hanging out with my team.

Their wives.

Hell, they'd fall on Emmersyn and suck her into their crew faster than vultures fall on prey and then never remove their claws from her.

"That is, if you think you'll be here longer than a couple weeks. If you need to get back to work..."

"I don't." She shifted the laptop and pushed her lips to one side.

"No?"

"I do a lot of volunteer work."

She didn't have to work? I was missing something to this saga, and something big.

Too damn bad I'd pressed her enough today and didn't have the time now to ask why. "That's nothing to be embarrassed about, Emmersyn. There are a lot of women who choose not to work."

"I'm not embarrassed."

Sure she wasn't.

But whatever. Again. She wasn't my problem to fix or a puzzle to solve. She was someone to help. I needed someone to clobber me over the head with that, though, so I'd remember.

"I'd say call if you need anything while I'm out, but..."

"I'll be fine." She smiled. "And if we could get a phone tomorrow, that'd be good. I'm okay for today, though."

"Good. Right. I'll get going. Keys to the car are on the counter—"

"I won't take it. At least not today."

"Oh, just so you know, in case there are any deliveries or anything, the security guards at the gate have to call it in. They'll buzz here first before calling me, and that's by the front door where the security system is."

"Thanks for the heads up."

He scanned his living area and kitchen. "Anything else you need?"

Because I was now making this weird. I really needed to get going.

"I'm fine, Kane. Truly. You can leave and not worry about me. I'll probably take a nap, watch some TV, maybe go for a walk."

"I know. It's... well, it's been a while since I've left a woman in my home. Feels strange, I guess."

Understatement.

"I promise I won't burn it down."

Another smile. Goddamn, this woman. She had a healthy amount of sass in her for a woman who'd been through enough. Still, I laughed.

"Make sure you don't. Oh, and I was planning on ordering groceries tonight when I get back. If there's anything you need, feel free to head to the grocery store link and add your own. It's saved under my favorites. I'll finish it when I get back."

"Oh. That'd be great. Thanks."

"Yup. All right, I need to take off. But have a good day, okay? And if you do need anything, whoever is on duty at the security gate has my number. I'll stop by and let them know you're staying here for a while so you can come and go as you please."

"Go." She pointed toward the door. "I'll be fine. I *swear.*"

I threw my hands up and stepped back. "All right. All right. I'm gone. But promise... if you need anything..."

"I'm a big girl and can figure it out." Her tone was slightly petulant. A little bit bossy. A whole lot of funny.

I stuck out my tongue at her like a child and she laughed.

"You look just like your sister when you do that."

I'd turned and started walking away. Forgot who I was talking to for a second. Because my mouth opened and I blurted out, "Then I bet she looks like one damn sexy man."

Fuckkkk. No flirting, dipshit.

"I didn't mean it like that."

"I... uh... I know. I get the joke."

"Right," I muttered.

I needed to get out of here.

Maybe, yeah... no maybe about it. I definitely should have had sex at least at *some* point over the last three years. I probably wouldn't be having these reactions at all.

Now I had a sexy woman in my townhome and was acting like a massive idiot.

And why, why now, of all times and with all the women I'd come across, was *this* the woman my dick finally seemed to notice.

"Not cool," I muttered.

ALIX PLOPPED down on the seat next to me. Kicking his legs out, he wasn't anywhere close to being dressed for practice. His head fell back, arms crossed over his chest, and he let out a sigh that didn't say good things.

"You okay?" I turned from where I was bent over, lacing up my skates. "You got home late this morning."

His eyes were closed, but his lips kicked up into a grin. "Aww. Nice to know you were worried about me."

"Not worried." I'd usually call him though, make sure he was all right. Alix liked to party. Nothing wrong with that. He was still in his mid-twenties and had no interest in settling down anytime soon. Still, I liked knowing he wasn't lost in a ditch somewhere.

"What happened to you? You disappeared as soon as we all hit the floor, and you missed it, man. Bromann can *dance*. Had the girls eating out of the palm of his hand."

"Think it'll help?"

He shrugged, eyes still closed, face tipped up to the ceiling. "I guess we'll see today, although we might all be too hungover, so maybe tomorrow. Oh, and Joey said Gabby wants to have a party this weekend at their place. You in?"

Joey's parties were the best. Huge pool, indoor faux skating area we could mess around and practice in. It'd been years since I enjoyed my time at one, though.

Although, if I brought Emmersyn with one of those new swimsuits I'd ordered for her? Not that she knew about that—yet.

Not that I'd bought it with her full tits in mind, either.

"Yeah. I'll be there."

"Cool. So what happened? Why'd you take off?"

"Aww. Worried about me?" I parroted back to him.

I was done, ready to take the ice, like half the team around us, but there were still a few who hadn't arrived yet.

He turned and opened his eyes into slits. "Should I be?"

My brothers knew me well. Alix more than most.

"I'm good. Heather called. Needed help with a friend." I should probably introduce them. Wouldn't want Alix scaring her someday when she stepped outside or anything.

"And she called *you?*"

"Fuck off. Who should she have called? You?"

"If your sister needed my help, I would have her calling me God in minutes."

This jackass. I punched him in the shoulder so hard he almost fell off his chair. Once he righted himself, he laughed. Along with half the guys still standing around.

"Don't be a dick. It's my sister."

"And Garrett's sister is married to Joey." He grinned like a savage. "The team likes to share. Keep it in the family, yes?"

"If you weren't one of my best friends, you'd have two fewer teeth right now." I stood, did a few squats to stretch out, and shook my arms. "I haven't forgotten how you blew me off, either. Where were you until mid-morning?"

"The blondes." He grinned and kicked out his legs, settling one ankle over another. Looked like he was ready for a nap. "Fantastic. At least one of them. Couldn't get enough of her."

"Yeah. Stop right there. I've heard enough. Keep those stories to yourself, all right?"

"Will do. How'd you help Heather's friend? She got one in here in Vegas or something?"

"Nah." I scanned the room, debating how much to tell him. It wasn't my story after all and who knew how much Emmersyn wanted her problems shared around.

"She's got some trouble."

"How much trouble?" Dom interjected. He'd been near us,

tugging on his jersey and ignoring the general mayhem of the locker room.

He was alert now, though. His sister, Lucy, was just getting back on her feet after a traumatic past. One that Dom spent a night in jail for to save her from.

Knowing exactly where his thoughts would go, I lowered my voice and grabbed his shoulder. "Not that kind of trouble. She just needs a place to stay for a while. Figure things out."

"Good. That's good." He worked his jaw back and forth and shook out whatever was going on with him. Couldn't blame the guy, though. Not once he started opening up and telling his family story.

Ugliest, darkest shit I'd ever heard.

I shoved his shoulder and grinned. "Nice to know you care, though."

He was a notorious prick until Holly and her son skated into his life. He hated being reminded he was a good guy. Probably better than most of us really, considering his life.

"Fuck off."

He shoved me back, and I stumbled into Alix's feet, over them, and almost landed my ass on the floor before I slammed a hand into the locker.

"You dick."

Dom was smiling though. It was good to see it on him.

"You going to get ready?" I asked Alix and kicked his shoe with my foot.

"Yeah." He shoved to his feet and tore off his shirt. "It is time I embarrass all of you old men."

"It's like you're just looking to get your ass kicked," Joey said from his other side.

"That blonde," he muttered. "I cannot stop thinking of her."

"Get her number?" Joey asked and propped a shoulder on the locker.

"No." Alix scowled. "As soon as I mentioned I had practice

today, she kicked me out. Got all... weird? Is what you say? Wanted nothing to do with me."

I threw my head back and laughed. The poor fool looked so confused. "Not all women are bunnies."

"Shame." He kicked off his shorts and started pulling on his gear. "They are the fun ones."

Speaking of...

"No flirting with Emmersyn either, Alix. I mean it."

"Emmersyn?"

"Heather's friend. She's staying at my place until she can figure out her next steps." So I didn't upset Dominick again, I leaned in. "Her ex is a complete dick, in the worst ways. She's here to figure out what to do next and get away from him. Let her heal without you muddling her head."

"Muddling?"

"Confusing. I know how you are. Hell, you just talked about sharing my sister."

"I would be offended if you were not right." He grinned and slapped my chest. "Okay, okay. She is safe from me."

"Good." I grabbed my helmet.

"But is she safe from you?"

I scoffed and took off, but the question lingered.

I hadn't been with a woman since Ava left me. I hadn't even had the desire to get involved with another woman. That was how messed up I still was over her leaving, over the kind of husband I'd been.

But Emmersyn... I was attracted to her. For the first time in years, my dick was working just fine around the opposite sex, and that was a fucking bummer.

Heather would kill me if I screwed her friend or screwed her over.

SEVEN

EMMERSYN

I brushed sweat off my forehead and shook out my T-shirt. Sweat clung to me in all sorts of disgusting places.

The air was stifling. I was never walking outside again after nine in the morning while I stayed here.

It was still well over a hundred degrees and the morning's breeze was non-existent. My face probably looked like a dripping tomato as I neared Kane's front porch.

I needed another shower and dinner. And then what?

A full day with nothing to do might have been relaxing in my own apartment, but I was already going stir crazy. No friends to see, no one to talk to, and I had yet to find a single paperback in Kane's home, not that I'd looked too hard. But after hours of sitting around and re-watching my favorite Netflix show where Vikings try to conquer England, and doing some shopping as instructed, I had no sit left in me.

The walk didn't help. As soon as I stepped out, all the moisture in my body was vacuumed out from the dry heat.

Twenty minutes later and I was back at Kane's, attempting to nonchalantly wipe my face off with my shirt that was clinging to every inch of my body.

As soon as I dropped the shirt, my jaw went with it.

"Holy shit," I murmured as I took in the piles of boxes stacked on his front porch.

Boxes labeled *Calloway* and *Titleist* and a host of other boxes with Nordstrom and Saks Fifth Avenue labels were stacked in massive piles.

"He has to be kidding," I muttered and went to one of the larger boxes that was over four feet high. I shook it, felt the weight and dropped it like the cardboard had burned me. "Golf clubs?"

Holy shit. Kane—or Heather—bought me fucking golf clubs. This was insane.

There was another large box, big enough to be a golf bag. More boxes with some of the nicest golf brands on them. Had to be shoes. Clothes?

What in the hell had he done? And how did he do it so quickly?

I unlocked his front door and propped it open with my foot until I'd dragged one of the boxes into the doorway so it wouldn't close on me.

After dragging in the rest of the boxes, my sweat that had already been bad was out of control. Hair stuck to the back of my neck, my chest, and every time I tried to cool down, it made it worse.

I needed a shower. And then I'd deal with this mess.

At the first sight of me in the bathroom mirror, I flinched.

I wasn't a tomato, I was a freaking eggplant. Good grief. Sweat pooled beneath my breasts, creating sweaty little smiley faces and lined through the shirt where my rolls were. I didn't dare check out my back. It was probably equally soaked through.

This was why I should have only bought black clothing. The sweat stains I created when working out were embarrassing, even if I didn't normally mind my larger than stick thin sized body.

Hell, in my experience, men loved my curves. At least my breasts and my ass. Perhaps they didn't like my thick thighs or the rolls over the waistband of my clothing if they didn't fit perfectly, but few had complained.

Although, I should have swiped deodorant on my thighs given the chafing currently happening in the workout shorts I'd bought.

There was no way Kane decided he needed a brand-new set of clubs and golfing equipment on a whim today.

He bought it for me.

Which meant he and I would need to have a conversation on the limits of help I was comfortable with.

It was too much. Way too freaking much, even if I couldn't wait to check them out and play a round...

As soon as I wouldn't turn into a sweaty, oversized mess on the course.

THEY'RE YOURS. *I don't want to hear any shit about it either. Take 'em. Use 'em. Or return 'em and get what you like. And I texted Heather for your sizes. Hope everything fits.*

The man was possibly, certifiably insane.

I found the card taped to one of the Neiman Marcus boxes while I brought the smaller boxes up to the bedroom. I doubted it was his handwriting, but I memorized it before I opened a single package. Now, it was lost beneath the massive pile of clothes on the bed...

Shopping was my favorite hobby, but I'd never been able to do this much damage in a weekend, much less in the minuscule time Kane had to do all this.

I'd opened the golf clubs first. Even if I thought he went overboard, curiosity won out on that one. Not only were they Calloways, one of their top-of-the-line models, but he was maybe crazier than I thought. Return them? I salivated over those clubs the first time I tried them in a store. There wasn't just a bag, either. Golf balls, tees, ball markers. Visors and hats, three different pairs of shoes, towels, and club covers. There was even a cute necklace with a magnetic ball marker attached to it. An umbrella, which made me laugh considering we were in the desert. Every possible accessory I could ever use and some I probably never would were stacked on the floor next to the bed, and none of that included the clothes.

Pretty sure the call Kane made went something like, *"Yeah, I got a size 10 woman who loves to golf and swim and play tennis. I need four of everything in your store in her size. Yep. Every fucking item of clothing you have. Pants, skirts, shorts, long sleeves, sweats, short sleeves, tanks, sports bras, you name it I want it."*

Hopefully the workers were paid on commission. Kane probably made their yearly salary with a phone call.

It was way too much, in both generosity and amount.

I wouldn't wear all these clothes over the course of a year. At least he wouldn't be pissed if I returned some. Or most of them. Who in the hell needed sweatpants and sweatshirts in Vegas when it was still over a hundred degrees outside?

Not this girl.

On the other hand... the pile of clothes was tempting. Grabbing the first golf dress I saw, I riffled through the pile to find the matching shorts that went beneath with pockets and small slits for tees to slide into. Perfect for a golf course with a dress code, which I assumed his had, the dress had a flip collar, modest V-neck, and thick shoulder sleeves. It'd be perfect for playing tennis, too. Minty green in color, I figured it'd look good on me, so I tore off the tank top and shorts I'd climbed into after my shower and pulled on the dress. And...

"Holy crap," I whispered and hurried to the attached bathroom. It felt like silk on my skin, cool, and even though it was skintight, it didn't feel clingy or like it'd suction to me once I got hot in the sun. I tugged at it and swiveled back and forth in the mirror. "I could live in this thing."

So comfortable. Not sexy, but Spanx must have helped design

the line because it hid my side handles that usually rested right above my hips, sucked in my stomach, almost fully flattening it. I could still breathe, though. Move easily.

"Maybe I won't return any of these," I muttered and hurried back to the pile to dig through and find the rest of them.

Seven of them. One for every day of the week. All different colors.

"Oh yeah."

Too bad I didn't have a phone to send a picture to Heather. She'd roll her eyes and laugh, but a dress that was comfortable on me? Made me feel good, and didn't make me feel like I was having to hold my breath to hide my thick stomach?

Absolute perfection.

I was hanging all of them in the closet when a heavy thump echoed through the townhome, followed quickly by Kane's voice bellowing below.

"Emmersyn, you here? I got an annoying little pain in the ass on the phone for you!"

That could only mean Heather. "Coming!"

I left the rest of the clothes I hadn't put away yet on the bed. A pile of swimsuits. Dresses. Skirts. Shorts. The man didn't know my style, but he did good even if I wasn't entirely comfortable with keeping everything.

I'd pay him back, though, every cent, as soon as I could get it out of my joint account with Lincoln and move the rest of my finances to someone else other than Lincoln's dad's friend.

That was a conversation that was going to be lovely.

By the time I was downstairs, Kane had Heather on his laptop FaceTime, and her smile turned huge as I stepped into view behind him.

"Ooohhh... cute dress."

If it was just Heather and me, I'd do a little shimmy shake for her approval but considering Kane was gaping at me, mouth open and his dark brows high on his forehead, I didn't.

"Oh. Um. Thanks... both of you." I glanced at Kane. "Even if it was all a little over the top."

"It's all good." He smiled easily. "How was your day?"

"Relaxing." I brushed at the sides of my dress and leaned over the counter so I could see Heather better. "You shouldn't have helped him, you know."

"You'll pay me back. No worries." She flipped her hand in the air like the thousands of dollars meant nothing, although considering she made good money and Kane was probably loaded, too, it wasn't to them.

Kane turned, grabbed something out of the fridge and while his back was turned, Heather whispered, "Did you ask?"

I shook my head.

"Ask me what?"

Great. The man had supernatural hearing.

"Heather—" Damn it. I'd told her I needed more time. I didn't know this man. I glanced back at Kane. "Nothing. Nothing at all."

He returned to the counter, standing behind me and off to the side, and settled a hand on the countertop. "Liars. What is it?"

"There's another way you can help Emmersyn."

"Is there?" Oh... he knew Heather well. Suspicion was thick in his voice, tinged with humor. Almost like he'd been expecting another bomb to fall in his lap.

Heather nodded. I slammed my hand over the screen to block her face. Like that'd do anything, but it was all I had. "Nothing. Really. You've done enough and—"

"You can marry her!" Heather shouted and damn her.

Water flew straight from Kane's mouth all over the computer screen, the keyboard, and my dress. "Oh fuck. Sorry. So sorry." He grabbed a hand towel and handed one to me. I wiped up the water and caught Heather laughing her ass off at both of us.

"I thought I just heard my sister say we should get married."

"I did, silly!"

He glanced at me. My lip found its way between my teeth. I

had no idea what cringy look I was giving him, but his nose wrinkled.

"You're serious?" he asked me and faced Heather on the screen. "Are you high?"

"No. It's perfect." Heather grinned and then it flatlined. "He can't come after you if you're married to another man. His dad will explain it away. Lincoln will have to get over it. I mean, what's he going to do, hunt you down and steal you back? Please. The man fucks strippers for fuck's sake, he's not in the Mafia."

What a pleasant reminder. I hadn't even told Kane that embarrassing discovery. Finding out your fiancé not only cheated on you but also hired women for sex, sometimes only hours before you had sex with him, was enough to make me vomit.

Thank God I'd done the smart thing weeks ago and went to the doctor for an STI panel. All clean, thank goodness, but also humiliating.

"Right," I muttered and rolled my lips together.

"Shit. Sorry," Heather mumbled, and behind me, a warm hand pressed to my lower back.

Oh God. Kane was still there. Touching me now and breathing so close.

And right, he'd just learned my fiancé fucked strippers like some kids devour candy.

Kane, somehow, so much more stable than I was ever going to be again, settled a hand at my lower back. If he was trying to comfort me, he failed. The touch of his burned straight through my dress and I flinched.

His hand fell and he grabbed his water bottle. "Why?"

He glanced at me. Then Heather.

"I have a trust from my grandparents. A lot of money I inherited. But they were old-fashioned, and I can't access it until I'm at least twenty-five and married."

"You're fucking with me."

"No, and I'm sorry. I told Heather I needed more time to ask, because it's a lot. And it's weird, but without a marriage, I only get a stipend to live off. And it's enough, more than enough, but I want what they wanted me to have."

"It's easy," Heather chimed in, sitting back in her chair like she was relaxed as relaxed could be. If she was in the room, I'd throttle her. "You get married. Lincoln goes away. His dad will make him leave you alone and then once you get your trust access, you get a divorce."

"You're talking about a divorce like it's a trip to the nail salon," Kane said and there was grit in his voice now.

"I know, bro. I know. But not all marriages were like yours or ended like yours, either."

She bounced her gaze from him to me in the screen. "It'll be fine. You two can do this."

I shook my head. For a moment, it sounded great. Until that divorce word. Until reality crashed down.

Marry a stranger? There was no way I could ask this of him.

I pointed at Heather. "I think you've officially spent too much time in front of a steaming oven, Heather. I love you, but—"

"I'll do it."

The. Fuck?

"What?" I froze.

Heather's jaw hit the floor.

Kane faced me. "She's getting carried away with some of it. But I can see it working. If he really expects you to move home and still be with him, it's the fastest way to get him off your back."

A clapping sound echoed, and I turned to the noise to find Heather bouncing in her seat and clapping. "Yay! See Emmersyn!? I told you he'd say yes and now we can be sisters for real! Or for fake... or temporarily—"

Kane spun the phone so I couldn't see the screen and his finger hovered over the end call button.

"Night, sis," he said.

"Night brother and future sis!"

He hit a button and tossed the phone on the counter loud enough to rival a gunshot.

Well shit.

Now what?

EIGHT
KANE

I blamed the damn dress. The way it hugged her body and showed off her curves.

The excitement in her eyes as she thanked me for her things before she got on FaceTime with Heather and me.

I blamed my lack of sleep last night and a long fucking day and then I blamed Emmersyn for showing up at my place, looking beaten, and having curves for days. My hand still felt the warmth of her back from touching her earlier.

Mostly, I blamed my damn dick that hadn't cared to be used by anything else other than my hand for three long ass years for this catastrophe.

Get fucking married?

Again?

I didn't even want to *date* a woman again. Much less love her. Marry her.

That's not what this was, though. Love had nothing to do with this. This was about keeping Emmersyn safe and giving her a chance to be free from an epic asshole.

"Um. I know I've been in the room for this conversation and everything, and I'm not stupid, but well... explain to me what's happening here? And also, I would like to understand what kind of drugs you're on as well."

Good question. Maybe the trainers spiked my after-practice smoothie drink with something.

"I'm not on any drugs." My hands slammed to my hips, and I inhaled a deep breath.

Calm. I need to be calm. Regain some rationality.

The scent of her perfume or body soap infiltrated my senses, making me dizzy. Jesus. This was not helping one damn bit.

I scrubbed my hand through my hair, down my face.

"Tell me about the trust Heather mentioned."

Her face paled, and she bit her bottom lip. "It's nothing. Stupid. I'll figure something else out, but I can't ask you to do this. Not when—"

"Ava." Her name burned in my throat. "I know. I get it. Now tell me about the trust."

Her cheeks puffed out, giving me a very vivid image of what... *nope*. Not fucking going there right now.

"I'm given a decent amount every month, mostly it was for school and basic living, but I stupidly put that all in a joint account with Lincoln once we moved in together. I can't get access to the rest until I'm married. There are provisions for certain instances, like abuse, but fidelity? No... like I said, my grandfather was old-fashioned. And truthfully, I'm pretty sure my grandmother understood. She never minded, and I'm not entirely sure she was always faithful either based on some of her stories."

Who *was* this girl? Engaged to a hospitality mogul's son. Trust funds that sounded straight from the pre-American Revolution time period?

"Who were your grandparents?"

"Rocky Lorenz. My grandmother's name was Colette... but everyone called her Coco. They were my mother's parents."

My brows furrowed. *Oh... shit...*

She saw when it clicked and nodded. "Yeah. Coco Rock Music Productions."

"Holy fucking shit. They're..."

"Were." She flinched as she said it.

"Shit. I'm sorry."

"It's okay. It was five years ago. Airplane ride when I was twenty. Strangely enough, headed to their house on Martha's Vineyard."

"Why is that strange?"

She laughed then, almost bemused by my confusion. "Did it ever occur to you... or did Heather never say how she got her job?"

"No." I shoved my hands through my hair and sighed. Holy fucking balls. Her grandparents were legends. They helped produce some of the most famous musicians. "That house..."

She nodded. "Their business partner's son, Graham Rawlings, bought it. He's running most of the business now. Good guy, but since they had a music studio in that house, and it was always a beloved place for him, he was given the option to buy it. He wanted it more than I did, so it was the one thing he received in their will."

"And that money went to your trust."

"Some of it. But yes, outside the funds needed for the business, all of their personal holdings and investments and other estates went to me, as the only heir they liked."

Which meant she was *loaded*. Or would be.

As soon as she got married.

"Okay. Okay." Shit. This was way more complicated than Heather's original call of *"hey, I got a friend headed your way and needs some help."*

I'd do anything for my sister. Take in her friend while she healed and figured out a plan and buy her golf clubs included. But this?

Yet...

I had no reason to believe she wasn't being truthful. Which

meant my desire to always be here for my sister might have just taken a drastic turn, because her idea wasn't a *horrible* one... just a crazy one.

"You have to admit, Heather's idea makes sense in some ways. And bonus, if you do get married, you get to shove a big middle finger in Lincoln's direction."

She headed straight for the wine fridge. Bottles rattled as she searched for the one she wanted and yanked it out. The glass made a heavy thunk on the counter and she turned to grab a glass.

Fuck it.

If she was having wine, I needed a drink, too. Alcohol might've made some people make poor decisions, but at this rate, what else could I screw up? Seriously, what in the hell was I thinking?

I met her in the kitchen where she poured her glass of wine and grabbed a Stella Artois from my regular fridge. After I popped the top and took a healthy swig, I gave us both a moment to calm down and process.

"I know Heather's idea sounds absurd, and I know you've been going through a lot. Hell, my sister is crazy enough, she probably didn't think of the idea until we were already on the phone with her. But the reason I think it's a good idea is because, like she said, it keeps you on the offense. If we get married, we can come up with a story. Maybe you and Heather visited last spring during playoffs. She was here for several of my games."

"I know. She was probably more upset than your team when you guys lost." Emmersyn gave me a soft smile that told me she wasn't going too crazy with the idea.

Good. Progress.

"She definitely was. I had to listen to her rant about the way we played for days after that loss. I'm pretty sure if my team hired her, she'd help us make it all the way."

"At minimum she'd keep you well fed." Another soft smile tilted Emmersyn's lips, and she took a sip of wine before setting it down. "Okay, let's say I join you and your sister on this fun little trip on the Tilt-A-Whirl ride, and not only agree to this, but that you two are right—"

"We usually are."

She rolled her forest green-colored eyes and smirked. "Of course you are."

I shrugged. Not much to say.

"So, we come up with a story like you said. Heather and I visited last spring, and what... I couldn't stop thinking about you? I cheated on Lincoln with you? I... maybe Lincoln and I were having problems and I went back to Boston and realized that I had fallen madly in love with you in three days?"

When she put it that way, it did sound unbelievable. Also, if she said that she cheated on Lincoln, that would make her look bad and gain him sympathy. Not what I wanted to have happen.

"Okay, so we change the story. Trust me, with some of the crazy things my teammates have gone through over the last few months and years, our publicity team knows how to spin a story that is beneficial to us."

"Like what?"

"I mean... there was the incident where Joey woke up married to one of our teammate's sisters. And they only realized they were married because a TikTok went viral and was blasted all over social media before they woke up the next morning. And then there's Dominick, who landed his ass in jail last year on Christmas Eve..."

As I retold the stories in their most basic form, her brows rose in surprise.

"Heather never mentioned any of this to you?"

She was usually quick to defend us to anyone, and she'd called me for the inside scoop, a.k.a. truth, when both of these things happened so she could squash any rumors she heard.

"No." Emmersyn shook her head. "I think I'd remember those conversations."

I laughed and took a drink. "Okay, so the story needs work, but picture this for a moment."

I spread my hands in two outward circles, pretending to craft a scene for her.

"Okay..."

"Imagine... we go through with us. We get married and invite photographers and hell, even some lifestyle and sports reporters or sports bloggers to cover this huge affair. With me so far?"

"Yep." Her giant gulp of wine proved her words a lie, but I soldiered on.

"All right, so imagine, the next morning, Lincoln and his father wake up in Boston and their phones are pinging off the hook with Google alerts of your name, or his dad gets a call from somebody on his PR team about your wedding and your huge affair to a professional hockey player, who they would know you know because of Heather, right?"

"They know that I know you, yes. And okay, so I like the idea of shocking the hell out of Lincoln like he shocked the hell out of me the other night. But what does this do besides piss them both off, and outside of never having to deal with Lincoln again, like I was planning on anyway, what benefit does this give me?"

"It gives you a fresh start."

"In Vegas," she deadpanned. "And I gotta say, based on today's weather, I'm not really loving it."

She had a point. Was it foolish to uproot her entire life? Hell, I could hire some guys, get her moved out of her apartment with Lincoln, and get her away from him. But that didn't take care of her inheritance.

"It takes a while to adjust," I said, in regard to the heat. "But let me ask you this. If you were to get on a plane tomorrow, pack up your shit and move out of the apartment with Lincoln? Where would you go? And would he be angry enough to follow you?"

I glanced at the cut by her eye. Couldn't help it. Her finger followed and ran along the stitches there, making her cringe.

"What do you get out of this?"

"I get to help my sister's friend."

She gave me a dubious look and fingered her wineglass. "I know about Ava. How hard you took that divorce."

Yeah. Shit. I figured this would come up, and for the first time since I'd agreed to this, I faltered. I swallowed down a gulp of beer to wash away the thickness in my throat whenever her name came up.

Hell, my parents had called me a few weeks ago and quietly, and reluctantly, told me they received her wedding invitation taking place in November. I'd already known about the wedding, but hearing my parents were invited was a stab to the gut I hadn't expected, even if I knew they'd stayed friends with Ava's parents.

She was doing it. Getting remarried. Moving on from me permanently.

"I promised myself after Ava left me I would never get married again. And you have to know that if we were to do this, I can make you two promises. The first is that as soon as you want out, we'll do it. We can live separate lives for this, you can stay here, or you can move out. I'm sure that we'll have to be seen together to make it look legit, at least for as long as Lincoln and his dad don't believe it or whatever. But as soon as you feel safe enough and you want your own life, then we'll sign the papers, we'll hug it out and we'll go our separate ways."

I had no idea how it was possible I was talking about marriage and divorce so easily. I reminded myself again that this had nothing to do with my life, or a lifetime commitment to someone. This was a short-term commitment for completely different reasons.

"Okay…" Emmersyn said. "What's your second promise?"

This one was easy. Still, my grip on my beer tightened. I made sure to look her in the eye, forced myself to not get lost in those huge swirls of green or examine any areas of her I was finding myself attracted to.

This was carnal attraction.

Nothing more.

"I will never love you. Ever."

Her eyes widened and she blinked away the surprise. "I'm not asking you to love me. I don't even want that. Hell, I'm still not even sure this is a good idea."

"I know. But if you do stay here, things could get... tricky... maybe. Maybe not, who knows. But being totally upfront with you, I'll keep my hands to myself. I'll take care of you in any way you need help getting a new life set up. Hell, I could even become a friend to you like Heather is. But love? I will never fall again."

Understanding registered. Must have been the grit in my voice. "You still love Ava."

"She's the only woman I'll ever love."

"Wow. That's..."

"It is what it is." I shrugged and acted like it was no big deal when I'd just bared myself more to an almost stranger, and maybe future wife, than I had anyone since the day I came home to a four thousand square foot home devoid of everything Ava. It was so empty, I knew she was gone the moment I opened the front door.

She didn't just leave me, she sucked the personality out of my home, the excitement and comfort I'd always found near her. Leaving turned our home into a shell of stucco and red tile shingles and my heart equally emptied.

"What would your teammates say?"

"They're my brothers. They'll go along with whatever they need to."

Her fingers thrummed on the counter. "Okay. And what about your parents?"

NINE
EMMERSYN

Chuck and Tracy Andrews were two of the best people I've ever had the privilege of meeting. I spent more time in their house and with them since I'd seen my parents when I was a teenager. The last few years before college, I'd moved in with my grandparents once both my parents took off. The last thing I ever wanted to do was lie to the Andrews when they'd treated me like a daughter from the moment Heather introduced me to them.

"We'll tell them what they need to know. Whatever you feel comfortable telling them is what they'll learn."

The very idea of telling Tracy and Chuck what happened between Lincoln and me made my stomach roll. Chuck could lose his mind if he knew that Lincoln laid a hand on me in any way, shape, or form. And since the Andrews were from the New England area, I could only imagine how much all of their friends have been looking forward to the invite to my wedding. It was supposed to be held in the ballroom of the Regal's flagship hotel in downtown Boston. The place where celebrities stayed, and presidents and foreign dignitaries. One night there cost over a thousand dollars alone with beds covered in the silkiest sheets imaginable.

My own parents, on the other hand, they didn't even know I was engaged.

"What about you and your family?"

Odd how easily he read my mind. I sipped my wine and set down the empty glass. "I haven't had anything to do with either of my parents since before I went to college."

Kane tilted his head and chewed his bottom lip. Probably shouldn't have made flutters erupt in my stomach. I grabbed the bottle of wine and refilled my glass.

"Do I need to know why?"

I smirked at him. "I mean, I guess if we're going to be married, you should probably know about my family, right?"

His answer was a chuckle and sip of his beer. For a moment I was distracted by the bob of his throat as he swallowed, the corded muscles along the side as he worked his jaw. It should be a criminal activity to be so goddamn attractive all the time.

"Cute." He tilted his chin. I took it as a gesture for me to spill all my dirty little secrets.

I dragged my finger down the stem of my wineglass. "My parents got divorced when I was twelve. Dad moved in with the woman he cheated on my mom with, and six months later, they had a baby, and he had a new family to start over with." A son, too. I used to wonder if that was why he had an affair. My mom didn't want more kids and he'd always wanted a boy. "I got a few birthday cards after he left, but they were always in a woman's handwriting. When I was sixteen, I ripped it up and mailed it back to her. Haven't heard from him since."

"Jesus. "

"It gets worse." I waited a beat for that to register with Kane and continued. "Mom, always willing to follow in my father's footsteps, remarried a man when I was fifteen. My grandparents, her parents, despised him. Said he was only after their money and if she married him, she would never see a cent. She apparently, and from what I heard from her, figured they were bluffing. She moved in with him and his two kids from a previous marriage, and she decided she was going to start a whole new family too. I haven't talked to her since I was twenty. She calls maybe once a year to see how I'm doing, but at this point, they're both strangers."

I didn't often speak of my family, why would I want to? What woman wanted to admit that she was so unlovable, both of her parents abandoned her for newer and better families. Better children.

A familiar lump lodged in my throat and I cleared it. I glanced out Kane's living room windows for a moment to clear my head except my thoughts were too loud. Too vibrant.

"Probably shouldn't be all that surprising," I said more to myself than him. "That I ended up finding a guy exactly like my dad."

Kane called my name on a whisper, but I shook my head. I didn't need to see pity and sadness in his eyes. They'd looked too much like Heather's the first time I told her, when she asked why I never went home for holiday breaks. I had to look my best friend in the eye, who came from such a perfect, loving, accepting, and beautiful family, and tell her *where would I go? I have no home.*

"I need a minute."

Kane called my name again, but I was already around the corner of the hall and up the stairs to my room. There, I went straight to the bathroom and flipped on the water faucet handles. Splashing my face with cold water didn't help soothe or minimize the rush of emotion rushing to the surface.

What horrible, selfish people would so easily abandon their daughter? And it wasn't like we came from some kind of stereotypical family you'd think of when you heard a story like that. My parents weren't alcoholics or drug addicts. They didn't gamble away their savings or live in some rundown, falling apart shack in the middle of nowhere. My mom was the daughter of some of the most famous music production company owners. She'd had everything she always wanted. Grew up with extreme privilege. My dad had always had to work for everything he wanted until they got married, but even then, he worked in pharmaceutical sales until he was vice president of the company.

And yet somehow, all of that meant nothing when it came to their ability to love me. Tears mixed with water and I kept rinsing and scrubbing my face to wash it all away.

Suddenly, the dress I'd been so comfortable in restricted my chest, made it difficult to breathe. I struggled out of it, twisting and turning to get the clingy fabric off my body, over my thick hips and jiggly ass and my oversized, ugly breasts.

I flung it to the floor and then I was left with only me, my reflection, and a thousand thoughts I'd worked so hard over the years to silence.

Too fat.

Too loud.

Too unworthy.

Too chunky with my cellulite and stretch marks.

Too stupid.

Too ugly.

That was probably why Lincoln fucked women on the side. He might have wanted me, but now I knew he played me. He found a woman he could marry who would probably help his family look even better. Hell, it was highly probable at this point he was only with me *for* my inheritance.

I'd seen some of the sexts he'd received. The way those women looked. He could probably bend them in all manner of positions he'd never want to see me in.

"Fuck," I chanted on repeat. I pressed my hands to my face, found my cheeks and face still wet from water and tears and grabbed a towel.

"Get control of yourself. You're not that. You're not."

Perhaps I was. Perhaps denying the truth hadn't brought me many favors. I flung the hand towel to the counter and went to my room. Enough with the stupid pep talks and self-examination.

Digging through the pile of clothes Kane bought, I heaved them all off the bed. Too tight. Too fitted. He'd seen and heard enough of my ugly past. He didn't need to be forced to see the body that went with it too.

In the closet where I'd hung the clothes Heather bought me, I tugged on an oversized T-shirt and grabbed a pair of pajama pants.

A hair tie sat on the dresser, and I pulled my hair up and off my neck.

I'd go downstairs.

Say good night and tell Kane there was no way I'd force someone as perfect as him to marry a mess like me.

I'd figure it out on my own.

And tomorrow, when I woke... I'd start doing it.

Find a job.

A new place to live.

I'd get my money out of our account, call an attorney and reach out to the executor of my grandparents' trust to see if anything could be done, and then I'd move on.

I'd move on alone.

After all, I was used to it.

I HAD no idea how much time passed while I was in my room, but once I was settled, my decision to start getting my shit together tomorrow worked out in my head, and I knew I wouldn't start crying at the drop of a hat again, I returned to the kitchen.

Kane was sitting at the bar, head bent to his phone and what must have been a fresh beer next to him.

As soon as I entered, he set down his phone and lifted his head.

"You okay?"

"Fine. Yeah."

I was anything but, and based on the tightening in his jaw, the way he worked it side to side, he knew.

"That why you been crying?"

My feet froze to his wood floor, and my hand stalled almost to my wineglass. "What?"

"Your eyes are red, and I'm not an idiot."

No, he definitely wasn't. I grabbed my wineglass and took a sip. It was warm, making me flinch as it slid down my throat. "Emotional overload. I think it's allowed after the week I had, isn't it?"

"Of course it is. Doesn't mean I like being the guy who caused it."

"You weren't." It was my family and my own failings that threw me into a tailspin. I shook my head. Tomorrow. I'd deal with it tomorrow.

I dumped out my wine and refilled my glass. At a minimum, I'd need a job to pay for all the wine of his I was drinking. The thought made me smile as I brought the glass to my lips. "Can we not talk about this anymore? I'm exhausted and—"

"*Intruder Alert! Intruder Alert!*"

An alarm blasted, followed by a loud screech.

I jumped, wine sloshed over the edge of the glass and over my fingers.

Kane laughed and stood. "It's all right. It's Alix. I have the code set to go off whenever he comes over uninvited." He turned toward the entryway. "Which is way too damn often!"

A blond man, tall, lean and probably chiseled on every inch of his muscles appeared in the doorway. Wearing a forest green polo shirt, collar popped, and most likely professionally pressed khaki shorts, he sauntered into the room like he owned the place and went straight to the fridge. "You never call. You never write or invite me. I missed you."

His accent was light, but noticeable.

And I was standing there, in the ugliest and loosest clothes I owned while these two species of male perfection laughed.

"I saw you two hours ago, asshole." Kane shoved the man out of the way and slammed the fridge door shut.

Fortunately, the man had good reflexes because his hand slid out of the fridge, fresh beer in his fist, right before the door slammed. "I cannot play if you break my hand."

"You can't play if I break your face, either. What are you doing here?"

He turned to me then. Smiled. A smile that could easily turn women's brains into scrambled eggs. "I wanted to see our new roommate."

Our?

I looked to Kane.

He sighed. Heavily. Annoyed but playful. "Alix, this is Emmersyn. Emmersyn, this is my teammate and former best friend, Alix Halvrick."

"You are beautiful," Alix said, his eyes scanning my body.

My own narrowed. Liar. At least, not in what I was wearing now.

He swung his head toward Kane. "And before you hit me, you told me I couldn't flirt with her. You did not say I couldn't be honest."

Kane sighed and shook his head like he was giving up.

For a moment, that little flutter of confidence I usually wore returned. *Beautiful.*

Just not lovable.

Shit.

"Nice to meet you." I held out my hand, expecting Alix to shake it. Instead, he brought my fingers to his lips and kissed them.

"You too, beautiful."

"Alix—" Kane said lowly.

"All right. All right. So. What are we doing for dinner tonight?"

He grinned at Kane. Then me.

I'd totally forgotten I hadn't eaten dinner.

"I ordered a boatload of Chinese," he said to Alix and turned to me. "While you were upstairs."

My stomach rumbled at the thought. Who didn't love Chinese? "Any chance you ordered pot stickers?"

He grinned. "Texted Heather and asked for your favorites."

That flutter in my stomach grew warm and stretched. "Thank you."

"Great," Alix declared and helped himself to the couch in the living room, throwing his feet up on the coffee table, crossing his ankles like he lived here.

I stared at him, then Kane groaned. "You're not invited, Alix."

"He can stay," I said quietly. If anything, he'd keep Kane and me from revisiting conversations best left alone.

"You sure?"

"I'm sure."

He looked doubtful, turned to Alix. "He's harmless, I promise."

"He seems fun."

"Stop talking about me like I cannot hear you. I am Swiss, not stupid."

"Huh." Kane brought his beer to his mouth. I yanked my eyes off those full lips. "Thought they were the same thing."

Something was going on with Emmersyn.

I didn't even know the woman, and I knew she wasn't acting right. Granted, two nights ago had been tough. From what Heather suggested to the talking about her family after. How she compared her dad to her ex had pissed me off. Made me want to throw her in front of a mirror and have her catalog every beautiful and lovable thing about herself.

She shut down once she returned. I felt it. Wall slammed firmly in place, she had no interest in discussing anything further. It went against every inch of my instinctual nature.

See a problem, solve it.

I lived for that shit.

Yet even before Alix showed up, I knew it wouldn't happen. And after Alix arrived, he helped lighten the mood somewhat. Chinese food was delivered. We all had a couple more drinks, and then we laughed at Alix choosing eighties movies on Netflix to watch because he said they were his favorite look at America before he came here.

Like red Solo cup keg parties in front of a booming bonfire and rusted out pickup trucks were every American's typical high school experience.

Eventually, Emmersyn had yawned, excused herself to bed. Alix went home shortly after, leaving me to clean up, which I did and went to bed myself.

There was no light shining beneath the door to her room, and once I entered mine, I did something I never did.

I kept my door open, left a pair of shorts at the corner of the bed in case she screamed or had another nightmare.

Neither happened, and when I woke up at nine the next morning, the house was quiet and I thankfully, didn't have a headache from the few beers. We went about our day barely talking and another night went by with no nightmares.

But this morning, she was still quiet. Had no interest in anything and it ticked me off when I sat down across from her and asked, "Did your clothes not fit?"

We hadn't even really talked about that much and yesterday she'd been wearing the clothes she brought with her.

"They fit fine."

Fine. It was the female's version of shut the fuck up and I don't want to talk about it, mixed into one simple word.

I dropped it, ate my breakfast, and got in a quick workout before an early practice.

Before I left, I turned to her, still staring at the computer. "Have you given any more thought—"

"No." Her head lifted quickly, the answer quick and sharp.

"No to the marriage or no to thinking about it?"

Why I was pushing so damn hard for it was anyone's guess. I didn't even *want* to be married again, much less to a woman I didn't know.

"Can we talk about it later?" she asked, and her voice was so soft, so sad, I let it go.

I could give her that. "Sure. I have the weekend off, you know. Want to go golfing or explore Vegas or anything?"

At least that could get her mind off everything. If she was anything like Heather, Emmersyn would probably start getting bored out of her mind if I didn't get her out of here for a bit.

Finally, a genuine smile lit her face. I ignored the squeeze in my chest. "That'd be fun. At least the golfing. I'm not really a huge fan of casinos or anything."

"Cool. I'll call and get us a tee time for tomorrow morning. Early, before it gets too hot."

"Perfect."

"And I know Joey and his wife Gabby planned on having people over to their house for a pool party. Would you be interested?"

I usually went and didn't stay long.

"You don't have to entertain me, you know."

Yeah, but it'd probably be more fun if she was there. And hell, maybe she'd make some friends. Meet the women, so she had other people to hang out with when I wasn't home. Many of the wives hung out all the time.

"Got other exciting things planned?" I teased. Hell, maybe there were other things she wanted to do I hadn't thought of. Or maybe she didn't like large groups of people.

"No." She laughed. "But you don't have to babysit me."

"No babysitting involved. You walk into that home and the women will swoop you up and I won't see you the rest of the time. They're good people."

"All right. A pool party?"

And did it make me an ass I instantly imagined her in one of the swimsuits I bought for her? She hadn't worn them yet, at least, not when I'd been home, but the color on her cheeks told me she'd spent some time outside.

Just the thought of what she'd look like, in one of those bikinis, made my body tighten.

"Good. I'll see you after practice then?"

"Yeah, and if it's okay, do you mind if I cook dinner?"

I loved to cook, although I hadn't done much of it this week. But my fridge was stocked with my grocery delivery, a whole bunch of items I didn't use so I knew she'd added her own things the other day when I suggested it.

"Cool. Anything else you need?"

"If I do, I can figure it out."

"THANKS AGAIN FOR DRIVING," I told Alix when we reached our doors.

I'd taken to riding with him to practice so Emmersyn had her choice of cars to drive. Not that I could tell if she'd used any of them yet, but today the golf cart was slightly crooked and her clubs were strapped in next to mine at the back, so I could tell she'd at least hit the driving range.

"You know it is not a big deal. I'll see you tomorrow?"

"Emmersyn and I have a tee time at seven. Assuming we're not too tired, we'll be at Joey's later."

They were having people over until five, so I figured we'd make it.

"Want to ride with us?"

"No. I am good on my own. Might head back to Piazza Romano."

"No luck finding the girl yet?"

"None. Went to her hotel. She checked out. They would not give me her name. Can you believe that?"

I couldn't believe Alix, king of one-night stands and short-term sex binges, was hung up on someone he met at a club. "It's called personal security and privacy."

"I know. I know. But..." He shoved his hand through his blond hair and groaned. "I cannot get her out of my head. Stupid, yes?"

Stupid is as stupid does in that case. My eyes wandered to my door. Where behind it, Emmersyn was cooking us dinner. Living in my space. Making it smell like flowers and girly shit all over the place. The amount of headspace I'd given her in the last few days was embarrassing.

But not, either, because I liked it all.

"Awww..." I shoved Alix into the wall. "My little boy is growing up."

He cursed at me in French. Or German. Wasn't sure which language, but Alix was fluent in several, so it could have been anything.

We said goodbye, and I opened the door to my home, immediately hit with a warm atmosphere that stole my breath.

Soft music played. Candles had to be lit due to the soft scent. More than that, were the sounds of cooking. Pots and pans. Bowl being scraped. Something clattering to my kitchen counter.

Everything Ava would have done years ago. Made a mess while cooking and always, always she had to be listening to music. And what was it with women and candles? I didn't have any at all, threw them all out after Ava walked out.

Shit.

Emmersyn wasn't Ava. She wasn't trying to seduce me in that soft, gentle way Ava had. She was cooking us a meal.

Probably because she felt the constant need to thank me.

And I'd pushed her about marrying me.

The thought flung me back to the present, and I released my breath, shaking it off.

This wasn't a woman in love with me, taking care of me.

My sister's friend was doing something nice. Maybe something she enjoyed in her own right. Still, that didn't stop the vision I had as I dropped my keys and stepped out of my shoes from ripening.

Us, together in the kitchen. Emmersyn in an apron and nothing but. My boxers tugged down past my hips while I had her bent over the counter. Her ass jiggling as I splayed one hand at the center of her spine, holding her down. My other hand at her hip, fucking her… no… she was rearing back into me. Taking what she wanted. Using my cock as her personal pleasure toy.

"Fuck," I groaned and adjusted myself. Wherever that thought came from it needed to take a hike in the desert and never return.

"Hello?" Emmersyn called out.

"It's just me!" I blinked away the remains of that vision, willed my dick to soften and headed toward the kitchen.

My steps stalled again, this time for a completely different reason.

She was fucking beautiful. Her dark, thick hair was in some complicated-looking braid thing, draped over one shoulder. She had makeup on, something I hadn't seen yet. And on her body? A new fucking dress. Not athletic in the least. It was soft and flowy, hitting her at mid-thigh. The V-neck deep enough to give me a glimpse of *all* that cleavage. At her shoulders, there were ruffles that bounced as she turned and smiled at me, a glass of clear liquid and ice in her hand, and I was pretty sure there was a lime in there, too.

"You found the tonic." My voice sounded rough. Almost pissed. Even to me.

Emmersyn glanced down at her glass, back to me. A tiny worry line tugged her brows inward. "Yeah… that okay?"

Of course it was. I'd told her to order anything she wanted but I hadn't expected to almost be knocked on my ass at the sight of her, and I couldn't exactly say, "*hey nice tits, wanna fuck?*" now, could I?

"Of course. Sorry. I…" I shook my head. I was being an animal. "Long day. Smells good in here."

"Thanks. You hungry?"

Yes. *Yes,* I was fucking hungry. Starving. And dinner was the last thing on my mind.

"Yeah." I cleared my throat and ripped my gaze off the buttery yellow dress that showed off her glorious curves and managed to look sexy and innocent at the same time.

Holy hot damn fucking shit. I needed to rethink that idea of marrying her, immediately.

"Good, it's almost ready. Nothing special, a chicken and spinach bake I found one day. One of the first meals I really learned to cook." Her nose wrinkled as she babbled, "I'm not that great at it, though, I mean, cooking in general, but this meal is good."

"I'm starving. But is there time for me to grab a quick shower?" I showered after practice. Should have slipped into the ice bath, although even that now would have been wasted.

"Sure." She blinked, and I swore a color rose on her cheeks. Probably from the wine, not my asshole self standing there, gaping at her. "It's warming in the oven. Want anything to drink?"

"Water would be great."

I'd had enough to drink this week. Would probably have a few tomorrow, on the course and at Joey's. Tonight I should probably keep my head clear, not to mention with the season starting, I needed to cut back anyway.

I made quick work of hurrying upstairs to my room. Glanced at my closed bedroom door.

Ground my teeth together.

That fucking dress.

That smile.

Why in the fuck did the first woman who turned me on in three years have to be my sister's best friend? A woman just getting out of what sounded like a seriously fucked up relationship.

But... fuck it.

There was no way I could go downstairs, not with my pulse racing. My dick so goddamn hard it could split the seam of my athletic shorts.

"Fuck," I groaned again and shoved off my boxers. Flipping on the water, I didn't even wait for it to warm before stepping into the icy cold spray.

Needles hit my skin, and I flinched from it, but still... nothing helped my erection, standing proud, long, and so damn hard it almost hurt when I wrapped my hand around it.

"Shit," I gasped as I ran my hand up and down my length. I worked myself fast and quick, the sudden desire to paint Emmersyn's breasts with cum whipping through me. The way I wanted to bite that area of soft flesh right above her hips. I wanted my dick sliding in between her tits, and I wanted those thighs straddling my shoulders as she sat on my face.

I allowed myself the moment of those visions pummeling me, making me throb, making my chest seize with a want I hadn't had in *years*, well before Ava walked out on me, and when I came, I ground down on my teeth and braced my free hand on the shower wall so Emmersyn didn't hear me grunting out her name from a floor away.

What in the hell had I gotten myself into?

I should have been over my physical attraction to Kane years ago. I mean, Heather had his picture up all over her place. Both in college and afterward. She spent hours forcing me to watch his games, to which, admittedly, I never understood. Throw me in front of a football game or baseball game and I got it. Could pick a team and cheer with the best of them. Hockey? It all moved so fast. Which meant I usually ended up spending my time reading books and drinking wine while she screamed at the TV, occasionally slapping my thigh and shouting, "Did you see that?" Either while she was pissed off at a ref, another player on a different team, or thought her brother had done something awesome.

So yeah. *Years.* Seven long years where it was normal for Heather to gush about how awesome her brother was, talk to him on the phone with me in the background, listening to his gravelly laughter through the speakerphone.

And when he got divorced? When Ava left him? I thought Heather was going to burn the world down, she was so mad until Kane told her it was okay. It was his fault. Ava did nothing wrong except want to be happy.

That was Kane Andrews. Even when his wife left him, he thought of her first.

But if my libido could seriously catch up to the fact that this guy didn't want me, wouldn't want me, and was only doing me a favor, it'd really help me out.

Needless to say, as soon as he left the kitchen earlier, I'd considered following him, dipping into my room and doing a little bit of self-love when he couldn't hear me so I could take care of the pulsing at the tops of my thighs whenever he walked into my vicinity.

Kane Andrews was one of the sexiest men I'd ever seen. One of the nicest guys I'd ever met.

Even Lincoln, on days when I thought he was handsome and good-looking and so damn nice and kind-hearted, never held a flame to Kane.

Probably due to the difference between the two. Lincoln acted like a good guy. Had spent his lifetime perfecting the mask he'd so quickly discarded along with me and probably the prostitute after he paid her.

Kane just was a good guy. Down to his core.

And I was the idiot who was now staying here, with nothing else to do with my life except hang out and cook a mediocre meal for him.

The dishes were done.

I'd switch from my gin and tonic to a glass of red wine after dinner, and I had my feet tucked up on the couch next to me, blanket I found in the guest room draped over my lap when Kane came into the living room after, insisting I sit down and he'd clean up the kitchen.

Which was now spotless. The faint scent of lemon-scented cleaning supplies in the air.

His phone rang and he looked up at me. "It's Heather. Again."

Probably wondering if we'd set a wedding date yet. "Great," I muttered, and rolled my eyes.

He caught it, chuckled, and said, "Prepare yourself."

Heather's blurry face cleared on the screen and Kane moved the phone so we could both see her.

"What's up, chica?" Perhaps if I pretended she hadn't thrown me out to sea the other night, she'd forget as well.

She clasped her hands together and laughed. "So... when's the wedding?"

Or maybe not.

Kane leaned in. His cheek brushed my shoulder, and I inhaled the crisp scent of his body wash. Clean, fresh.

All man. Goose bumps burst on my arms and I crossed them over my stomach so he didn't see.

"If this is the only reason why you called, I'm hanging up."

"No you won't. You love me too much."

"Not that much." Kane scowled, his face on the screen so close to mine, and lifted his finger.

"No! Don't. Okay, okay, I won't be crazy. I promise."

"You can do that?" I asked and stuck out my tongue.

She hmphed and threw herself back into her chair, returning the look. "Of course. And I actually didn't call you tonight to tease you."

Kane's brows rose. "No? I'm shocked."

"Shut up. I'm serious." As her tone changed, a chill slid down my spine. "I turned your phone on again today to see if that asshole called again and he has. And he's not mad, Emmersyn. He's *big* mad. Like, I'm glad you're halfway across the country or I'd be super terrified for you."

The phone was torn out of my hand and in front of Kane. I had to lean in far to see her face, but the fury in Kane's tone was unmistakable.

"What do you mean? What's he saying?"

Another shiver, this one warmer took place of the chill.

"It's not so much what he's saying, but how he's saying it. Mostly he keeps saying you've thrown your tantrum and you need to get over it, get back home. There's some gala or charity event you're supposed to be going to next week—"

"Oh shit. I totally forgot about it. No wonder he's pissed."

"What's it for?" Kane asked.

"Fundraiser for Doctors Without Borders organization. It's mostly for the governor to start gearing up for his campaign next year but it's being held at their flagship hotel." My chin trembled and my stomach rolled. "This will make Lincoln pissed if I'm not there with him. Totally embarrass him."

"When is it?"

I looked at Kane. "Next Saturday."

"It'll be okay, sweetie," Heather said through the phone. She was chewing her bottom lip, which grabbed my attention.

She never hesitated. "What is it?"

"*His* mom called."

"Irena?" She had always been kind to me. A former supermodel from Germany, she wasn't Lincoln's birth mom, but she was the only mother figure in his life since he was ten. His mom died in a car accident when he was three. She welcomed me into their family from the first time we met, and unlike his dad, who I knew saw my familial connections and approved, she simply liked *me*.

"Yeah, her message said Lincoln called her. She wants to talk to you."

She might not have been Lincoln's birth mom, but they'd never had their own kids, either by choice or complications. I never thought it kind to ask, but she always loved Lincoln like her own. She was fiercely protective, although frustrated when he went through hard times. I figured this was one of those hard times. But whether she'd call me to talk me into going back or would even listen to why I left, was something I didn't know.

Wasn't sure I was willing to risk that conversation either.

"Great. I don't know what to do with that."

She smiled shakily. "That's what I figured you'd say. That choice is yours though, you know?" A buzzing sounded in the background, like an old oven timer. She glanced right and frowned. "Hold on a sec. Security is buzzing me."

She stood and hurried to her security panel. She could probably fly to Mars with as high tech as the security at her guest house was. And that didn't compare to the main house's either.

I'd spent so many summers at the house growing up and staying with my grandparents, back when I thought my life was perfect, I shouldn't have still been blown away by the security they had. Of course, when Graham bought the house from me, he'd also added additional security.

She pressed a green button on the flat screen and instantly, the guard's face was shining on it. "Hi Steve. How can I help you?"

The guard, with a graying mustache, hat tugged down low, glanced to the left and his blue eyes came back to the screen. "Hi Miss Andrews. I have a Mr. Lincoln Powers at the gate for you."

"What?" I gasped.

Next to me, a hand settled at my back, startling me. I glanced up to find Kane, peering at the screen intently. If he realized he was touching me when our eyes met, he didn't show it.

Heather turned to us and muttered, "Looks like you were right about that phone tracking thing."

"Or he knows I'd run to you."

"Shh." She pressed her finger to her lips and turned back to the screen.

"Hi Steve. Can you please tell Mr. Powers to leave and if he ever tries to step foot on this property again, I'll fill his ass with buckshot?"

"God, she's psychotic," Kane mumbled. "Since when do you have Dad's shotgun?"

She winked at us and whispered with a smile. "He doesn't know I don't."

I shook my head. "So much for not acting crazy."

"Let me talk to her!" Lincoln's voice screamed through the speakers and a bucket of cold water couldn't have chilled me more.

I couldn't see him, but he must have been close to the guard's station because his voice was loud and clear.

"It's okay, Steve," Heather said. "I wouldn't mind hearing what Lincoln here has to say."

"You sure?" he asked, and he took off his hat, revealing a shiny bald head before he swiped his forehead and settled it back on.

"I'm sure," she called out louder. "Hi Lincoln. How can I help you?"

"Let me in, you fucking cunt. I know Emmersyn's in there and she and I need to talk."

Heather's smile turned feral. "Well, hello pencil dick. I have no idea what you're talking about. You and Emmersyn are having problems?"

"Fuck you. Where is she?"

Somehow, Heather's voice took on a southern belle accent straight out of *Gone with the Wind*. "Well, I just don't know what you're talkin' 'bout, darlin', but I suggest you turn that fancy car of yours around and head back to where you belong."

Next to me, Kane chuckled. "She's fucking crazy."

"I'm not sure making him madder is the way to go," I mumbled, and my thumb found its way to my teeth. I nibbled on it, a nervous habit I could never quite kick, but listening to Lincoln's voice, so damn angry, not the same patient man I used to know, burned through me.

How could I have been stupid for so long? So blind?

Kane's hand on my back tensed, like he knew my train of thoughts.

"You know, Heather. I've always thought you were a whore. A beautiful one, but a whore nonetheless. When Emmersyn stops throwing a fucking tantrum, I'm going to make sure she never sees you again..."

"Oh..." Heather said, voice now normal. "Does this mean you'll pay me to fuck you, too? I hear you like worn out, used pussy."

Poor Steve. The security guard's face blanched as Heather and Lincoln volleyed back and forth.

"Asshole," Kane rasped. "If he calls her a whore again, I might lose my shit."

"Fuck you." Came through the line loud and clear right before Heather laughed.

Loudly.

"Hey pencil dick. I know you think you're such a hot shit and all, but I should tell you something."

"What?"

"I have Emmersyn on speaker on FaceTime and she's heard every lovely, beautiful word you've just said to me." She smiled at me, made me think she might actually make good on her eunuch threat. "Say hello, Emmersyn sweetie."

Before I could, Lincoln's voice changed. Immediately turned back to the voice I'd known and loved for so long, but this time, as he spoke, I felt nothing but regret. Three long years of it. "Emmersyn, hey. I'm sorry, I'm just upset, and I miss—"

"Save it." My words came out sharp and strong. So much at odds with the turmoil racing through me. "I've heard enough and you can save your breath. I'm never coming back to you."

"You bitch," he seethed through the line, and that was when Heather had enough because she turned back.

"Steve, please escort Mr. Powers off the property. Call the cops if you have to. He's one hundred percent never allowed back here. And Lincoln? Toodle-loo, motherfucker." She pressed the red button. Ended the call and turned back to me. "You okay? I told you he was *big* mad."

"I'm fine." I wasn't. My fingers were shaking and all the blood was rushing to my brain, making me dizzy.

"Did you just quote *The Hangover*?" Kane asked.

Heather grinned. "It's the best. But seriously, that was intense."

"I'm fine," I said. "Really, or I will be, and I don't know... hearing all of that helps? In a way? I had no idea..."

"None of us did." Her smile fell. She glanced to Kane. "Take care of her?"

"Of course."

"Do you need me?" she asked. "Because I can get out there, Emmersyn, if you need me. Graham will understand."

"No. Stay there. I think I'm just going to drink the rest of the wine Kane has on hand and I'll be good in no time."

"That's my girl." She fluffed her dark hair. "So, now that that's out of the way, I have a date tonight. Wish me luck." She winked.

I laughed.

This girl.

Kane might have thought she was crazy, but I loved it about her. She'd always been so much freer than me, so wild. So daring.

It didn't surprise me one bit she could flip her switch that fast, and God love her for it. A valve released in my chest as we giggled, and I blew her a kiss with my fingers. "Be good."

"Well that's no fun! I'll call you later, okay?"

"Of course."

Her screen went dark and Kane stared at his phone for a beat before dropping it to his side. "I had no idea my sister was such a lunatic."

"She's the best."

"Yeah." He shook his head and chuckled. A low, rasp laugh that stopped just as quick as it made me smile. "How are you? She's not wrong. That was intense."

I was already on my way to the kitchen, grabbing the bottle of wine. I hadn't lied about any of it. "I think I've decided something." I poured my glass and took a healthy swig.

"What's that?"

I turned to him, gathered up my courage into a nice little ball and tipped my glass in his direction. "I think you're right. We should get married."

My head was spinning. I'd taken worse hits into the boards than the dizziness brought on listening to my sister and that *pencil dick* trade threats and insults back and forth. So much so I was debating whether or not to book a flight, fly my ass out to Boston and let Lincoln know exactly what I thought of him and the way he talked to my sister.

How in the hell did Emmersyn appear so calm? She was trembling moments ago when I'd pressed my hand to her as soon as she heard Lincoln was there.

Now? She was smiling at me, vibrant green eyes as bright as the grass outside.

I was still seeing red.

Whore. Cunt. Bitch... that guy was a dead man next time I was in the Northeast.

"What?" I choked out the question. She couldn't have just said what she did.

Not now. Not after that.

Her head tilted to the side, long, braided dark hair draped over her shoulder. "I've spent most of my adult life volunteering, and I've been waiting a long time in order to be able to get that money.

To be able to do good things with it. To start organizations for kids who don't grow up in circumstances I was fortunate to have."

She said the last part quickly, almost like she was trying to reassure me she deserved it, but hell, that wasn't even my call.

"So... Lincoln's a dick, a complete and utter asshole, and now you think Heather's idea is a good one."

"Frankly, I'm pissed. And yeah. I mean, I'd love to be able to rip off his balls and throw them in a fire."

It was instinct that had my hand going to my crotch while choking. "Fuck, Emmersyn."

"Too much?" She laughed and took a drink.

It took me a second. "Not even severe enough for what he deserves."

"Then we're on the same page." She gulped audibly and her green eyes flared. "We're getting married."

Shit. A couple of nights ago, it'd seemed like a good idea. I helped her out. Kept her safe.

But after all of this, after a day to think about it, not to mention how my dick reacted happily to the sight of her or thought of her, now I was the one hesitating.

"Yeah," I finally managed to mumble. "We should make some rules though."

"Rules?"

"So there's no confusion. I mean. A prenup, obviously. So you know I'm not after your money and everything."

At that, she laughed. "I think you probably have enough you don't need mine."

"True." God, I needed a drink. I'd have to slow down soon, but a man getting married again could drink, right? Fuck. My head hurt.

I rubbed my temples as I headed to pour a glass of bourbon and groaned.

"So a prenup. I've got lawyers who can draw that up." Which reminded me of her finances. The fact she came with nothing.

"What about money, until then? Are you okay, or..."

"Lincoln and I have a joint checking account. My savings and my trust are all wrapped up and held by his father's best friend, Glen Hayes, who's also their family's financial advisor. I didn't want to touch anything or call Glen until I was somewhere Lincoln couldn't come get me."

Right. Because she didn't want him finding her.

"How about this. Let's change our tee time for another day and tomorrow, before we go to Joey's, we'll swing by the bank and finally get you the phone I've been promising all week. I want you to be able to call Heather. Or... his mom?"

"Yeah. Maybe that'd be smart. As far as Irena, if I think about that part, my head will explode. I like her, don't get me wrong, but who knows what Lincoln called her for or why she wants to talk to me. Hell, she might not know a damn thing and have questions about next week's gala or our wedding." She snorted and took another sip of her wine before she pushed it away. "Let's get back to these rules."

Right.

Our marriage rules.

"Sex," I blurted out.

Red wine spewed all over my white marble counters. "Oh shit, I'm so sorry. It's just... that's not at all what I thought you were going to say."

"Yeah, me either." But I couldn't help myself. I looked at her and I thought about it.

I touched her and for the first time in three years, I *wanted* it.

These rules were as necessary for me as for her.

"Um... well..." Her cheeks turned the stained color of my counter while she frantically grabbed paper towels and tried to mop up her mess. "I guess you're right. There's the consummation and everything."

"Pretty sure that doesn't *have* to happen for everything to be legal."

At least, I hoped not.

"Right. Of course. So... does that mean...?"

God, she was cute.

Too damn bad my dick worked just fine around her. Any other woman I'd met in the last three years this wouldn't have been a problem. "No. I think we take that off the table. If you want it, or find someone, be discreet is all I ask. We don't get recognized much, and you probably will less, but if you get caught..."

"Right." Her nose wrinkled and I suddenly felt like scum.

She'd just been cheated on, if she thought I was offering this so I could do the same as Lincoln...

"I'll be fine," I told her.

So I had to live with a woman I wanted to fuck. Big deal. I'd honed my self-control years ago.

"And discreet," she whispered, nose still wrinkled like she smelled something sour.

"I'm not him," I told her as nicely as I possibly could. "Trust me, I haven't been with a woman since Ava left. I'll be fine for another year."

Shit. The truth came out before I could stop it.

"Right," she whispered again, and this time looked sad. "I'm sorry. This is a lot for you and it's not fair, and..."

"It'll be fine. You get the urge, be careful. That's all I'm asking."

"Okay." She chewed her cheek. "What other rules?"

I drained my bourbon. We'd dealt with the two big ones. I wasn't sure I had any more rules in me. "I think that's enough for now, don't you? When do you want to get married then?"

It was a miracle I didn't stumble over the word.

"Well, Lincoln's expecting me back in Boston for that charity event on Saturday..." She trailed off as a wicked gleam twisted her lips and hit her eye. "So, I'm thinking... Friday?"

Holy shit. "So the news will hit and he'll be a fucking wreck the day of the event."

She brought her fresh glass of wine to her lips and smiled. "I think he deserves it."

Damn right he did. Bonus: Me getting married in a week meant I didn't have time to panic over what the fuck I was actually doing.

"Friday it is. Cheers." I moved toward her and tried not to inhale that scent of her perfume. Tried to not drop my gaze to her breasts. Tried not to notice the heat stirring in my stomach.

Three years I'd gone without sex. What was one more?

"Cheers." She tapped her glass against mine. "Let's find a chapel, then, shall we?"

<hr>

"YOU'RE WHAT?!"

"That was subtle," Emmersyn said, standing next to me. "Just like we discussed."

So I hadn't gone with the plan of easing people into the idea.

We took one step into Joey's house, I hugged Gabby. Joey slapped me on the back and in a house full of my teammates and friends, happened to blurt out I was engaged.

"We're getting married," I repeated.

Gabby's dark lashes blinked rapidly. Repeatedly. "Um."

"Congratulations?" Joey asked. His tanned skin paled and next to him, his wife Gabby reached out and curled her hand around his elbow.

"I know it's a shock," I told them all, the men behind them with their brows raised, and the women, some with champagne glasses frozen at their mouths. Others with their jaws dropped wide open. "But it's not what you're thinking."

"Um." Gabby's dark brown eyes continued to bounce back and forth faster than her husband could dribble a puck. "Hi. I'm Gabby," she said, and held out her hand to Emmersyn.

"Nice to meet you," she said, and they shook hands.

It took Gabby two point three seconds to break into a smile. "Welcome to the crazy family. It seems like you'll fit right in."

Leave it to Gabby to break the ice. There were chuckles, awkward ones that fell flat, and Emmersyn shifted back and forth on her heels as she stepped back.

So maybe I could have handled this differently, but what the hell was the point.

I glanced down at her. "Sorry. Maybe we should have stuck with the plan."

She shrugged and tugged at the end of her braided hair that was draped over one shoulder. That shoulder was bare and showed off a tan she'd started to get in the last few days from spending the afternoons while I was at the gym and with the team laying out by the pool. "It's okay. Really."

She grinned up at me, back at Gabby and that smile wobbled as she realized everyone was still staring at us.

"Right," I muttered. Yeah, I'd fucked that up. But what the hell. We had to get married in less than a week, and we needed my team's help along with their spouses and girlfriends in order to get it done. "How about you all stop staring at us, get Emmersyn a drink, and we can explain everything."

"Oh no," Gabby said and she was joined by Garrett's wife, Lizzie. She had a toddler on her hip and I had no clue if it was Archer or Gavin, their twins. "You, my dear, are coming with us."

She reached out and grabbed hold of Emmersyn's hand and tugged her away from me.

"Nothing to worry about, Andrews! She's in good hands."

Emmersyn's eyes were wide, partly with fear, based on the twist of her lips, and equal amusement.

"Take care of her," I told Lizzie and received a snort from her in response.

As soon as Gabby and Lizzie were gone, and the other women filtered toward the kitchen where I assumed they went, twelve sets of eyes turned back to me.

"Want to explain?" Garrett asked. "She's got stitches on her face."

Stitches I couldn't wait until she could get removed so I didn't have the constant reminder of what happened to her. "Caught her fiancé cheating, and he didn't take it well."

"No shit?" Garrett's eyes widened right before his glare darkened and he turned in the direction the girls had gone.

"The hell?" Joey seethed. "What kind of piece of shit—"

I held up a hand and stopped. "It's worse than that."

Emmersyn and I had talked about what she was comfortable with everyone knowing since we agreed to this. They were my brothers, they'd have my back one hundred percent. It still didn't stop me from hesitating, scanning each of them, wondering who would believe this.

"You know the hotel chain and cruise lines? Regal? He's the president and CEO's son—Lincoln Powers."

Eyes widened. A few swiveled toward the kitchen and back to me.

"I thought she looked familiar," Braxton said. He was one of our wingers. Blond-haired, blue-eyed, thin and fast, and hadn't been playing so great lately. While he grew up in Wisconsin, he'd lived in New Jersey for several years before joining the Vipers. "Fuck. That's a mess and a half."

"Exactly."

Ryder scratched his cheek. "Isn't he that Doctors Without Borders dude? Gives a lot of money to them? Has donated some of his cruise ships to carry supplies to Africa or some shit?"

Of that, I had no fucking clue. But maybe I should do some investigating of my own. "You know him?"

"My dad's a doctor, Mom does a lot of volunteering. I swear they've mentioned him."

"It could be him. But even if not, trust me, if you would have heard the shit I heard him say the other night when he was screaming at my sister, you'd want to kill him about as much as I do."

It was Dom who stepped up, fury rolling off in pulsating waves. "Don't need to hear any more. But that doesn't explain why you're now suddenly engaged."

Because I was fucked in the head. And I'd opened my mouth before I could think clearly and it was too late to take it back.

"She's got inheritance issues. Old school grandparents and parents not in the picture, so everything they had goes to her. But most of it's in a trust she can't access... unless she's married."

"Jesus," Garrett said. "Who is this chick?"

"The granddaughter of CocoRock Music Productions founders."

Silence landed in the entryway like a bomb. Hell, I was still *in* Joey's entryway.

"Anyway. Wedding is going to be Friday."

"We have our first preseason game that night," Joey posted out cautiously.

"Then I guess we're going to pull a move like you and Gabby and get married after."

I smirked at him.

"You're an ass," he teased.

"And in desperate need of a drink."

IT WAS Dom who approached me at the beer cooler, stepping back while I shook ice-cold water off my Heineken.

He hadn't been the one I expected to make a move, talk some sense into me, but it shouldn't have surprised me, either.

After Dom opened his life story up to us and fell in love with Holly and his soon-to-be stepson, Ben, he'd become one of the most dependable guys on the team.

He grabbed a bottled water and twisted off the top.

It also didn't surprise me he dove right in. Dom wasn't much for bullshit or surface-level talk.

"Okay. So I get it. You're helping out your sister's friend. But is that all this is?"

I took my first drink, squinted from the sun where I'd headed outside to the backyard. From my view into the house, the girls were still crowding around Emmersyn, but there were smiles and laughter. She seemed to be doing okay, so I refocused on Dominick.

"What else would it be about?"

"You're the one who told me about Ava, remember? On that bus?"

"It's not about Ava." I'd changed after she left. Closed myself off to everything but being there for the guys and playing the best hockey I could. Watching Dom struggle with a woman he cared for had loosened some of the mortar I'd built around myself. He also wasn't entirely wrong. "At least not in the way you're thinking."

"Which way am I thinking?"

That I was still in love with my ex-wife.

He wouldn't be wrong about that either. But it wasn't entirely about that.

At his silence, I sighed. "Fine. It's about Ava, but only because she's getting married soon."

He dropped his water down to his side and his features tightened. Dom had the ability to be one of the meanest assholes in the league. Hell, he'd battled with his own team once or twice.

Even I took in the scary look on his face and had to look away.

"It's just..." The conversation with her from months ago was so bright and vivid I couldn't kick it out of my head. "I want her to think I'm happy, is all. It'd make her happy."

"You getting remarried will make your ex-wife happy?"

He didn't get it. Didn't understand Ava. How even after we got divorced, she still texted after a game. I'd never told her to stop. It made her feel better to.

It made no difference to me if every communication from her was a shiv to my chest. It was the same even if I didn't hear from her.

No one knew she called me to let me know about her engagement *before* she called anyone else. *"I didn't want you to hear it from your parents or anything. I'm sorry."*

I'd told her not to be. Wished her well. Gotten off the phone as soon as it was done and a cement wall of awkward silence slammed through the phone line right after she said, *"I want you to be happy, too, you know."*

Of course I did. It's all Ava had wanted. And I wanted it for her, too.

"Woman doesn't have a mean bone in her body," I told Dom. "But I know she still feels guilt for leaving, even if she shouldn't. That was all on me. But she knows she walked away, so she feels bad for hurting me. If I told her I'm happy, moving on... it'd give her some peace."

He was silent for a moment, brought his beer to his mouth at the same time his gaze stalled on the women inside. "You still love her."

"Always will."

Even if I was attracted to Emmersyn, that was all it'd ever be.

Made it easier to remember to keep my hands off her.

I'd already hurt one good woman. I didn't need the mark on my soul of doing it to another.

"All right. So, I get it, kind of, in a fucked-up kind of way."

I drained my beer. "Isn't fucked up right up your alley?"

"It's why it makes sense. Not like I haven't done some pretty messed up shit to protect the people I care about."

"Emmersyn knows the score," I assured him, because while Dom dealt with all that bullshit he mentioned, he had a protective streak a mile long. And I figured it'd extend to everyone he met, especially a good woman. "We've talked about it. She's been friends with my sister for years. Knows about Ava. She knows I'll never love her, but I'll help her."

His gaze stayed on the women inside, a muscle jumped in his cheek.

"It's just a year," I reminded him. "Then we go our separate ways."

I swear he smirked at me, disbelieving right before he clinked his water bottle to my beer. "If you say so, man."

The girlfriends and wives who yanked me into the kitchen, shoved a glass of wine into my hands, and then demanded I explain were some of the most hilarious women I'd ever met in my life.

It took about three minutes for them to get over their surprise, and possibly their doubt.

It took five minutes for me to explain what was going on.

Two minutes for me to explain Kane was only helping me out. This didn't mean anything, but if they'd help us, we'd appreciate it.

Ten minutes.

And suddenly I was in a kitchen, surrounded by women who could easily become a group of friends I'd love forever if this arrangement wasn't temporary.

"Okay. I'll call the girls at the salon. It's Friday night, so most will have plans, but I can sweet talk them into helping out." Gabby was already on her phone, texting the stylists at the salon she owned to see who'd help with last-minute hair and makeup after the game.

"We need a location," someone else said, and I think her name was Sophie, but there were so many in the room, I wasn't certain.

She was cute, though, with shining, long brown hair, and she'd managed to grab paper and pen from somewhere in Gabby's kitchen, writing down a list of everything we'd need.

"A park," someone, I think it was Paige, no... Holly, said. "It'll be late, dark, so we won't attract attention and it'll be better than any wedding chapel. That could make it all seem last minute."

"Don't knock last minute chapel weddings," Gabby said and tossed a chunk of cheese into her mouth. "Best damn thing to ever happen to me."

She winked at me, and I was thankful Kane had filled me in on most of his team's recent drama.

"This isn't that," I reminded her and then the rest of them with a look.

Holly nodded. "I know, but if you want to fool people *and* really piss off that ex of yours, you'll need to make it look special."

"Houghton Park," someone blurted.

Oh, the irony. They had to be kidding. "Houghton?" I asked and felt a pink heat growing on my cheeks.

"Yeah." Paige. *This* was Paige, and I knew that because she had a very young toddler on her hip. "It's a super cool park, and it has a stage and covered shelter. That could be kind of cool. It's also close to the arena, but it won't be crowded with fans or anything. We could get there easily after the game."

"My last name is Houghton."

Gabby chuckled. "Perfect. Emmersyn Houghton being married in Houghton Park."

"Okay." Paige clapped her hands together and pointed to Sophie. "Write that one down. We'll see if we can use it, but it's public, so I don't know why not, but maybe check for permits or whatever else we'll need."

"I'll be in charge of decorations and flowers," Holly said and she must have seen the overwhelmed look on my face because she leaned over the counter and filled my wineglass. "Maybe you should just keep drinking. We're a lot. I get it, but you get used to it."

"This is all really sweet of you."

"We're family." A slender but warm arm wrapped around my waist and Lizzie hugged me to her side. Her son, Archer, reached out and tugged on my braid. "Even if it's fake or temporary or whatever. But for now, we're all yours."

Emotion burned my eyes as I scanned the kitchen. These women were something else. They'd wrapped me in acceptance and slathered me with help as soon as they heard Kane's outlandish claim we were engaged.

Took a beat and kept on moving, instantly jumping into plan.

It was wild.

"Okay. What else do we need?" Lizzie asked. She squeezed my hip and stepped away, smiling softly like she'd read my train of thoughts.

Sophie tapped her pen to her lips. "Dresses. A maid of honor? A band or DJ could be cool if we held the reception out there, but maybe that should be someplace private. Eventually the ceremony will grab attention."

She was right. I wouldn't want pictures posted or shared without my control of the timing.

"What about here?" Gabby swung out her arm and gestured to the outdoor patio. A large portico shaded one area, but it was a vast space with an outdoor kitchen, another seating area off the far right of the pool. To the left was the pool house, but there were already solar lights draped over and across the backyard and I imagined a dance floor over by the pool house. An open bar. The sun long since set and dancing away and sipping champagne long into the night with Kane on my arm...

No. That was a line of thinking I needed to bring to a full halt.

We'd do that, sure, but it'd be a show. If only he wasn't so damn handsome, standing outside that exact moment. He'd dressed in a black polo shirt, gray golf shorts. Slid his bare feet into black Birkenstock sandals. I'd almost swallowed my tongue when I met him at the top of the stairs after we both got dressed and ready. The outfit was so casual, yet he wore it like a three-piece suit.

I'd spent several days trying to forget how attracted I was to him, how the few moments I swore I caught him checking me out and liking what he saw had to be my own mirage. My own confusion after everything I'd been through in the last week.

"Perfect," someone else said.

"Are you sure?" I asked, but I was still looking outside, imagining. And it was that moment Kane turned to me, caught my gaze and his thick, black brows rose in question.

Damn, he was hot.

I flashed him a wink, letting him know I was okay, and turned back to the girls.

I held up a finger. "We have one little problem."

"What is it?" Gabby's brows furrowed.

"I'll need a dress. In a week."

IT WAS late afternoon when we returned to Kane's house, but with the sun and the drinks and the constant activity, constant talking and meeting new people, all while everyone tried to act like our announcement of getting married wasn't the strangest thing they'd ever heard but were happily going along with it—I was exhausted.

I needed a nap, a shower, and a long night with a really good book to make up for all the conversation and extroverted energy I'd had to exude.

Today would be my last chance, because tomorrow, Gabby and Lizzie were picking me up to start a wedding dress shopping extravaganza where we were planning on touring every wedding bridal shoppe in Las Vegas in hopes we could find something I could wear, something that wouldn't look like this had all been planned last minute *and* could be altered in six days.

Just thinking about it made my head spin.

"You all right?" Kane asked, as I rubbed the tension pulsing at my temples.

"Overwhelmed," I admitted, and covered a yawn. "And tired. I need a nap."

"Things went okay, I take it. Based on Sophie's notes she showed off to everyone with names listed by to-do items, it looked like the women helping us plan a wedding was the highlight of their year."

"Yeah." I couldn't help but chuckle. "I think Gabby's getting into it, too. She said she gets to plan this one since she doesn't remember everything about her own."

Kane shook his head, laughing along with me. "Happens when you get drunk, I guess."

"She cracks me up." Another yawn hit and I covered my mouth, shook my head to clear away the cobwebs. "They were all really wonderful. You have good friends here."

"They're the twenty other brothers I never had." He raked a hand through his hair and sighed. "And they're good friends, which is why I knew we could trust them."

"I'm glad you have that."

We stopped at the top of his stairs. My bed was feet away, pulling me toward it, and yet, the way Kane looked at me, his dark brows furrowed, that intensity in his dark eyes prevented me from moving toward it.

"What is it?"

He opened his mouth. Closed it. "They're yours now, too, you know."

"Who?"

"My teammates. Their spouses and partners. Even when this is done, they'll want to stay in touch."

"Oh." I was knocked back a step. I hadn't been expecting that. Or why it looked like the admission cost him. "That's... well... that's sweet of them. They're good people, too."

"You are, too, you know." His lips twitched. Just one twitch of his lips at the corner turned up. "Good people. And I hope, I hope when this is done, we can remain friends, too."

A warmth shouldn't have flooded my veins. Friends. It was all he'd offer me and I knew that, respected it. Yet every time Kane looked at me in that way he was looking at me now like he wanted something more but wouldn't reach for it before he pulled back. I felt something entirely unfriendly about him.

"I suppose it's good for a husband and wife to be friends, isn't it?"

"Yeah. I suppose it is."

Another yawn forced itself from my throat and before I could say anything, didn't even know what to say, Kane squeezed my shoulder and passed by me. "I'll let you nap. We'll talk later."

About what, who knew. What else needed to be said?

Still, I felt that brand of his hand on my body long after I stripped out of my flowery summer dress, slid into a tank top and shorts, and climbed into bed.

Stupid Emmersyn. Stupid.

I couldn't be getting a crush on my soon-to-be husband.

It'd be the second worst mistake of my life.

***

"OH. THIS ONE," Gabby sighed happily, almost enviously, as I twirled on the small stage, a handful of mirrors fanning out in front of me. "You look incredible."

The dress was mermaid-style, flaring out slightly south of my hips. It had a corset top, white lace overlay and a thin layer of satin. A modest V-neck that still showed ample cleavage because no V-neck hid my girls completely. Reinforced lace straps, thick enough I wouldn't have to worry about them breaking. A completely open back meant I was thankful for the built-in bra and the sweeping train, only a few feet long to barely dust along behind me was all tulle and lace.

Amazingly enough, it fit almost perfectly, and after spending five hours trying on dresses that were either okay, or beautiful but would need way too many adjustments in a short time to fit properly, Gabby was absolutely right.

This was the perfect dress.

One hundred percent opposite the Vera Wang ballgown style dress I had on order in Boston for my wedding to Lincoln, which made it all the better. I'd never put this on and think of him, or at minimum, not think about the wedding day to him.

"You're right," I whispered, and reverently swept my hands down my hips, across my stomach. A quick twirl showed off my bare back. Somehow, the dress made every curve of mine look perfect while hiding the small bulges that always hit my insecurities.

"I love it too," Holly said, sipping a mimosa and walking toward me. "I might steal it from you for mine when you're done with it."

That brought a laugh from me. That silly woman. The petite blonde was at least six inches shorter than me and six sizes smaller. Still, I appreciated the compliment and the threat.

"This one." I glanced at myself back in the mirror, tried to forget why I was wearing this and who would be seeing me in it and nodded. "Definitely this one."

"Yay!" Gabby cheered. "Now we can finally go eat. I'm starved."

I met her gaze in the mirror. "You know I'll be paying you back for all of this, right? Everything you guys are doing for me."

"You can try," Gabby sang. "But we'll see who'll win that battle."

"And Gabby doesn't like to lose," Holly said. She helped me off the small stage and squeezed my hand. "But yes, of course we know you'll offer. Until then, let us help you."

"Thank you." Emotions bubbled and I choked them down.

What a whirlwind of a day. Nine months ago I'd stepped into my first bridal shop to try on dresses for an entirely different wedding.

I had my best friend with me and we'd giggled ourselves silly with mimosas and snacks while trying on a gazillion dresses and laughed over how I imagined the rest of my life would go.

Now, it was all fake. Pretend. And all of it was to get over that man I'd been so certain of.

"Do you think I'm making a mistake?" I asked these women who were essentially strangers. "Doing this to Kane?"

Gabby ushered me toward the dressing room. "Sometimes in life we have the luxury of doing whatever we want and sometimes we do what needs to be done. If Kane wasn't ready for this, he wouldn't have offered, so don't worry about him. He's a big boy and he can handle his own self and emotions."

She gently shoved me into the dressing room and closed the door behind me.

The problem, I figured, as I took one last look in the mirror before unzipping my dress at the side, was that I wasn't so worried about Kane being able to handle *his* emotions.

But me being able to handle mine.

"You're still kicking my ass."

Emmersyn's tee-off drive was straight down the fairway. Mine was somewhere lost in a sand trap, twenty yards closer to us.

The sky was overcast, and I had the day off from practice until this evening when we would meet up to watch films for the upcoming game on Friday.

Our first preseason game.

Then after, immediately following, my wedding.

To this bombshell of a goddess whose fluid and perfect golf swing left me looking at her plump ass on her follow through and having to hope like hell she couldn't see how much her body in that golf dress affected me.

"You're not as bad as you told me you were," she said, dropping her club to the tee box, bent over to grab her tee.

And *fuck me*. Twelve holes into the round and that move, where she kicked up her foot to grab the tee, had me fighting back a damn groan every time.

She wasn't even trying to be sexy. As soon as we stepped on the course, she was focused. Yeah she was having fun, but there were calculations behind her vivid green eyes I could only dream of having. A knowledge of the game, *her* game, that came from growing up on the course and having professional instructors.

All things she'd confirmed by the fifth hole when she was still hitting from the ladies' tees, scoring eagle and birdie, right after the other and beating me by twelve strokes in the first nine holes.

At the turn to hole ten, she joined me at the men's tee box. While her eagles and birdies had switched to pars and birdies instead due to the extra distance, there was no way in hell I'd catch up to her.

Not that it mattered. I came out with her for fun, to give her something else to think of.

Because yesterday, bright and early on Monday morning, she called Glen Hayes, after we'd opened up a bank account for her on Saturday.

Afterward, she'd gone to withdraw money from her account with Lincoln and found there was nothing in it.

Unfortunately, Glen was on vacation, or so his office claimed because Emmersyn didn't believe a word of it. Said the guy's last vacation had been in the year two thousand and five, and he worked fifteen hours a day, even on holidays.

Regardless, there was no hope of her getting access to the funds she was allowed to have while he was gone since there were strict instructions—set in place by Lincoln, she'd admitted with gritted teeth—that no one else was to access the account.

Which meant, until Glen returned to work, she couldn't switch the bank account where the monthly allowance from the trust was sent to and she had nothing except the money Heather had given her.

She'd looked thirty seconds from chucking her new iPhone off my balcony and into the pool after that phone call, so I suggested the only thing that'd take her mind off it.

And it worked. For her.

As soon as we stepped up to the first tee box, she was completely focused.

Me?

I kept being distracted by her resolve, her laugh, and her ass.

Cool. Cool. I was perving on my soon-to-be wife, but it was getting harder by the day—no pun intended—not to act on the growing attraction to her.

In four days, we were going to be married, and I wanted to fuck my fiancée.

Except I couldn't... because she wasn't a real fiancée.

I was currently living in hell and had locked myself in there on my own volition.

I swung the golf club, and afterward, debated. If I slammed it into my face, would it knock sense back into me? Or better yet, help me stop gawking at her ass?

I climbed into the golf cart and checked our scores instead of watching Emmersyn swish and sway her hips back and forth in that skintight dress. Which I wanted to pull off with my teeth.

"I'm still down nine."

"But only two on the back nine." She leaned closer in the golf cart and her nail slid across our scores. Fresh air and a slight breeze slid across me, coupled with the flowery scent of her perfume. My dick perked up, liking the scent and I shoved my jaw forward, to stop myself from leaning in, inhaling more deeply, searing her scent into my brain so I'd never forget it.

"You're impressively good," I ground out, fully aware my voice did not sound normal.

Her brows pinched, and she glanced up.

We were inches from each other. She was close enough I could reach out, wrap my hand around the back of her neck and pull her in for a kiss that would leave us both breathless and desperate for privacy.

I was certain of it.

Worse, killing me further, her tongue appeared through her parted lips, swiped along her bottom one and a hue of bubble gum pink rose on her cheeks.

Like she wanted my lips on hers as badly as I wanted to taste them.

Fuck!

I tore my eyes off Emmersyn's mouth and glared down the fairway until the fist gripping my chest loosened.

"You okay?" Emmersyn asked.

I flexed my fingers, loosened the white-knuckle grip I had on the steering wheel, and nodded. "Yup. Let's go see how badly I can lose to you."

Her soft chuckle echoed in my ears long after we were done playing.

After we returned to my house and we'd both showered.

Long after I'd taken care of myself in said shower.

And long after she went to bed that night.

Because for a moment, albeit a brief moment, I swore she wanted me just as much.

***

"GOOD PRACTICE TODAY." Bromann settled himself into his chair and ripped off his gloves. "We ready for tomorrow?"

"As ready as we'll ever be." Tomorrow's game should have been the first thing on my mind. Only, right after, there was a wedding.

Where I was the groom.

It was the wedding that had mostly consumed my thoughts this week. Not only because it was all Emmersyn talked about. Apparently that moment we had on the golf course on Monday was enough for her because ever since, she'd barely looked at me.

Tomorrow, we'd stand in front of our friends in a sham of a wedding and I was still waiting for the part where I'd be told, *"you may kiss the bride."*

Would she hesitate? Would it be a quick peck? If, once I got my mouth on hers, would she lean in? Exhale a surprise little burst of warm air against my lips? Would she sink into it, become overcome by my touch, or would she be steel straight? Uncomfortable and my touch unwanted...

I shook my head, cleared it, and shoved my sweaty, thick hair off my forehead.

Next to me, Ryder was still stripping out of his gear, unfazed by my lack of excitement.

The rest of the guys were laughing, joking around.

I needed to get my head on straight, my focus where it needed to be.

My marriage to Emmersyn would only last a year... I had way more left in my career if I could keep my shit together.

Hockey was my priority.

Would always come first. Women might come and go from my life, but hockey was the end goal.

"Hey. You ready for tomorrow?"

I knocked Joey's fist as he walked up to me and held out his fist. Knocking it, I nodded. "Yep. Definitely ready to get this season under way."

His thick brows furrowed before he smirked. "Cute. Obviously you're ready for the game. I was talking about your post-game performance."

"It'll be good."

"Sure?"

Joey Taylor had been in my life when Ava and I were happily married. As one of the oldest, and longest playing players on the team, more than two dozen men saw my happy ever after turn to my demise. And they'd been there through all of it.

Been with me for all of it.

"You doing okay with all of this?"

I swiped my hair back and to the side, shoulders slumped. No. No I wasn't. And for all the wrong reasons.

"I keep debating if I should tell Ava. Give her a heads up."

"Ava?" His dark brows rose.

"She called me. When she got engaged to her new fiancé."

"What the hell for?"

"Because she didn't want me to hear it from my parents, and she wanted to make sure I was okay."

Fuck. How pathetic. Three years after walking out on me and she was still checking in.

I should have changed my number. Ended all contact with her.

"What'd you tell her?"

"I told her I was glad she was happy. And I wished her well."

"Shit, Andrews. Why didn't you say anything then? I could have taken you out or something."

"I didn't need to get drunk, not like you did."

He laughed and shook his head. He'd come home from a game one night to find his wife cheating on him. He'd met up with Max and Alix and I at the bar he now owned and gotten so shitfaced he'd spent the night on Alix's couch.

I'd understood the need then. But drunkenness wasn't what I thought of when Ava had called me.

It was sadness. Melancholy. It was the sense of loneliness I hadn't been able to shake.

At least, until Emmersyn fell into my life.

"So are you going to call her?"

Talking to my ex-wife the night before I married someone else felt cold, even for me, because I knew like that phone call Ava gave me, it'd hurt her. Even if she was happy with someone else.

"I don't know. If I do..."

"You might not go through with this. You don't have to, you know. There has to be some other way for Emmersyn to get her inheritance."

"Nope." In addition to wedding planning, and still unable to get a hold of Glen, thanks to that snake Lincoln, I'd called my own contract attorney. Emmersyn sent him a copy of the will and testament of her grandparents and it was pretty clear.

Upon their death, or the age of twenty-one, she would receive eight grand a month for living expenses. Upon turning twenty-five, that would increase to ten thousand a month.

Upon marriage, she would receive a lump sum of eight figures, and that same figure to be paid out every year after the marriage lasted five years. Should the marriage end early, but not before one year, that figure dropped to a *measly* three million dollars a year. If the marriage ended prior to a year, the lump sum was all she received and the rest was to be donated to charities of their choosing.

Granted, that amount was vastly higher than most normal people, but Emmersyn wasn't normal, hadn't grown up with it. Besides, she deserved that money.

Of course, she'd also received the house she already sold. She had to have a pretty decent nest egg invested and in savings which was being held by that asshole financial advisor and taken from her joint account with Lincoln.

My lawyer was going to work on that as well, already getting in contact with lawyers he knew in the New England area to help her out.

But that meant for now, until she had her money in her own capable hands, she didn't have much. At least, not for her.

But she had plans for that money. Ideas, businesses she wanted to invest in and non-profits she wanted to start.

"Anyway, it doesn't matter." I shoved to my feet and returned to the business of stripping out of my gear. "I already committed. It's done, and I'll be fine."

"Vegas weddings sometimes work out," Joey replied.

He'd know since he got married one night to Garrett's sister, Gabby and didn't remember a thing the next day.

"It's not like that," I told him.

And it'd do me a world of good to keep remembering it.

"SEE YOU TOMORROW." I slapped Alix's shoulder when we reached our doors. We'd both been quiet on the drive home, him leaving me to my thoughts, I figured.

"Tomorrow will be good. The game and after."

"I know."

He opened his door while I punched in my code. "She is nice, though. And very pretty."

What was it with my team tonight?

Did they all need to try to set me up with the woman I was already going to marry?

"Drop it, Alix," I warned him, but like usual, he either didn't get the hint or didn't care.

"We are worried," he said and he put his back to his door, holding it open. Far enough out of my reach, I couldn't shove him through it without letting go of my own door. "And have been. I know... I know this is not real, but a year is a long time. And you've had three..."

"Stop. Right now, stop."

He closed his mouth, rubbed a hand over it. "You do not need to keep carrying guilt that does no longer matter, Andrews. We all see it. So you messed up. It happens, to good guys like you even. But that does not mean you have to be alone forever. That does not mean you can not be happy." He nodded his head, gesturing behind me. "Even if it is not with her, it is okay to move on."

A piercing, heated pain seared my chest. "Fuck you."

I turned and slammed the door behind me, and once inside, rested my back against it.

Screw them all. Every single guy who had the nerve to bring up Ava, tonight of all nights.

Fuck them, too, for having a point I was only *slightly* willing to consider.

I had bigger, more important things on my mind.

Like how in the hell I was going to go through all of this and not lose my shit.

"Score! Kane Andrews lights up the lamp..."

My head snapped up. The hell? What was Emmersyn doing? Or watching?

I headed around the corner and found her in the living room. A laptop perched on her thighs, legs bent to her side. The lights were muted, and her reflection was as clear in my dark windows as the reality of her was in my living room.

Dressed in a white tank and bright blue leggings, the bright colors set off her quickly darkening tan. She had her hair curled, a thick mass of it fell over her shoulders.

And her teeth were nibbling on the side of her thumb, eyes furrowed and narrowed on the screen.

Looking damn sexy, like she was concentrating on what must have been one of my games.

"You're watching my games?"

"Oh! Hey!" She jumped, grabbed the laptop as it slid off her lap and snapped it closed. "You're home. Hi."

The anger and frustration from Alix and Joey and what was coming drifted to the background in a heartbeat as her cheeks turned a dark shade of pink.

Curiosity had me grinning, and the fact she was clearly embarrassed about being caught.

"What are you doing?"

"Oh... watching an old game?" She nibbled on her thumbnail, a nervous gesture I picked up on last week.

"*My* old games?"

Shock, surprise, of the happy kind forced me to move forward and grab the laptop.

Emmersyn unkinked her legs from where they'd been bent out to the side of her on the couch and stood, brushing her hands down her thighs and settling them at her hips, stretching her back.

"Well, you know, I don't know much, and I figured since we're getting married tomorrow..." As she said it, she swallowed thickly, struggling to get the words out. "I figured as your wife, I should know something."

Well, that was nice. Unnecessary, but nice.

So why was she so embarrassed about it?

She shuffled away from the couch as I moved toward it, almost in a hurry to get away from getting caught, not that I cared.

My chest squeezed in a warm way as I grabbed the laptop, held it in one hand and typed in my code with the other to pull up what she'd been watching.

YouTube. Well, this was a surprise. "You watched the last game we played last year?"

We'd lost in the playoffs, but I'd had a hell of a game. Two goals, great defense. Colorado just wanted it more. Simple as that. They played harder, both on the road and at home and we were always on our back skates, playing catch up. Even Garrett had a record amount of goals blocked for a playoff game, and Dominick and Max hadn't been able to stop apologizing enough after that loss for their defensive struggles, even though the loss was most definitely not on them.

We won as a team, and we lost as a team.

But me? I'd had one of my best games of the playoffs that night. "What'd you think?"

"Oh. Um. You were great. Fast and..." She flipped out her hand, fingernails now painted a fire engine red, so different than the pale nails she'd sported all week. "You know. Great."

I closed the laptop again and set it on the coffee table. "You don't know anything about hockey, do you?"

"Heather made me watch. All the time."

I stepped closer to the island. With a game tomorrow, preseason or not, I couldn't drink, but that didn't mean I didn't fight back a laugh as she poured a healthy glass of white wine.

At least she'd finally made herself at home and stopped asking my permission for everything.

"That doesn't mean you know anything."

"I know Heather thinks you're the best guy in the league."

A bark of laughter burst from me. "Of course she does. She's my sister and loves me. My parents also think I'm the greatest player to ever play the game. So tell me, you who knows so much..." I waited until she drank her wine and set down the glass.

"What?"

"What did you think of that shitty tripping call the ref made in the first period that ended up with my ass in the sin bin?"

"Sin bin?" Two beautiful dark eyebrows rose in confusion.

"Penalty box. Nickname for it. So, what'd you think?"

"Well, I think he was wrong." She took another sip, brows puckered, and looked off to her left.

This girl. I learned something new about her.

She was stubborn as hell.

"You don't know anything, do you? And before you say you do, I'll have you know you used the word *great* at least twice to describe how I played."

"Are you saying you're not great?"

"Oh no. I am great."

"Fine," she huffed. "Heather made me watch, but everything moves so fast... and that puck... I can barely watch it, much less understand all the rules. So no, I don't understand, but the pre-game stretching isn't a bad way to spend a few minutes."

"Of course you liked the stretching. Come on." I laughed and headed back to the couch, threw a pillow on my lap and settled the laptop on it. Bonus, if I got an erection while she was next to me, she wouldn't see. "Let me teach you."

"Heather tried. Put me in front of a baseball game or football game and I'm good. It's just, it moves so *fast*. And I'm sorry, it stresses me out trying to watch the puck, learn the rules, and well... everything."

I patted the cushion next to me, grinning at her over my shoulder.

Tomorrow, we'd have to kiss, and I'd have to deal with that.

And everything that came after. But tonight, she wanted to learn about my job, and I was a hell of a good teacher.

She paused at the couch, slowly making her way closer.

One more thing I learned about my future wife—she was curious. Hesitant, but curious, and stubborn as hell because she tried to sit down on the chair at the end of the couch.

"You can see the computer from there?"

"No..." She paused, halfway into her squat, and stood. Finally taking the seat next to me. "Okay. Teach me, Mr. Hockey."

Teaching her, I could do.

It was kissing her that was scaring the hell out of me.

He moved faster in person than I watched on the small laptop last night. Kane Andrews skated across the ice like he was flying in air, and that puck? I was having at least a slightly easier time keeping my eyes on it from the family's suite the team allowed the wives and girlfriends to have for their first preseason game.

Around me were toddlers babbling, babies crying and giggling, and women talking, but I was so focused on watching the game, I barely paid anyone any attention. Mostly because I kept thinking of what was going to happen *after*.

My wedding to the man currently hunched over a blue circle at one side of the ice for a face-off after San Jose was called for icing. And thanks to Kane's lessons last night, I now knew what that was.

Movement came from my left and then Lizzie was taking the seat next to me, hands free of her twin boys but holding two glasses of wine.

"Need one?"

"Thank you." I hadn't had a drink yet, but I could use one to settle my nerves.

"How are you holding up?"

"I'm trying not to think about it," I admitted and took my first sip of the crisp, white wine. "To be honest, I keep thinking this is good. It gets Lincoln off my back and if Kane's willing to help me out with getting my trust, then it's cool. But then I think about what it's doing to him, and I think who cares about the money."

"You care about him."

"He's my best friend's brother, and she loves him more than anything, and he's a great guy. Of course I care about him."

I slid my eyes off Lizzie and back to the game where the men on the ice were a blur of white and teal jerseys, fighting for the puck, sticks clashing I could hear from up here. And the roar of the crowd in the arena? Eighty percent filled with Vipers gear but enough San Jose's fans had made the trip the arena hadn't fallen below a dull roar all game.

"Is that all he is?" Lizzie asked. "Just your best friend's brother?"

Of course. I wanted to be adamant.

The lie stuck in my throat and Lizzie grinned. "He's not a bad guy to have a crush on."

"Having a crush on a guy you're marrying because he's helping you out isn't a smart idea."

"Anything could happen. I mean, Gabby and Joey barely knew each other and woke up married and they worked it out."

"Not everyone gets their happily ever after."

My parents were the perfect example. So was Kane's first marriage. It wasn't that I didn't believe in love, or soulmates, but I figured humans were more flawed than most wanted to admit, and therefore, a successful marriage built under the best and most loving terms could still crumble.

"No, that's true." She sighed and took a sip of her wine and another whistle was called for a penalty I missed—and probably wouldn't understand—when she continued. "Kane's a great guy. He's loyal with a huge heart and I know Garrett and the guys who are on the team who were around during and after his divorce just want him to be happy again."

"That's what Heather wants for him, too. And, yeah, I can't lie. The guy is hot. I mean, I've had to see pictures of him for years. Of course he's sexy, but I don't want to get my hopes up, or try anything that could ruin this either. So, maybe for my sake, tell all your friends to stop with the matchmaking?"

It was said as nicely as possible, but it wasn't the first time I'd heard something like that this week. *Everyone* wanted Kane happy, and I wondered if he knew how much the team cared about him—not as a player, but as a friend.

Lizzie laughed and glanced back at the group of women scattered around behind us. "Point made, but if you ever need anything, we're all here for you."

"Thank you."

"And speaking of Heather. Have you talked to her?"

"No. I've been trying to call her since yesterday. I know Kane called his parents and explained everything, what was going on, and obviously Heather knows, but I figured she'd give me an update about Lincoln, or I don't know, talk to me and give me more shit about marrying her brother."

Or you know, fly out for it, but I hadn't heard from her and that had me worried in more ways than one.

I'd tried hard not to listen to that conversation with his parents, too, and mostly succeeded while he paced around his living room and kitchen area, phone to his ear. It had seemed to go really well until Ava's name was mentioned, and then Kane got off the phone quickly thereafter. He'd left the room, and a few minutes later, I'd heard the clang of weights slamming to the floor upstairs, almost above my head.

So there was that... I needed to remember not to get hung up on a guy who was still so very much hung up on his ex-wife.

"Maybe she's just busy—you said she has a crazy schedule, right?"

"She does, and it's not uncommon for me to go weeks without

talking to her, but I'd still think I'd hear from her this week. Makes me worried about Lincoln. If he's shown up there again."

Or if Heather ended up buying a rifle and filling him with buckshot. Wouldn't surprise me at all.

A buzzer blared through the arena, startling me and I looked up to the Megatron in the center.

"They won." I grinned from cheek to cheek as the guys on the ice lined up and all slapped Garrett's helmet before skating back to their bench and lining up.

"Of course they did. Our guys kick ass," Lizzie said, and she pulled me to my feet. "Which means we need to get going—and fast."

We headed back to the interior portion of the suite and everyone else was there, gathering purses and scooping up kids and car seats, all smiling at me.

Holy shit.

Reality slammed into me as hard as Dominick had hit them earlier.

I was about to get married to a guy in love with someone else while my own love life fell apart and was now marrying me as a pity favor.

That he'd starred in my dreams, some of my awake fantasies in the last week which would never be mentioned out loud didn't matter.

I was getting *married.*

"Ready?" Lizzie asked.

I forced a grin. "Let's do this."

THESE WOMEN WERE MIRACLE WORKERS. Thanks to Sophie's organizational skills, Paige's park idea and Gabby's stylists being willing to help out at the last minute, we were now in an enclosed tent Sophie had a company come and erect for both the ladies and another one for the guys.

They'd had to stay for the post-game talk and meeting and shower. But Gabby had assured me they all had their own tuxedos so they'd look nice.

The women were wearing dresses they'd previously worn for other black-tie events.

I was in my dress, my hair curled in loose waves and pulled back at the sides. No veil, but the stylist, Kelsey, who happened to be a coach's daughter and also worked for Gabby, had found some white baby's breath and tucked it into my hair as she made an elegant twist with the upper half of my hair.

I was standing in the mirror, hands trembling as I brushed down my dress. My makeup, done by me while other girls were having their hair curled and swooping into dresses, was at risk of running if I let my emotions rise to the surface, so I was trying to keep everything locked up.

In less than a month, I'd found out the man I loved was cheating on me and had no problems backhanding me in his anger. The man I'd loved had somehow become completely psychotic and I'd missed it. For *years*.

And now, I was in Vegas, planning an altogether different kind of wedding to a completely different man for a vastly different purpose. If I examined any further how my life had changed in the last four weeks, I'd crumble into a pile on the floor.

"You okay?" Gabby stepped up behind me, worry lining her eyes and tugging down at the edges of her mouth. "I'm sure this a lot."

I ran my finger down the small, light scar at the edge of my cheekbone. I'd been able to have the stitches removed yesterday but it was still healing.

"I'm okay."

She squeezed my other hand, a gesture saying she understood and like the others, wouldn't push me toward Kane or trying to make me think this was anything other than what it was, and bit her bottom lip. "We have a surprise for you. Well, Kane does."

"What is it?"

"Turn around."

She grinned and tugged on my hand. I swiveled around to the opening of the tent where Lizzie and Holly, the sweet blonde who was engaged to Dominick, stood with their hands at the white flaps of the tent opening.

"Guess who's here to see you?" Both of them sang, smiles wide, possibly more excited than anyone else in the tent.

They pulled back the flaps and my knees shook.

"You didn't think I'd miss this, did you!?" Heather swooped in, arms outstretched, and all those emotions I'd tried to ignore rushed to the surface, making my skin hot and my body shake.

I barely got out a cry of surprise before she was wrapped around me, hugging me tightly. "I'm so sorry I didn't answer your calls this week. I knew if I talked to you, I'd ruin the surprise, but you had to know there was no way I was missing this."

"I'm so glad you're here." I squeezed her back. My lifeline. My best friend.

The girl who'd come up with this insane idea in the first place —hmmm... maybe I needed to reevaluate more life choices.

"I love you. Thanks for coming."

"You didn't think I'd let you marry my brother and not make it, did you?" She stepped back, flicked her hand down the length of her silky champagne colored dress. It had to be new. "Besides, you need a maid of honor."

"And that's you?" I laughed. "You're the one who put me in this mess."

"I know. And you love me for it. Or you will. Trust me." She winked. "And besides, the best part about tonight is getting to stick it to the douchebag of a loser who won't be named."

At the mention of Lincoln—not by name, of course—reality slammed right back into me.

Right. This whole wedding had a purpose. "Have you heard from him this week?"

"He hasn't stopped by the house again."

"That's not what I asked."

She tucked her glossy brunette hair, almost as dark as her brother's, behind her ear. "We'll talk tomorrow. But essentially, it's no different. But he has gone from pissed off to pleading, begging you to come home, so whatever." Heather gave my hand a squeeze and then reached for a small bouquet of flowers. "Forget about him. At least enjoy the fun party tonight." She smelled the flowers and smiled. "Everyone did such an incredible job of putting this together." She grinned up at me. "He's going to lose his total fucking shit."

Something that didn't exactly thrill me. Mostly because now he'd know where I was—and how to find me.

"Hey," a deep, masculine voice rumbled in the doorway.

"Hey! Get out, you idiot!" Heather shouted as Kane stood in the entryway to the tent, flaps closing behind him. He stole my breath. Dressed in a well-tailored black tuxedo and vest, he looked like a man who wore suits for a living and not pads and skates and a helmet. The white backdrop behind him also gave him an ethereal glow even as Heather hurried to him and pressed her palm over his eyes.

"You can't see the bride before the wedding. It's bad luck."

Of course Heather would be concerned about superstitions.

He reached up and took his sister's hand, pulling it off his face, and flashed her an amused grin. "You need therapy." That amused smile turned to me and changed.

Darkened.

My ankles wobbled in my heels as I took in his expression, the way he filled out that tuxedo. "I need to talk to Emmersyn." He glared at Heather. "Alone."

She shrugged, smiled at both of us. "No probs. I'll go find Mom and Dad. Tell them we're about ready?"

"Five minutes," Kane confirmed and nerves lit up like fireworks in my belly.

Five minutes.

"Your parents are here?"

"Of course they are." Heather smiled. "They never miss one of Kane's weddings."

I bit back a laugh. As rude as it was, it was also kind of funny.

Kane gave her a little shove and rolled his eyes. "Not nice."

"See you in five!"

She danced around her brother and disappeared out of the tent.

"What's up?"

"You look beautiful," he said, and came toward me. He moved slowly, like a predator, inspecting the length of my dress and stalling at the neckline, the cleavage, before slowly bringing his eyes to mine. "Absolutely stunning."

"Thank you, but that's not why you came. Are you...?"

"Not backing out. I just have a question. Something I haven't been able to stop thinking about for days."

"What?"

As he continued moving closer, my chest warmed. That heat spread through my limbs until my fingertips buzzed with warmth, a need to reach out and run my hands down his lapels. Settle my hand at his heart to see if it was racing as much as mine.

"Before we go out there and do this, I wanted to know how you wanted to handle something."

"The ceremony?"

"No." He stopped directly in front of me. So much taller than me normally, with my high heels, I barely had to tilt my chin up to meet his gaze.

His dark eyes slid back and forth, scanning my face, my own eyes. He smelled like spice and pine trees and a crisp, fall day in the Northeast.

"What then?"

"The kiss."

He swallowed as he said it, and I swore his eyes dropped to my mouth before quickly flipping back up to meet mine. That heat running through my veins grew hotter, until that burn crept up my throat to my cheeks.

Oh God. I hadn't considered. I hadn't even thought of the kiss. He'd brought up sex, quickly kicked it off the discussion table.

And yet... "Well, I guess, friends can kiss? Maybe on the cheek."

"That won't work."

"Why not?"

He lifted his hand, brushed his knuckles along my jaw. I swore he leaned in even closer. A hair's breadth away from me. Inches. So close I could see his pulse at the base of his throat.

"Because I haven't been able to stop wondering what your lips will feel like."

"Oh."

Ohhh... I blinked rapidly. Several times. That meant he... he thought of me. Like I'd thought of him?

His hands cupped my cheeks, thumb brushed along my chin and he was there, bending down, lips kicking up at the corners once his mouth was almost to mine.

"Breathe," he whispered, and then his lips brushed against mine and time stopped.

And *wow*. The earth spun and stopped. It tilted and righted itself. Everything inside of me shook and settled as our lips pressed together, learned the feel of each other. It was barely a kiss, but soft and warm and the heat that had begun dissipating earlier returned full force until I reached up and wrapped my hands around his forearms. Braced myself against him while he knocked me off my axis.

Until Kane's thumb brushed over the spot where my stitches were removed.

Oh *God*. I was kissing a man who didn't want me, even if this kiss made me believe different.

Hadn't I wasted enough years with a man who wouldn't want me, and only me, forever?

I pushed against him, dropped my hands from his, and stepped back.

He did the same, eyes wide and glassy, lips wet from me.

My hands drifted to my own mouth, covering it. Oh *God*. That wasn't supposed to happen. I definitely wasn't supposed to *feel* so much while it did.

"I'm sorry," Kane said, wiping the taste of me off his lips. "I'm so sorry if that was unwanted, it's just—"

"It's fine." Because it had been fine. But there was a cost.

And I was starting to think when it came to Kane, the cost was my heart.

Again.

How many times would I let mine shredded?

I'd thought I read her right. Thought that while I was moving toward her earlier that her breathing had picked up to nearly match the racing of my heart. I'd thought that when I touched her, and she shivered beneath me she wanted to kiss me as much as I'd been craving her.

Until she pushed me back and ran out of the tent, mumbling something about how it was time for us to get married, and now we were saying our vows, this sham of a wedding to a woman I was actually starting to like who could barely look at me.

Our hands were held together, hers clammy and tense. When I tried to calm her down by brushing my thumb over the back of hers, she'd tensed, swallowed, and squeezed her eyes close.

So I'd stopped, because apparently what we'd done earlier was too much for her. Too wrong for her, and of course it was.

Her ex-fiancé was practically forcing her into this position by terrifying her, cheating on her, and backhanding her like a little bitch.

Of course she wouldn't want to be touched by another man.

I cleared my throat, trying to get her attention while our offici-ant, an ordained minister Holly had found, who had a thick head of graying hair and kind eyes and could wear a suit almost as well as any of the guys on my team, guided us through the declaration of intent.

It was then that she finally glanced at me, and I spoke the vows, guided by the minister.

"I, Kane Andrews, with this ring, I thee wed, and I do promise to love, honor, and cherish you, in good times and bad, for richer or poorer, in sickness and health, until death do us part."

Emotion clogged my throat as I spoke vows I didn't fully mean, so different than the last time I'd done this, and yet with Emmersyn in front of me, held no regrets I was doing it again, to this woman, for this reason.

That kiss had knocked me on my ass even if it'd scared her and had her barely unable to look at me. I turned to Alix, my best man, and took a simple gold band from him.

I squeezed her hand as I slid it on her finger and whispered, "Hey, look at me."

Her eyes dragged up like she was walking to a guillotine, and damn, okay, wouldn't make the mistake of kissing her again. Or at least—not after this kiss coming up.

"We'll figure this all out, okay? We can do this."

She smiled softly. "Okay."

Emmersyn spoke her vows, sounding a lot more confident and aware than she looked earlier, and then we were sliding a matching gold band on to my finger I once believed would never wear a ring again.

And then the minister was declaring us husband and wife, announcing we could kiss.

"We can skip this part," I whispered, leaning in and cupping her cheeks. No one would know if I kissed her or not if I bent her over and put my back to the crowd. The photographers we'd hired for the event would hopefully catch just enough to throw Lincoln into a tailspin.

"It's okay," she whispered back as I moved closer. "We've got this."

I admired the hell out of a woman with confidence despite her fear.

"Hell yeah, we do." I slid my hand to her back, bent her backward into a dip, and then I pressed my lips to the corner of hers as she clung to me, laughing in surprise.

"I won't kiss you again unless you ask for it," I said, moving my lips to her ear and then bringing her back to her feet. "But if you ever want it, I'll be ready."

Her jaw dropped, pink filled her cheeks, and then she shook her head, laughing.

"You're something else, Kane Andrews."

I held her against me while we smiled and lifted our free arms in a faux celebration. "That's husband to you, wife."

"OH MY GOSH. My feet are so sore I won't be able to walk tomorrow," Heather groaned as she collapsed into the chair next to me.

I was fucking beat. Besides the game and then the ceremony and now the party where we all decided it'd be more fun if we celebrated our win instead of a sham of a wedding that'd make at minimum, the bride and groom uncomfortable, I needed a half hour in a sauna, a gallon of water, and to sleep for twelve hours.

"Hell of a surprise you pulled off, showing up here like this."

"It hurts me you think I'd miss it. Besides, Lincoln would never believe I wouldn't be here." True. Odd how I hadn't even considered my parents and sister being here. I just figured since this wasn't real, they wouldn't come.

"I'm glad you're here. Mom and Dad are really okay with this?"

They left the party earlier, claiming the time change exhausted them and they needed sleep. They'd been kind to Emmersyn and me, although my dad took one look at the cut on her cheekbone and threatened to kill Lincoln himself.

"I think they're more worried. About both of you."

"Nothing to be worried about."

"No? Because I think you like her."

"Of course I like Mom."

She shoved my shoulder. "Don't be obtuse. You know what I mean."

"She's your best friend and you're a good judge of character, what's not to like?"

"Nothing. She's sweet and perfect."

She lingered on perfect, and I shook my head. "Please tell me you didn't set all this up, fly her out here just to have this night happen."

"No, of course not."

She spoke way too fast and gave me wide eyes.

My sister was the top five worst liars on the planet. But dear God. She had to be kidding me.

"Heather."

Heather shrugged, looked out to the dance floor where Emmersyn was dancing with Gabby and holding one of Garrett's boys on her hips, holding his little hand and laughing her head off.

"I mean, it wasn't when I sent her here. That was just me panicking, but after I had some time to settle down and think about it..."

"Are you sitting here telling me you are actually trying to set me up with your best friend?"

She gave me a sassy grin. "It worked, didn't it? You're married to her now." I opened my mouth to tell her this was all fake, that we'd end it in a year, just like Emmersyn and I agreed to, but she pushed to her feet, wincing as she did. "And don't get me all of this, this is *fake* crap, I know you, and any marriage would mean way too much for you to not at least give it your best effort."

She hobbled off, leaving me reeling.

My fucking sister had just trapped me into a marriage.

And the bitch of it was—she wasn't that wrong.

MY ALARM WENT off at eight, hours later than I normally get up to start doing day after post-game stretching, but after the late night, I figured my body would need the rest.

A groan slipped from me as I rolled over and hit the blaring app on my phone, only to have it more quietly followed with the sound of laughter.

I shoved the heels of my palms into my eyes and laid back in bed, groaning for a reason that had nothing to do with the soreness in my thighs and calves.

Last night, Heather declared she was staying at my house until she flew home.

Normally, not a problem, but I'd wanted time to talk to Emmersyn, take her pulse after the kiss, the wedding, and waiting for the downfall of what was sure to be a shitty day for her.

Instead, Heather had all but kidnapped her as soon as we got home, and she took charge of Emmersyn, ushering her up to the guest room.

I'd stayed downstairs, gripping my keys in my fist. I wanted to go there now, throw my sister out of there but found the strength not to be a dick.

None of this was real, despite Heather's plotting and feeling pretty damn good about herself for it, too.

Whatever.

I'd catch up with Emmersyn eventually, but a hot shower and some stretching was currently more important. Pre-season sucked. It was good for the team, finalize lines and who'd play where and with who. It was good to test the mettle of new players or new additions to the team like Bromann, but it was hell on our bodies. After not playing daily for months, getting back into the groove always took a few weeks to settle, for our bodies to remember they were trained for this.

And since I was older, I was feeling it more and more. My guess, twenty-two-year-old Arlo had hopped out of bed at the crack of dawn without a single creak or groan or cramp.

Scents of garlic and sugar and other delicious concoctions drifted upstairs, perking me up.

The benefit to having a sister who was a self-trained incredible chef?

Free food whenever she was in town, and she always made sure she fed me well.

I shoved out of bed, took care of using the bathroom and a quick brush of my teeth. As I headed downstairs, their laughs grew louder, more carefree than I'd heard from Emmersyn yet.

Good to hear, given what lay ahead.

Hell, I was surprised her old phone Heather brought wasn't already exploding with texts and calls.

Thankfully, I walked into two happy women in the kitchen, Emmersyn sitting at the kitchen counter, sipping orange juice—probably freshly squeezed, knowing Heather—and Heather where she loved to be, in the kitchen flipping what looked like crepes in a skillet. Next to the stove, on a cutting board, was spinach and mushrooms, some thinly sliced onions and garlic. Loads of garlic.

"Go to the grocery store this morning?" I asked.

"Hey." Heather grinned up at me. "Good morning to you too, grumpy. And no, I didn't."

"The food fairy deliver all of this then?"

At her perch on the stool, Emmersyn covered a laugh with her fist.

"No." Heather scrunched her nose. "Well, sort of. I made a plan last night after you two went to bed and ordered everything to be delivered today."

"You're the best." I kissed her temple as I moved past her. "You can crash my wedding any day if it means you cook for me." I winked at Emmersyn and headed toward the coffee. "Smells delicious. What else are you cooking?"

"What? Crepes aren't good enough for you?"

They absolutely were, I just knew her. I poured my coffee, arching a brow as I took my first sip.

"Fine. Cinnamon rolls are in the warming drawer, already done, and I have homestyle potatoes in the oven."

"Also a fruit salad," Emmersyn piped in. "In the fridge, and she already has steak marinating for dinner tonight."

"Traitor." She shoved a spatula in Emmersyn's direction.

I barked out a laugh. "Perfect. How long are you staying?"

"Early morning the day after your game tomorrow."

"Another game already?" Emmersyn asked. "Don't you like... need time to heal?"

Heather and I both laughed. "Welcome to the hockey season. We have about three games a week from now until April—"

"June or July because this year you're taking it all," Heather cut in.

"That's my favorite cheerleader." I fist pumped her and turned back to Emmersyn. "Like I was saying, yeah. We don't get many days off. We'll have a break. There's the all-star weekend, a few days around Christmas, that kind of thing, but for the most part, once the season starts, we're off and running for a while."

"Wow. I didn't realize. How do you recover so quick?"

"We train for it. Ice baths and bikes after games to release the lactic acid to keep us from getting sore. Saunas, which is why I have one installed in my bathroom, and a lot of stretching. Yoga. Eating as healthy as possible. That kind of thing. And then we hope like hell we don't get injured badly enough we have to miss more than a couple of games, if any at all."

"And the most important part of that is nutrition," Heather

piped up, shoving a plate with four crepes on it almost into my gut before I grabbed it from her.

"Sit. Eat. Both of you. And then we'll get online and search for all your wedding pics and learn what Lincoln has to say."

"Oh yay," I muttered.

Exactly how I wanted to start my day with my new wife.

The crepes were probably delicious because everything Heather cooked was, but since she'd tossed down the gauntlet right before dishing out our breakfast, I didn't say a thing.

Last night, reasons for getting married aside, was an absolute blast. There was dancing, drinking. I laughed with Gabby and Holly almost constantly. His friends were wonderful.

Gabby knocked my socks off with a completely decorated backyard patio. Lights strung. A dance floor brought in with a DJ who'd had so much energy, I wouldn't be surprised if he was still awake and dancing.

We'd come home, accompanied by Heather and after she and I changed out of our dresses and washed off our makeup, I was beat and told her we'd hang out more today. Then I collapsed into my bed, the night of my wedding—alone.

And then I'd cried.

Because I'd thought, hoped, that kiss with Kane had meant something, but I was a fool to think so.

He'd promised me he'd never love me, and I needed to remember that.

The last thing I needed was another broken heart by being a

fool to fall for someone who'd made it very clear he was willing to be my friend, but that was as far as it would go.

Even if temptation or curiosity or maybe even attraction had him acting out of character.

I shoveled a bite of potatoes into my mouth, ignoring Heather cleaning up, even after cooking.

"Did you bring my phone?" I asked her.

"It's off. Might need to be charged." She glanced at me over her shoulder, her straight, jet-black hair that matched Kane's pulled up and clipped into a twist at the back of her head. "And at this point, your voice mail could be full."

"Awesome." I slid off the stool and scraped my remaining food into the trash.

Kane seemed to have no problems eating, shoveling food into his mouth like he wasn't going to eat for another week. "Probably a good call. Not sure I need to hear the shit he has to say again." He pointed his fork at me. "And maybe you should let us listen first, especially if news of last night has spread."

It would. Gabby said she made sure the photographer knew to blast it everywhere and Lincoln's a sports fan. He'd see it soon if he didn't late last night.

I faced them both. "No. He's my problem. I appreciate you wanting to protect me, but I think I have the right to know."

"Of course you do." Heather rubbed my back.

Kane grunted something I couldn't make out and shoved another bite of food into his mouth. "Your call."

"I'll go get the phone. Unless you want to wait? For like an eternity?"

"No." I was still curious about Irena calling me, and if she heard if he'd called me again, too. Besides, I wanted to see what I was dealing with. There was a high probability that if I pissed him off, I'd have an even harder time getting Glen on the phone, but that was the risk I was willing to take in order to get full access.

Besides, Kane had his lawyers looking into things. Hopefully this coming week we'd get everything straightened out and I'd finally get access to my trust. Then Kane and I could discuss the new marriage slash non-relationship we had and how we wanted to handle it.

"Go get the phone," Kane said and pushed off the stool. "Let's get this shit over with so I won't still be pissed when Mom and Dad come over later."

"Your parents are coming over here? Today?"

"Yeah." Heather nodded. "When they bailed last night early, they said they'd be here. Wanted to talk to you two, see how you're doing."

"They're not mad, though, right? Because they were quiet last night and left early…"

"They're not mad. They're worried, about you mostly, and me, admittedly, but they're not mad. And you know they love you."

"I know." That didn't mean I wasn't nervous to spend time with them now that I was married to their son, fake or not.

"And we don't have to know if Lincoln's heard anything yet," Heather said and held up her phone. "Because it's *all* over social media, along with the surprise since you and Lincoln looked so happy together a month ago out to eat."

Kane

"SHIT," Emmersyn muttered. "This is bad."

She shoved her hands through her hair, paced back and forth through the living room where I'd turned on the television after Heather's announcement.

She was right. We were a hot topic numero uno in the sports world and I'd checked my phone to see calls and emails from our team's reporter. Granted, she'd been there last night. She was the one who dropped the story in the right hands, but it seemed it'd taken on a life of its own.

Social media was being absolutely *vicious* toward Emmersyn, something I hadn't considered a possibility but the fact she jumped from one mogul into the arms of a hockey player didn't seem to be sitting well with either hockey fans or those who were enamored with public faces like Lincoln's family.

"I hadn't considered this part," she muttered, and took another lap down and back the length of my house. "Are you sure the reporter we talked to shared the story correctly?"

"She wouldn't fuck us over."

We'd lied a shit ton during the interview, and Alicia had coached us through everything. Yeah, she'd mention there could be some negative comments, but I hadn't anticipated things like Emmersyn being called a whore so blatantly to be the main reaction.

We'd told Alicia that Emmersyn and Lincoln have been separated since spring. That they'd paused their wedding plans and had spent time trying to see if they could work things out, but that they'd both been free to explore during that time. We'd met during the playoffs last year when Heather flew out for my games, and after they separated, she reached out to me. We started talking. She wanted to fly out to see me, and so she did. We fell hard. Fast. And decided to get married.

Except we'd forgotten about all of the other pictures of the two of them during this supposed separation time. A vacation she'd taken in May to Miami. Events with his family. Those we could easily brush off as Emmersyn feeling the need to do her duty for the family despite their problems.

But the pictures of them kissing on the pub streets of Boston or holding hands, tucked away in quiet romantic restaurants, with smiles?

The only thing that would save her from those pictures would be if the women he cheated on her with ever came forward, and who in their right mind would do that? They'd be thrown into the fire right along with Emmersyn.

"Shit. I'm so sorry. I should have considered the public flogging you'd get for this." Heather wrapped her arm around her friend's waist and tugged her tight to her side. "I didn't even think about this."

"It's fine." Emmersyn stepped away from Heather and shook out her arms. "It's temporary, right? And maybe this might help. Lincoln can play the wounded fiancé. Maybe if people feel sorry for him, he'll use it to his advantage, right?"

She glanced at both of us.

I didn't trust Lincoln as far as I could drop kick his lame ass, and I didn't know him.

"Who knows," Heather admitted. "Based on his behavior the last couple of weeks, I think he's pretty much an unknown right now."

"Helpful," I told my sister with a baleful look.

She shrugged. "It's true."

She'd been upstairs, digging through her things for Emmersyn's phone and once it was plugged in, and she finally turned it on, Emmersyn's old phone started chiming and beeping and lighting up like one of our victory celebrations after a home win.

Damn thing went berserk, and with every ping and ding on the screen, Emmersyn paled a little more.

And there wasn't a damn thing I could do to help my wife through this.

"I need a minute," she said, and ran up the stairs. Her bedroom door slammed close, followed by what I assumed was her bathroom.

I looked to Heather.

"Stress release. She'll be fine."

Fucking great. What a way to start my day as a husband.

EMMERSYN CAME BACK DOWNSTAIRS twenty minutes later. She'd showered, changed out of her pajama shorts and tank and into another summer dress.

"You look good," I told her, and she did. Hair straight as a sheet, mascara and blush on and a shimmer of lip gloss. If this was how she dealt with a stress release, I was impressed.

"I figured if I was going to have a shitty day, I might as well look good."

Women. I'd never understand them.

"Okay." Heather grabbed the phone and plopped down on the couch. "Let's get this over with, shall we?"

In the time Emmersyn was gone, I'd helped Heather finish cleaning up the dishes. I'd gotten on my own social media accounts and then immediately deleted Twitter. Why was everything so much worse over there?

Regardless, since I hadn't posted any photographs of me since the spring, there were few comments on any of my actual pages, but there were requests for quotes from a number of online blogs and sports sites. I copied and pasted the link Alicia had us use for them to reach out to her.

She'd take care of it.

In the meantime, I'd avoided checking Lincoln's social media even though I saw him tagged all over.

Yeah. He clearly knew. Had to.

"Do you want me to start with the oldest voice mail or go to the newest?"

"Newest," Emmersyn said, nibbling at the edge of her thumb. "Let's tear off the Band-Aid."

"All right."

She unlocked the phone, pulled up the app, and every second that waited my rage pulsed like a feral beast. Until his voice, the one I'd heard through the security camera, pierced the air.

"You fucking cunt. You have no idea. No goddamn idea what you've done. I swear to God, Emmersyn, you fucking slut. I will ruin you. Enjoy him while you have him, because I will destroy both of you."

"Pleasant," I muttered.

On the couch next to Heather, Emmersyn's face scrunched up. "Not as bad as I was expecting."

"What in the fuck? You goddamn fucking insane bitch! I knew. I should have known that's where you went. Goddammit, Emmersyn. You shouldn't have done this. You have no idea the mess you've made, but I swear to God you'll regret this. If you think marrying that fucking two-bit player will keep you safe from me, you better think again. I cannot believe this. Jesus... you have fucked everything up for me. I swear to God, Emmersyn. You better call me, tell me this is some kind of goddamn joke—"

"I think that's enough of that," Heather said, and then cringed. "Except his mom called a couple of times too. You want to hear those?"

"He could be with her," I said. I didn't put it past him, and my blood wasn't just boiling at how this man spoke to Emmersyn.

It was the edge to his voice. The panic in it. The ultimate, absolute unmitigated fury and it had nothing to do with his embarrassment. She'd *ruined* something for him, more than his ego.

And that worried me.

"Let's try one." Emmersyn nodded decisively. "I need to know."

A few seconds later, a woman's accented voice came through. "Emmersyn, dear. I don't... I don't know what's going on, but I'm happy for you. Wherever you are, whatever has happened." Her voice lowered, like she didn't want to be heard, and my pulse kicked up in my chest. "Do not come back here. Lincoln is... he is not angry, Emmy, he's losing his mind and there are things I've learned recently that you don't know... but whatever happened between you two, whatever he did to you... stay safe. He is... he is not okay right now. I just wanted you to know, I am not upset this happened. Elias is well... Elias is Elias, and he is not happy, but he is not happy with Lincoln either. I only called to let you know that. That we are thinking of you and we understand, I think I know why this happened. Stay safe, Emmy, and take care."

She hung up, and Emmersyn stared at the phone, bug-eyed. "What does she know that I don't? What in the hell is going on?"

Pretty sure that was the hammer that landed we were all wondering, staring at each other, slack-jawed and confused.

And Emmersyn? More than a little terrified.

"Is it too early to start drinking?" Heather asked.

She tossed the phone onto the counter. Emmersyn stared at it while Heather helped herself to my wine fridge.

"You okay?" I asked Emmersyn quietly.

She shook her head, not taking her eyes off the phone like Lincoln could jump right out of it and slash her throat. Given his panic and the worry and intensity from his stepmom, it wouldn't surprise me.

"No," she finally said. Slowly, hazy green eyes rose and met mine. "I don't know if I am or not."

EIGHTEEN
EMMERSYN

Lincoln sounded like a man at the tail end of a five-day bender strung out on meth or cocaine. His stepmom sounded like she'd been fearful of her own life while she spoke to me in rushed, hushed whispers. What in the hell was happening? Neither of them sounded like the people I'd known and loved for so long. And Lincoln? I could practically see him pacing, his tie askew, shirt unbuttoned and half pulled out of his waistband, dress pants wrinkled like some frat bro who'd partied all weekend and slept in his clothes for two days straight.

This wasn't *Lincoln*. Not the guy I knew, but as I was quickly realizing, I didn't think I knew him at all. Whatever version this man was, was not the man who held my hand on walks through the city, who always made sure he stood on the street side and who hadn't let me open a car door in three years. He was not the man who took me shopping at a furniture boutique before we moved into our place *"just to look"* and then special ordered everything that had caught my eye, surprising me the day we moved in together with everything I'd wanted. This was not the man who bought store-bought cakes for any small or large celebration and then neatly scripted whatever we were celebrating with icing on top by himself.

This was not the man who made me feel like a princess, who bought me flowers just because, and admitted he spent three months trying to find the perfect engagement ring for me.

I did not *know* this man, and that was stunningly terrifying.

Heartbreakingly sad.

I gaped at the phone, practically gnawing a hole in my bottom lip until Heather plopped down next to me and slid a glass of wine in front of me. It blocked my view of the phone, but barely. I brought it to my mouth without thinking, without caring it was something like eight in the morning and yeah... day drinking the day away seemed like the best idea she'd had since I met her.

"He'll cool down," she murmured and rested her head on my shoulder. "Keep focused on what this means for you. Once you get your trust fund you finally get to start looking into those nonprofits you've been talking about for so long. Or maybe you can do something for kids this winter still, like organize a donation drive for Christmas presents, surprise a family with gifts. Your heart is huge, Emmersyn, and all that money you have will do great things."

Tears welled in my eyes. Across from us, Kane watched us closely. Too close.

"Toy drive?" he asked.

Heather kissed my shoulder and sat up. "You haven't told him what you wanted to do with the money?"

She was surprised, with good reason. I told everyone I was close to what I wanted the money used for.

"I mentioned nonprofits for kids who didn't grow up with my privilege, just not specifics. And until I can get Glen to call me back, none of that really matters. Shit." I dropped my head into my hands. I knew this would be bad. I knew Lincoln was *pissed*. Hell, my side still ached and the bruise he'd left in memory of him was fading, but still a pale yellow.

"It'll be okay," Kane said and the cushion next to me depressed with his weight.

His hand rubbed up and down my back. Yesterday, that might have made me feel warm, today all I felt was shame.

For bringing him into this. For going along with it. I shook my head and groaned. "I'm so sorry."

"Hey." His voice was a whisper, kind, like he was trying not to scare me. "Look at me."

I refused. I couldn't. I'd already run upstairs and puked this morning when the stress got to me. The only option after that was to shower to feel slightly human, I hadn't been joking—if I was going to have a shitty day, I thought it would help me feel better if I didn't look like a drowned rat. Wishful thinking.

Something warm and firm settled at my chin. Then pressure hit, lifting my chin and turning it at the same time so I had no choice but to lift my head. Kane's knuckle was at my chin, and his dark, steely eyes were on me as soon as I blinked away my surprise.

"What did I tell you? I don't do anything I don't want, and right now, after seeing how freaked out he is and how insane he's sounding, I'm glad you're here, okay? Don't apologize for something I volunteered to do. As far as your trust, I'll give my lawyer a call. There has to be something he can do to make sure we get you what you're owed, okay?"

I stared into his dark, rich eyes as he spoke and felt the twisted knot in my stomach uncoil. "Thanks Kane. You're a good man."

His mouth kicked up at the corner. "As your husband, it's now my job."

I laughed softly and then his smile vanished. "Go. Go outside, hang in the pool with Heather. There's nothing we can do about Lincoln's tantrum or what his mom said until we know more." His brows tugged in, wrinkled with worry. "We'll figure the rest out later, okay?"

"Come on." Heather pulled on my hand until I stood with her. "Kane has a point. We now know he's pissed, but he's still almost a full country away. There's nothing else you can do until banks and businesses open Monday anyway, so let's go see if we can have some fun."

"Just don't get drunk and drown in my pool, please," Kane called out, and by the wink he gave me, I figured that was more directed at Heather.

"Geez, bro, you're always ruining my fun."

These two. Even while I was still on the verge of tears, they could still make me smile.

HEATHER DUG out two floating pool chairs from Kane's garage along with a floating cooler where she settled our bottles of wine and that was how his parents found us when they showed up, Heather and I lounging in the pool, me three drinks in and wearing a teal one-piece suit Kane bought for me.

He'd needed to go into practice. A light day he said to stretch and recover and watch game film, so he wasn't home when Tracy and Chuck showed up, apparently having a key because they walked right in.

For being in their late-fifties, Tracy Andrews didn't look a day over thirty. Her hair, black and sleek like both Heather and Kane's, was cut in a severe bob that rested at her shoulders. It shone in the sunlight as she stripped out of the cover-up she wore, revealing a fire engine red bikini and a svelte body. Her features were like Kane's, all sharp-edged and lines that gave her a serious look where Heather had the softer features of their dad. But Tracy's heart was larger than all of Massachusetts, and I'd always felt welcome by them. Especially her.

She waved at us as she headed straight to the hot tub and then called to me. "Come here, sweetheart. Let me love on you a bit."

"You better hurry," Chuck said, entering the backyard with a cooler filled with, I assumed, beer, considering he had a simple

Coors Light in his hand, navy-blue swim trunks and a white T-shirt on. He looked as healthy and built as Kane and always wore a deep farmer's tan from working in his fields and with his cattle all day long.

Their son might have made it to the NHL and they could have easily retired, leaving behind a lifetime of hard work, but when Kane offered them a chance years ago, Heather said they laughed their asses off at him.

"No one is taking my farm," Chuck had said. "Until I can't work it anymore and I'm ready to let it go."

And that was that. They lived a simple life in a small town in the northeast corner of New York where the largest city was Albany, almost an hour south of them.

"Go," Heather whispered, grabbing on to my float to stabilize me. "She's worried about you."

"Right." I pushed the float to the pool and scrambled out of it on all fours. Once I was on my feet, Heather handed me my wine.

"Better bring the bottle, too," Tracy called out. "We're probably going to need it."

I tossed a scowl at Heather. "You're just like your mother."

She blocked the sun with a hand at her forehead and grinned up at me. "Best compliment ever."

If only we were all so lucky.

Hell, even Irena had been a better mom to me in three years than my mom had been in my first eighteen but since I was ignoring reality today, I kicked that thought to the curb and drowned the lump in my throat with a sip of wine.

The hot tub was hot, despite the heater being turned off, and I flinched as I went from the cool pool to the heated water. Once I was settled in and Chuck handed Tracy her own fresh glass of wine with a kiss at her temple and a squeeze of my shoulder, she tossed one arm around me, pulled me tight to her and squeezed.

"Come on, sweetheart. Tell me everything."

It might have been the sun. The heat. The emotions or the fact

I caught sight of my glimmering diamond shining on my left ring finger.

Whatever it was that flipped my switch, I buried my forehead into the crook of her neck and sobbed.

CHUCK'S FACE was red as a tomato and he'd crushed the empty beer can in his hand before replacing it with a fresh one. While I told Tracy everything, he'd joined us in the hot tub, keeping his distance, but his anger boiled as much as the water.

Eventually Heather climbed in as well and sat next to her dad. Once I was done, Heather and I filled them both in on Lincoln's erratic behavior of late and Irena's concerned phone call, his dad turned to Heather.

"It's a damn shame you didn't bring that phone to me. Five seconds. Give me five seconds with that boy and it wouldn't have come to this."

"If you'd let me have your Remington when I asked for it, I could have taken care of him when he showed up at Graham's," Heather chimed in.

"There are no deer there," Chuck said and patted his daughter on the head. "But you are a hell of a shot."

"See?" Heather grinned at me. "Buckshot would work every time."

Goodness gracious. I didn't need to envision Heather walking around with a shotgun slung over her shoulder, even if I knew she could handle it just fine. She grew up on a farm. Hunting was a way of life, as was shooting coyotes and other predators to keep their cattle safe.

"It's sweet you're all so protective."

"Nonsense." Tracy rubbed my shoulder before finally pulling her arm from behind me. "You're family. It's what we do."

Heather smirked. "And now she's really family."

"And speaking of..." Tracy sipped her wine and set it on the ledge. "Be kind to him, okay? And be patient. We all know he thinks he's still wrapped up in Ava, but as his mom, and I shouldn't even be saying this probably—"

"When has that ever stopped you—" Chuck muttered.

Tracy rolled her eyes. "He's over her, he's just not over the guilt that he didn't give her what she needed. That's Kane's problem. He's a protector to his core, a problem solver, and he knows he put hockey in front of his relationship. Don't get me wrong, we adore Ava. Absolutely still love her and we're so thrilled for her with this new man she has, but Kane's problem isn't that he still loves her, it's that he didn't protect her."

My gut flipped as she spoke. I wasn't so sure she was right about that, not based on the look Kane made when her name was mentioned.

Plus, there was the ardent expression he gave when I realized he still loved her. *I always will.*

Yeah, didn't sound like Mama Andrews knew what she was talking about, but considering Chuck and Heather both nodded, I didn't argue.

"Okay," I said instead.

"And I know this isn't real," she kept going. "I know you two will become great friends, though, I'm sure of that. And if it ends, or *when* it's set to end, just make sure you two are truly on the same page with it. Don't walk away if you don't want, and without fighting for it."

"You're making it sound like I wouldn't *want* to walk away. He's helping me, I know the score. And I know where I'm at."

"Do you, though?" Her brows arched in a classic Kane move.

Of course I did.

I wasn't going to fall in love with Heather's brother. Not when he'd so succinctly told me he'd never love me back.

But if Tracy was right...

"Room in there for me?"

I jumped at the sound of Kane's voice. "Hey. You're home."

He must have seen my red and swollen eyes because he glared at his mom. "What'd you do to her? Or say?"

"Nothing." She shrugged and grabbed her drink. "Just a girl talk. Climb on in, honey."

Kane's hot tub was large enough for eight at least, but he and Chuck weren't small men and since Heather and her dad were on the opposite side of Tracy and me, Kane climbed into the hot tub and slid into the seat next to me.

"Fuck, this feels good," he moaned, and closed his eyes. He tipped his face to the sun and spread his arms out to the side.

I forced myself to remember how to swallow. With his arms out, muscles in his biceps flexed. Water rolled and bubbled over his chest, a dark smattering of hair that wasn't too much, but definitely not bare. He inhaled deeply, and as he blew out a breath, his corded throat made my mouth water.

Next to me, Tracy patted my thigh beneath the water and when I turned to her, she winked. "See?"

Good god. Yeah I saw. I saw her sexy as hell son sitting next to me, totally oblivious to the fact I was checking him out—but his mom didn't miss a beat.

I stared at the water, my cheeks warming that had nothing to do with the water or the sun and felt both her and Heather's eyes on me. And I was pretty sure they were feeling pretty damn pleased with themselves.

Heather squeezed my hand as we followed Chuck and Tracy down the arena's hallways to the locker room area. There was a family waiting room around the corner where we could hang out while the guys showered. The family room, I'd learned the other night, also had a small, staffed daycare area so wives of players with kids could drop them off and enjoy watching their guy play in peace.

Lizzie and Paige had both taken their babies there the other night for the first period so they could watch a little bit of the game without distraction.

"And the game was incredible."

The game was equally confusing as it'd always been for me. Moved so fast, and changed direction so often, I wasn't exactly sure how they could have named positions when it all looked like madness and mayhem. Yeah, I was learning a few of the rules, and every time Kane had the puck, my hands curled into fists with excitement.

But *incredible*? It'd be a while, a long while, before I understood the game enough to call it that.

Chaotic was the only word I could use to describe it.

"It was good they won."

Beating Seattle by three, however, I guess was a good thing.

"You crack me up." Heather bumped her shoulder into mine playfully. "And we haven't had a lot of time alone the last couple days to really talk. You doing okay?"

She dropped her hand and grabbed mine, giving it a squeeze.

"I'm still in denial mode until I can talk with Kane's lawyer tomorrow and give Glen another call."

"Good. Then I hope you two can finally enjoy a night alone."

"You're not staying there again?"

"No. Mom and Dad fly out early tomorrow too so I'm riding with them. I'm staying at the hotel with them by the airport."

My bottom lip pushed out into a pout. Ever since Heather started working out at Martha's Vineyard, I hardly saw her. These last few days with her, despite the reason, had been a surprise blessing I needed after the last couple of months.

"I'll miss you," I pouted. "Too much."

"I'll make sure I get back out here this fall. Graham's talking of leaving the Vineyard at the end of October, so my schedule will be more flexible. Oh, and guess who's coming out next week?"

"Who?"

"Zack Walters. His band and their entire families."

"Holy crap. Why?"

"Graham says they've decided to do a reunion tour, but first they want to re-record old music."

Zack Walters had been one of the largest rock stars several years ago. He'd been under CocoRock Productions ever since the beginning. One of the nicest guys I'd ever met, and I'd spent some time with him when he was just getting started. Granted, back then I was a gangly teenager going through some awkward years and he was a hotshot in his early twenties, but he'd been cool to me. He got married to an even kinder woman named Nicole, and then the rest of the band slowly did as well. After they started having children and didn't want to tour ten months out of the year, they slowed down on the music production.

My grandma had been heartbroken but understood.

"No way! For real?"

"Scout's honor. Graham's team is planning on announcing as soon as they get the album done."

"Tell him I said hello, and make sure he gives me good tickets and backstage passes if they tour this way."

"What are you two ladies squealing about?" Tracy asked, and I realized we were now stopped outside the locker room.

I glanced at Heather. I wasn't a part of CocoRock in any form outside of being an heir, but since I didn't have anything to do with the business, it wasn't my news to spill.

"Graham won't care. He trusts me." She turned to her parents. "Zach Walters and his band are coming back for a reunion tour. Plans to start right after the holidays."

"Oh. Well, that's... nice."

Heather and I both laughed at Tracy. If her music didn't have the class country squawk in it, she wanted nothing do with it. "I hope that goes well for them."

"Sure, Mom. Right."

Heather and I collapsed into each other, laughing, while Tracy's brows furrowed in confusion. "What'd I say?"

"Nothing, Mom." Heather peeled away from me to give her a hug. "You are perfect just the way you are."

And wasn't that the truth. I wasn't sure they made them better than Tracy Andrews.

"Emmersyn?"

I turned at the sound of a woman calling my name and smiled at Alicia. "Alicia. Hi! How are you?"

"Good. Good. Just leaving the media area. We, uh, talked to Kane. About the game. Someone brought up your marriage and wedding."

"Oh?"

And with a snap, reality was slamming back into me. "Was... did everything go okay?"

"Great." She smiled, and that relieved tension settling between my shoulders. "But since you're here, and his whole family is, I'm thinking I could get some pictures of you and have Kane post them on social media pages?"

Heather snorted. "My brother never uses those."

"Well, he might want to. It will help the public perception of everything." Her eyes slid to me, an apologetic look on them.

Which meant there were still unflattering things being said about his new wife. Me.

Great.

"If his fans see he has his family's support, it could help them get behind you both. As it is, they're not being kind, and my job—"

"I know. I get it. And if it distracts him, his game could suffer. No one wants that," I assured her.

She exhaled, relieved I understood. "Exactly."

"Where do you want us?"

"Right here is great. Waiting outside the locker room for him, together, if that's okay? Fans always love a little backstage look even if it's a cement hall."

"Perfect." Chuck came up and tugged me to his side, and Tracy rounded my other side. "And if you could get us some pics of the wedding, we'd love that too. Our friends will want to see and we have quite a few followers who think following us on The Facebook or The Gram will be a way into Kane's life."

"It's not *The* anything," Heather laughed at her dad. "You're so *old.*"

"Watch it," he warned her with a loving glare. "I'll say and do whatever I want." He turned to me and side-hugged me tighter. "And that includes supporting my new daughter, too. Any way she needs."

Tears burned my eyes.

Gosh. This family was incredible. "Thanks, Chuck."

"Nonsense." He grinned and turned to Alicia. "You can call me Dad."

KANE YAWNED ALMOST AS SOON as he entered his home. "Damn, it feels good to be back."

He kicked off his shoes after we shut the door, alarmed the system behind me, and slid his shoes beneath the sideboard table near the entry.

He'd had to head to the arena at two in order to prepare for their seven o'clock game and I might have only been around him for two games, but already I could see what he meant about the intensity of the season. There was always something to be doing, somewhere to be going, or a late-night return home. Once they finished in the locker room and the media room, and then Alicia declared she had enough pictures once he came out of the locker room, there'd been chatting with some of the guys on the way to the car, Gabby and Paige talking about their first away game later this week.

It all made my head spin, and even if it was only eleven, he'd had nine hard hours of work.

"Do you need anything?"

The house was quiet, a drastic change from the last couple of days with Heather and their parents around. I missed all of them already and my goodbye to Heather might have included alligator-sized tears on my part.

Now, real life was coming to a head.

Where Kane and I could no longer pretend we weren't married, that we weren't going to have to be seen together when we could, being all happy and lovey dovey. Alicia said that'd be important on his home game days and off days so his fans would get used to seeing us together. Not that Kane cared about that, it didn't seem to be affecting him at all... but what if it did eventually?

I couldn't handle it if he didn't play his best because his head was filled with the knowledge people were giving him shit for who he was basically tricked into marrying.

"No, I'm good." He yawned and covered it with his fist, hanging up his keys on the wall by the kitchen counter. "Some water, and then I'm going to hang out in the sauna before I head to bed. You doing okay?"

"I will be."

He glanced around his dark living room, lit up only by two lamps by the couch. "House feels weird with everyone gone."

"Your parents are good people."

"The best. I'm sorry you didn't grow up with that."

"I had my grandparents. They made up for it."

"Then I'm sorry you lost them so soon, that they put you in this position."

The sincerity made my chest squeeze. Because of course he'd truly care. About me. About a loss that occurred years before we ended up in this predicament.

I'd experienced enough range of wild emotions lately. I didn't need to handle any more tonight.

"Well, there are worse men to be married to," I teased, and then realized what I said.

That he'd been a shitty husband to Ava—or at least believed he'd been, and that I'd truly almost married a worse man. "Shit. I'm sorry. That sounded funnier in my head. Forget it."

"I'd like to apologize to you, again, for that kiss."

"What?"

It came out of nowhere.

"That kiss before our wedding. I shouldn't have done that. It was just..." His voice trailed off, and I was left wondering. A mistake? A curiosity? Some deep-seated attraction to me he didn't want to admit to?

"I'm struggling with the fact I want to do it again, too, and that I promised you I wouldn't until you asked for it."

"Kane..." This time I was the one who lost their words.

"I know. I get it. It'd be a dumb thing."

"Not dumb. Nothing you do would be dumb, but it might be... dangerous?"

"Dangerous?" His eyes widened with surprise.

"I don't know if I'd want to stop at kissing," I admitted. "And knowing how you feel, I don't know if I'd walk away unscathed at the end of this, if that's all it was."

He sighed and looked away from me, staring at the dark kitchen cabinets while his jaw tightened. "I said things could get complicated if we did this."

"You did."

"Looks like I was right."

He turned, hurried up the stairs, and I stood with my feet glued to the kitchen floor.

Complicated was right.

TWENTY

KANE

"John. Thanks for meeting with us so early." I shook my attorney's hand and introduced him to Emmersyn.

"Mr. Banks. I can't thank you enough."

He shook her hand and stepped back, inviting us into his office with his arm outstretched. "Not a problem at all. I figured it'd be best to meet as soon as we could, so I could let you know what I've learned this last week."

Next to me, Emmersyn swiped her hands down the front of her thighs. She'd been nibbling the side of her thumb all morning and I was thankful I didn't have to be at the arena until after dinner before we flew out to San Jose, so we had time to meet with John when he called us.

I'd worked with John Banks since Ava and I moved to Las Vegas. He handled my contracts for sponsors. When Ava left, he'd set me up with a divorce attorney in the same firm to make sure it went through as seamlessly as possible. Banks's firm had attorneys that handled every kind of law imaginable, and I was thankful he was on my team.

"I suppose first, I should say congratulations to the two of you."

"Thank you," we both said at the same time. I turned to

Emmersyn and smiled, but she was focused on the attorney, stress straightening and tightening her spine and every other muscle I could see. I reached out and took her hand, held it softly in mine.

I hadn't been joking one bit last night when I admitted I still wanted to kiss her. I wanted to do more, in every room in my house and outside for that matter, but the terrified look on her face as she admitted I had the potential of breaking her heart pulled me back.

Until I could get my own shit together, I needed to keep my mouth, and other parts, off her. But we said we'd be friends, and friends held hands, right?

I drifted my thumb over hers and slowly, the tension in her body relaxed as John tapped a stack of papers on his desk.

"So. I read through your grandparents' will and testament along with their trust agreement you gave me last week."

"Okay..." Emmersyn's voice wobbled.

I hated we were here. Hated she kept having to relive this nightmare and getting money she was entitled to wasn't so easy and Lincoln was still only making things worse.

"You had another trustee handling everything originally, correct?"

"Yeah." Emmersyn's nose scrunched. "Yes, sir. Bob Dickerson. He had been my grandparents' attorney for years, and they trusted him, but he was retiring. Lincoln and I had just gotten engaged when Bob called me for a meeting. Introduced me to the partner at the firm he wanted to take over my account with them, but Lincoln talked me into moving everything to the firm his family uses. Said it'd be easier long term if everything was together." She pushed a piece of her curled hair behind her ear and frowned. "Stupid, I know. I should have kept it separate like Bob suggested."

"Hindsight is always clearer," he said with a kind smile. "However, and I'm surprised Bob didn't catch this, or maybe he knew and did it anyway, but there's a clause in the trust."

"What?" She sat up straight and her hand gripped mine tighter.

I followed suit and leaned forward. "What clause?"

"The trustee is supposed to always be a part of Dickerson, Barton, and Booth."

"No." Emmersyn shook her head. "That can't be right. Bob had always protected me. He would have known about that. He wrote everything."

John nodded. "He did. I'm not sure why he would have allowed the trust to be violated. Maybe he didn't trust the partner who was taking over his accounts, maybe he trusted you and this... Lincoln Powers." He glanced down for the name and back up. "But regardless. This actually makes the position you're currently in pretty easy. You'll need Mr. Hayes to sign over the trust, but if he doesn't, you can absolutely sue the firm and take him to court. If they fight it, they're looking at a pretty substantial lawsuit on their hands."

He grinned and clasped his hands on the desk in front of him. "I'm not sure how it happened. Perhaps Mr. Dickerson simply forgot and knew you so well he didn't feel the need to review the trust before you approached him for a new trustee. It could be that simple, but irrespective of how the error occurred, if the trust isn't placed back in the original firm, Mr. Hayes can be sued, and I am one hundred percent betting on the fact that Mr. Elias Powers isn't going to want that made public any more than he's wanted news of your wedding made public."

Emmersyn bit her lip. "Right."

He glanced at both of us and I saw that look in his eye, that knowing look that said he knew exactly why we'd gotten married. I kept my mouth shut about it. He'd seen me after Ava left. He'd known me for years.

But things were changing too. Because I couldn't stop thinking about Emmersyn and right then, thinking of Ava didn't create that burning hole in my chest like it always did.

"It's that easy?" I asked, because finally, something seemed to be going right for her. And usually if it sounded too good to be true, it usually was.

"I wouldn't say easy. I'd suggest you call Dickerson's office, talk to his partner or someone else there, explain the situation and ask them to review the documents. I'm certain they'd still have them. Or if you'd prefer, I'm happy to handle it for you. They'll need to file for a trust return and everyone will need to sign documents, but yes, assuming we can get in contact with Mr. Hayes, this issue should be rectified rather quickly."

"Wow," Emmersyn sighed. Her smile wobbled as she glanced at John and me. Her hand trembled in mine. "I didn't know I didn't... how could I have been so stupid? Or Bob? I mean..."

"Like I said, there are lots of reasons why this happened. I wouldn't beat yourself up over it, and I'm assuming you had your own reasons for trusting your ex-fiancé which you've learned are no longer valid. We all make mistakes, Miss Houghton." He shrugged and raised his hands, palms up. "Even the best lawyers."

"Right. Okay. I know you said I could call, but if you could... at least Dickerson's firm, I'd appreciate it."

"I'll do it before my next appointment and can let you know as soon as I hear from them."

She smiled then, and it was a true one that made her green eyes sparkle. "That'd be wonderful. Thank you."

He stood and pushed away from his desk, smiling at both of us. "That was worth the last-minute trip in, wasn't it?"

"Absolutely it was." I held out my hand and shook his, he gripped my arm firmly, gave me that same knowing look as earlier and squeezed my bicep with his other. "Let me know if there's anything else you need."

"Oh..." Emmersyn said and looked at me. "We never did a prenup."

Shit, she was right. We'd talked about it. I trusted her, one hundred percent. We'd walk away from his eventually with what we both had. No harm, no foul. And yet, for the first time, the thought of her actually walking away twisted my stomach. We were *married*. I knew the exact reasons why, but that didn't mean like Heather said, I wouldn't take a marriage seriously.

Fuck me.

I turned to John. "A post-nup? Is there such a thing?"

"Yeah." He cleared his throat. "I can get a family attorney working on that and get back to you. If that's what you both want?"

"It's for the best," Emmersyn said, nodding. "I think. Don't you?"

She glanced up at me, nibbling on that damn lip again. I had to force myself to swallow to stop thinking about how she'd tasted. How soft those lips were and how warm.

"Yeah. We walk away with everything we brought into it. I can't get access to your trust, you're not entitled to any sponsorships or anything I might get while we're married, right?"

"Right." She blinked and looked away. Hell, it'd been her idea, but she didn't look all that happy about either.

Which meant, hope was on my side—as soon as I figured out where my heart and head were. Because I wouldn't take another step toward Emmersyn until I was absolutely sure I wouldn't end up breaking her heart.

***

"WE SHOULD GO CELEBRATE," I said once we slid back into my Land Rover after leaving John's office.

"Isn't that bad luck? Celebrate before anything's official?" She pulled lip gloss from her small purse and swiped it over her lips, pressing and rolling them out into a pout. Done, she slipped it back into her purse and flipped back the mirrored visor. She glanced at me. "What? Am I wrong?"

There wasn't a damn thing wrong with her. Or what she said.

"Fine. No celebration. Let's go grab some lunch. Be visible."

Alicia had suggested we spend time out and about, walking the

Strip, being seen. The more pictures that popped up of us happy and in love, the sooner people would stop calling her a slut or whatever they were still calling her on social media. Emmersyn and I had both deleted our social media apps on our phones, so we weren't tempted to look at them, but Alicia had a point.

This needed to be real. At least real enough we could, at some point, convince Elias to get his son under control if he kept being a manic asshole.

"Right. Any suggestions?"

"I know just the place."

And fortunately, since we'd dressed nice to go meet with my attorney, we'd fit the dress code.

I pulled my car out of the parking lot, turned left, and drove through Vegas until I turned on Las Vegas Boulevard and we headed south, dodging tourists and Ubers and drunken assholes not giving a shit about the crosswalks, stumbling across the streets even though it wasn't even yet noon on a fucking Monday.

I pulled into the north side of the Bellagio, up to their valet service area.

"The Bellagio?" Emmersyn asked, an excited smile lighting up her face as she took in the fountains.

"Thought you'd enjoy lunch overlooking the fountains."

"I would. Definitely."

I climbed out of the car, taking the tag from the valet and handing over my keys and helped Emmersyn out of the SUV. She was wearing a casual but classy peach colored dress. The straps were wide, and the neckline was modest. Most of it was tightly fitted and showed off her curves, but the dress flared out at her hips and she'd paired it with nude heels that almost brought her up to my chin. She'd looked so damn gorgeous when she met me at the bottom of the stairs this morning, I'd almost dropped to my knees right there and begged her to take a chance on me.

The same thoughts slammed into my chest as she took my hand and climbed down from the SUV like she'd been born in high heels. Elegant and classy and sexy described Emmersyn to perfection.

I forced myself not to gawk at her. Remembering the earlier promise I made to myself, I slid her hand to my forearm and escorted her inside.

"I was thinking the LAGO. They not only have delicious small plates, but we might be able to sit outside on the patio and watch the fountains. It's one of my favorite brunch or lunch restaurants, but if you'd prefer something else—"

"It sounds perfect," she replied as the doors were opened for us and we stepped inside. The air conditioning cooled me almost immediately, but thankfully it wasn't yet scorching hot. Sitting outside wouldn't be unbearable and we'd be fortunate to get a light mist from the fountain show to keep us cool.

We strolled into the Bellagio, and Emmersyn's eyes went wide with wonder. Harry Winston was straight ahead of us and as we turned to pass it and head toward LAGO, Emmersyn's head swiveled backward.

"It amazes me sometimes, the obscene wealth people have, even if I grew up with it."

"You don't live like it."

She shook her head. "No. My grandparents did a really good job of trying to keep me grounded, especially after both of my parents went off the rails. My dad had money he earned, and threw his cash around like pennies, and my mom was so used to living off her own trust fund they'd set up for her I'm not sure she ever lived with two feet on the ground. I wanted to be different than them, different than the people I went to school with."

It was probably only one of the few reasons why Heather loved her so much. Emmersyn was probably one of the top twenty wealthiest women in the country, at least she would be once she got her trust, but she was right. She absolutely didn't live like it, and considering I'd grown up a farmer's son and never had more than a few quarters to my own name growing up, I'd tried really hard not to let my own fortune get the better of me.

But hockey players and most professional athletes were smart with their money if they listened to advice in the beginning. Our careers could end in a second. One wrong hit, one career-ending injury, and our millions vanished so it was important to invest and create different streams of wealth. Some of that came from simply investing in the market, some came from purchasing real estate. Others started non-profits or owned restaurants. Me? I'd put most of mine in real estate and rented out properties on the East Coast. All under a handful of different LLCs that'd be difficult to trace back to me.

Essentially, even if my career ended tomorrow, I'd be fine for life.

We were seated quickly, and fortunately, were able to be given a table right by the glass railing outside. As soon as we did, the fountains went off to the music and the show began.

Emmersyn smiled with glee and it was one more thing I was starting to like about her—how the simplest things could bring such a huge smile to her face.

She was right. She didn't at all live like someone entitled to their wealth and it only made me more curious about her, especially since she said she did a lot of volunteering, but hadn't mentioned a job.

After drinks were ordered, water for me and a mimosa for her, I rested my forearms on the table, pushing away extra glasses and the blue napkin and silverware.

"Tell me more about what you want to do."

She'd still been watching the show, and my question took her by surprise. "What I want to do?"

"Yeah. You mentioned nonprofits for underprivileged youth, and Heather mentioned clothing or toy drives or something for Christmas, but you haven't really said. Do you have plans?"

"Nothing concrete." A wistful look took over her face, softening every one of her perfect features from her slim, pert nose to her high cheekbones and pillowy lips. "But yeah, I have some ideas. Mostly about the education system, but in general, helping them. It's not a child's fault they're born into poverty or abusive homes or ones filled with neglect, and while I think there are a lot of great systems in place to help, a lot of them are also funded by governments and rely on lawmakers and taxes to support them. I'd like to be able to support some organizations where donations don't factor into being able to help."

God, she was beautiful. So elegant. So intelligent, and so damn kind it stole my breath away and I had to work to gather myself. The bar, Malley's, that Joey took over had always helped support youth baseball leagues for underprivileged kids in Las Vegas. Dominick had gotten into coaching youth hockey back for community service, but he enjoyed it so much he was doing it again this year, once again coaching Holly's son, Ben, but he also bought uniforms and new skates and gear for every single child who registered to play. There were a lot of guys who did good things like that with their money, especially for youth and while I'd donated my money and time when I could and easily, I'd never found a cause that I could throw my full support behind that would include my name in it.

"Like what?" Because this was interesting. She wasn't talking about sports, but education and meeting needs that could be done everywhere. In every city of our country and hell, even suburbs and small rural towns similar to the one I grew up in.

"I graduated college with a teaching degree in early education. When I had to do my student teaching, I chose one of the poorest schools in Boston."

"You chose that?"

"Yeah. I had some options on what schools had openings, but most of them were private schools or upper middle-class suburbs. I grew up in the city but had never really lived or seen the poorer side outside homeless people on the street. So I figured, why not?"

Why not. She said it with a shrug and such nonchalance. Like every major heiress in the world would simply walk willingly into one of the poorest schools in a major city.

"You're something else," I told her, and by the way she blushed, I figured she knew how impressed I was.

Our server came, and we ordered several small plates each. I'd be fed on the plane later by our team's chef with lots of protein and whole grains to keep us healthy for tomorrow's game, so I kept it light, knowing I wouldn't get a normal workout in before we flew out.

Once Pierre refilled my water and left us, I gestured for Emmersyn to continue.

"Tell me more. What's your starting point? What's your ultimate goal?"

She blushed again, and pressed her lips together, gazed out to the fountains while they danced to "Bad Romance."

Fitting, I figured, and hoped she wasn't thinking the same thing I was. Were *we* a bad romance? Hell, so far, we weren't a romance at all, we were more likely to end up being a cautionary tale.

She cleared her throat and gathered her courage, rolling back her shoulders and meeting my gaze dead on. "Eventually, I'd like to run charter schools. Fully funded, with all the technology private schools get. Chromebooks and laptops, smart boards in every room. I'd supply them with hotspots, or anything else so those who couldn't afford Wi-Fi could still get access at their homes. All three meals a day would be included, uniforms paid for, for every student. They'd have updated textbooks, supplies on hand. Basically, I want every student to have access to the same technology and teachers I did. And I don't want teachers spending their own personal income on extra supplies for their classrooms."

Her eyes glazed over as she spoke and my heart thumped an erratic rhythm.

And all I wanted to do was lean forward, slam my mouth to hers and when she was breathless for me, ask how I could help.

"They'd be lucky kids," I said, a thickness growing in my throat.

"Yeah, well, I need to start small, I think, grow to that with connections and working toward that. That's why Heather mentioned the donation drives and things. But schools have already started and Lincoln and I weren't supposed to be married until Christmas anyway, so I had time to think. If I can get access earlier though, I like the idea of a toy drive. I did a lot of volunteering in Boston, working with organizations that were similar and have several contacts already, but now, I don't know if I'd want to go back there. Not with the way things are..." She trailed off, and I again had the urge to punch that piece of shit baby Powers in the face and then leave my own shoe print on his hip.

"You could do it here. A lot of the wives and guys on the team volunteer and have their own non-profits. I'm sure any one of them would be happy to help you get started. Or help out."

"You think?" Excitement lit her eyes, making her vibrant greens sparkle.

"Yeah, Emmersyn. After everything they've already done to help us, you think they wouldn't?"

Me included. I was starting to realize I'd give her anything she needed—in business or for the rest of her life.

Kane stood at the bottom of the stairs with his rolling suitcase handle in his hand, carry-on draped over his shoulder.

It should have been illegal for a man to look so damn good in a suit. His was blue, too bright to be navy, with black pinstripes running through it that had a slight shimmer when the light caught them just right. A black dress shirt with the collar opened at the base of his throat, and black shining dress shoes with no socks, I'd almost swallowed my tongue when he came downstairs.

There I was, in sweat shorts and a short sleeve, oversized white shirt that draped off one shoulder.

We got back from walking around the Bellagio and down to Caesar's Palace. Kane stopped to play a few games, won a thousand dollars in fifteen minutes at the craps table, handed me two hundred and I walked away with five hundred from a roulette table. Around us, people had occasionally clicked our picture. Whether they recognized him from playing hockey, or me from my relationship with Lincoln, or all of the above, I wasn't sure, but Kane made sure we put on a good show.

His hand was either holding mine or at my lower back. He

smiled down at me and wiggled his brows and silently requested I play along.

I'd rolled to my feet at one point when he won at craps, kicked one up behind me and placed my hands on his shoulders as he bent down and kissed the corner of my lips.

"Here you go, baby," he'd muttered and settled his winnings into my hand.

Oh, if only he could get over Ava. Although, I was so turned on, from being around him so much, from living with him and getting to know him, I was starting to think that might not even matter.

We'd live together for a *year*. Yeah, he'd told me I could go elsewhere and be discreet... but who would I ever find that was better than the man currently in front of me, dark hair styled and swept perfectly to the side, checking his phone before sliding it into a pocket in his suit coat.

"I need to get going."

I hoped like hell he didn't see the lust shining like a neon light all over me. "Good luck."

His lips twitched. "You'll be okay here? You've got the cars, and I know the wives get together sometimes to watch the games."

"Sophie already texted me."

"I'll be home Thursday night, late. I think our plane lands at two in the morning or something. So Friday, I guess."

"I know." He'd already left me his schedule for the week on the counter. "You can go, Kane. I'll be all right, you know. And if I didn't thank you for today, thank you. I had a great time hanging out with you."

"You did. At least a dozen times." He smiled then and his gaze fell to the hem of my shorts that were way too short and raked slowly back up, stalling at my chest, my throat, and when our eyes met again, his dark brown eyes were narrowed.

Heated.

Damn. If only he didn't still love his ex. As it was, I felt that look from across the room. The pull of him was undeniable, and before I knew it, I was taking a step toward him.

Then another.

This could be the death of me.

Or maybe... wishful thinking and all... the beginning of something?

Who said it had to be forever?

"I hope you have a good flight," I whispered, and surprised myself with the depth of my voice, the grit in it. "And a good game tomorrow. I'll be watching."

"The whole thing?"

"Every moment you're on the ice, my eyes will be on you."

"Good." He cleared his throat. His voice was as gritty as mine. I was closer to him now, so close I could reach out and touch him, and yet that last step was difficult, leaden with fear and hope and mixed with lust and tinged with oncoming regret.

"What are you doing to me, Emmersyn?"

"Probably the same thing you're doing to me."

Confusing the hell out of me. Spinning my world off its axis. Giving me hope I could still find a decent guy to love me—or at minimum, care and respect me.

"Fuck it," he muttered. He dropped his suitcase and before it crashed to the floor, his lips were on mine, hand at my lower back, and pulling me to him.

"Oh." I gasped in surprise and then hummed in pleasure as our mouths touched, his tongue slipped out and tasted mine.

The kiss was soft, gentle, but the hand at my back was tense, fingers pressing into me and holding me against him like he couldn't walk away. Couldn't let me go.

If only that were true.

I prayed a prayer of fruitless hope that maybe things could be different between us, could become real, and kissed him back, hoping to hide that hope for fear of him pushing me away, but then his mouth opened and he didn't just kiss me, he devoured me like he was as hopeful as me, and I stopped giving two shits about potential heartbreak and regret.

I had this man for a year and we were both clearly fighting attraction.

Would it be so wrong to throw my hands in the air and enjoy the ride?

"I need to go," he rasped, lips at mine and his chest heaving, his arousal evident at my lower stomach. "I need to get to the arena to get the rest of my gear ready for our crew to load on the plane, but we'll pick this back up when I get back."

I huffed a laugh and then was silenced by another breath-stealing, hard kiss.

"Fuck, Emmersyn." Kane's forehead settled on mine as we both settled ourselves down. "I'm kind of pissed I'm riding in with Alix. He's going to give me so much shit if he can see how hard I am right now."

A laugh burst from me, and I gave him a kiss. "You'll manage," I teased.

"Until I get back," he assured me, and after another soft, lingering kiss, he bent down and picked up his suitcase, resettled his carry-on and grabbed his keys.

"See you soon," I told him and gave him space to get to the door.

"You bet your sexy ass you will."

He left, and long after the door was still closed, I was still attempting to pick my jaw up off the floor.

SOPHIE LAID BACK and rested her head on the float. "This was the best idea you've had yet," she said and lifted her bottled water in the air.

Sitting next to me in the small wading area of the pool, Paige laughed. "I think maybe marrying Kane was a better idea. I mean, without it, we wouldn't be able to pre-party for tonight's game in this lovely little oasis."

I wanted to point out I was sure they'd done this dozens of times at Gabby and Joey's house, or even Sophie's because I knew she and Braxton had a pool as well, but I kept my mouth shut.

Mostly because before I could speak, Sophie splashed water at us, kicking it with her feet. "Shut up. You know what I mean. And besides, that's all pretend anyway." She tipped up her sunglasses. "Right?"

"Right." I sipped my own water. We had wine for later, when Gabby would join us after she got off work. Lizzie was staying home with the twins, said she'll need help and company later in the season once she reached her wit's end, but for tonight, she was looking forward to relaxing alone.

Other women were coming, too, and how it'd turned into everyone meeting at Sophie's to me hosting in a house that wasn't technically mine, kind of snowballed.

Mostly because I'd hesitated when Sophie asked me to come, and she invited everyone over here, instead.

I was pretty sure she was trying to make me feel included and comfortable, but the question she asked made me feel anything but.

Because what would happen in a year and Kane decided we were over?

"Uh-oh…" Paige poked me in the hip. "Problems."

"No. No problems. None at all."

I spoke too fast. My cheeks heated too quickly.

Sophie clamored out of her float so fast she ended up falling into the knee-deep water. "What happened? Did something happen? Because you're all blushing and you have to tell us… WAGs' rule."

"Wags?"

"Wives and girlfriends. There are sites devoted to us," Paige explained.

"Websites? For wives and girlfriends?"

"Of all professional athletes on all teams. You should check it out." Her nose scrunched. "Or maybe wait a while."

Great. More reminders that all Las Vegas Vipers fans despised me.

"Enough of the dictionary," Sophie said and climbed out of the pool. "Forget all that stupid stuff. We're here for the good stuff. Now spill the tea. What happened?"

We kissed. He didn't seem to immediately regret it afterward and then he called me sexy.

Just thinking of the way he'd looked at me in that moment was enough to make me squirm in the pool. "I like him, okay? A lot. And it confuses me and makes me scared and excites me all at the same time."

"I don't blame you," Paige said. "You've been through a lot lately."

"Exactly. And what if this is just a rebound thing for me? Like, a good guy is there, in front of me, and I'm still just pissed about Lincoln cheating and becoming a psychopath or something that I'm not thinking straight."

Sophie grabbed her hair and wrapped it up in a bun. Her mascara was now smeared beneath her eyes and she was shaking water off her sunglasses. "Do you *think* you like him because all of that?"

There were so many years I stared at photos of Kane and wished a guy like him would be attracted to a girl like me, slightly overweight, definitely not thin, and see more to me than the thickness of my hips.

Now I had him, and every time Kane looked at me, he definitely liked what he saw—unless that was my imagination working.

"I didn't kiss him for revenge or anything—"

"You kissed him!" Sophie shouted and slapped her hands on the water. "When? How?"

Paige chuckled. "*How* did she kiss him?"

Sophie shoved a finger at her friend. "It's a valid question. Like a little goodbye peck? A friendly little cheek kiss? Or was it…"

"It was more," I admitted, and then shut my mouth. These were his friends first. Wives of men he called brothers. I wasn't sure gossiping about our relationship, fake or otherwise, was smart. "But that doesn't matter. It's that I know he still misses Ava. I don't want to be some temporary placeholder."

"Yeah." Sophie frowned and swam to the side of the pool where the cooler was and grabbed another bottled water. "That sucks, but I don't think Kane's the guy to use someone either, unintentionally or not, so if he kissed you back…" She turned and raised two blond brows in my direction.

"He kissed me back," I confirmed, and couldn't meet her gaze. He hadn't kissed me back, he'd taken over the kiss and devoured me completely.

"Then I think you have your answer, at least on his part. He has to be attracted to you, I mean, you're gorgeous and have tits I'd kill someone for. Real relationships have started with less."

"Less than perfect tits?" I asked, choking on my water.

"I mean, yeah." She pointed at her own. "Like these small little B-cup babies. They're not even tits. They're like tit-lets."

"Tit-lets?" Paige asked, and I was trying so hard not to laugh and completely failing.

"Yes. Like the Chiclets gum? Those small little things? That's what these itty-bitties are, and I'm pretty sure Braxton was attracted to me, and everything I *didn't* have… so why can't Kane be attracted to you and everything you *do* have?"

She made it sound like a valid question. But Sophie was crazy.

"Enough tits talk," Paige said. "Ilsa's waking up." She grabbed the monitor she'd set next to the edge of the pool and climbed to her feet. "I'm going to go get her and be back in five." She pointed at Sophie. "And you'll leave this poor girl alone. Let them figure out their own relationship drama. You and your tits need to let them work it out for themselves."

She grinned and her face was full of mischief and fake innocence. "Why? No one else on the team lets the guys do that."

Awesome.

I pictured Kane getting his own brand of personal relationship therapy and cringed.

Not sure that'd go over well at all.

TWENTY-TWO
KANE

My ass plopped down on the bench and I grabbed a green Gatorade bottle filled with water in front of me. "Your ass is done for the game," Coach Vik said as he paced behind the team, sweat drenching down the sides of his face and onto the collar of his dress shirt.

Pretty sure our coach was the only man who could sweat in an arena built for ice, but whatever. "Got it."

We were up by three, with only ten minutes left. Sure, we could still lose, but I'd had my time on the ice. The other lines needed some work, so no harm, no foul.

Bromann slid down next to me and tapped his stick between his skates. "Good game. Really good game."

"You're better than I thought you'd be."

"Fuck you." He shoved into my shoulder. "Don't be a dick."

I laughed and squirted him in the face with the water bottle. "You know I'm shitting you. But you played a good game. Smooth and focused. Just what we need to make it."

"Damn straight." He slapped the water bottle out of my hands and we both leaned forward.

Braxton stole the puck from San Jose's winger and took off,

passing it to Seth McCabe right before he got tripped by their defense.

"Come on. Come on." I wanted Braxton to do well. There'd been some quiet chatter in the off-season about him being traded for Sven Klemmons from New York. So far, it hadn't happened, but he wasn't as sharp this season as he had been previously. I didn't know if our team could survive losing him and Max all in one season.

McCabe passed it back to Braxton, but San Jose got there first, slapped at the puck and our third line defenders, Calix Weekes and Ryan Easton, charged after it. Easton grabbed it first, and I was surprised with how strong he'd been. As a new recruit, the kid was only twenty, but every time he got on the ice, he didn't show a single ounce of hesitation.

He passed it to Seth who took off with it before passing to Arlo. Arlo swung toward the goal.

"Shit," Bromann muttered as the goalie blocked it and the puck bounced straight to Braxton. He used a slap shot, crouched perfectly, hard hit, and *yes!*

The buzzer went off and I was on my feet next to Bromann, our gloves pounding against the wall.

"That's it! Damn straight, Brax!"

He skated by us grinning and as he did, wiped faux sweat off the front of his cage.

Yeah. He knew he needed that too.

The game ticked down in time, and San Jose never managed to get another goal. We clamored off to the locker room, high on our first win on the road and how the team played.

We were doing it. Executing every single play we needed and so far, we'd kept control of every game, every possession. We'd had few errors and even fewer unnecessary penalties.

This was the kind of team talent and focus that could take us all the way to holding that cup again.

I knocked my stick against the wall for good luck and headed to the locker room.

As soon as I reached my locker, I grabbed my phone. Habit, from years of being with Ava and my parents and sister always watching my games. There were always texts before I got back to the lockers, whether it was bitching about my play, worried if I'd been hurt, or congratulating me.

I ignored the ones from my mom and dad and Heather, because Emmersyn had texted.

A grin split my face before I could hide it.

Great game. Good win. Also, I liked those pre-game stretches.

She ended the text with a wink and a wineglass, which made me hesitate in my reply. Was she playing this off as being drunk?

Who gave a shit. I was pretty certain I'd made myself clear before I left, which meant I didn't think she'd mind a little flirty texting.

After all, she started it.

Just wait and soon you can learn how flexible I am in person. Get some sleep. You'll need it.

I tossed my phone back into my locker and tugged off my helmet. As I shook out my hair, I caught Dom looking at me, an odd look on his face.

"What?"

"You're smiling." He pointed at my face. "I'm not sure I've ever seen that kind of smile on you."

"Shut up." I slapped his hand away with my glove and tore them off. "I smile."

"Yeah, but that's a happy smile. Not sure you've known what that is for some time. Married life treating you well, huh?"

I tried to scowl. Failed.

Dom laughed his ass off and turned to his locker area.

"What is this?" I asked. "Getting me back for the shit I gave you about Holly?"

"Nope. I don't think I need to give you any shit. You'll figure things out on your own."

I started to ask him, *yeah? Like what things?* But I didn't need to actually discuss anything.

So I was attracted to my new wife. So I actually liked spending time with her. And yeah, I was starting to like her in a way that didn't entirely mean friends-only, but big deal.

We had an agreement, and we both understood.

At least I hoped so, because I could give Emmersyn every single thing she wanted, my body included, but I was still pretty sure my heart would never work right again.

I DROPPED my bag in the laundry room and scrubbed a hand down my face. It was two o'clock in the morning and I was as exhausted as I was on edge. We'd won tonight's game in Los Angeles, but barely, and it'd been our hardest pre-season game yet. Dominick lost his cool and ended up with two unnecessary penalties which allowed LA to tie it up with five minutes left in the game.

Fortunately, Joey and Arlo and I were faster than their defense and managed to sneak one past the goalie on a lucky shot when I passed it to Arlo behind their net.

An assist wasn't bad, but I didn't have a goal and that always pissed me off.

The flight home was short, and we'd hurried through our post-game routines in order to make the flight, but Alix and I were so keyed up on the way home, I'd almost invited myself over to his place for a drink to calm down.

Because Emmersyn was in this house—probably sleeping—and I hadn't been able to stop thinking about her since I walked out the door after that kiss.

We'd texted a few times, but there was no more flirting. She'd texted she'd had a call from John earlier but was too nervous to listen to the message he left, and she'd also had a call from Dickerson's law firm she also didn't listen to. I didn't blame her, but I wanted her shit figured out so she could work on her goals and I wanted her drama with Lincoln in our rearview.

Mostly, I wanted her, and I was getting sick and tired after using my hand to take care of my unending and growing need to have her.

Which wouldn't happen now since she was probably sleeping in her bed and the last thing I was going to do was wake her up.

I left my gear in the laundry room and headed to the kitchen for a beer. We only had a light practice tomorrow afternoon and another film day.

One might not knock me out, but hopefully it'd calm me down. I had just grabbed the beer from the fridge, the light from it brightening up the kitchen enough I caught sight of Emmersyn.

She was on the couch, and I was right that she was sleeping. She was also curled up on the couch, head to the back cushion. A blanket was draped over her and there was a book in her lap, facedown and opened like she'd fallen asleep reading, or took a break to close her eyes and didn't open them again. Screw the beer.

I wanted her and since I needed to wake her up anyway...

I moved on quick, light feet to the couch where I flicked on the lamp next to her to its softest setting. She didn't stir while I took the book from her and set it as it was on the coffee table.

My hand went to her cheek and I brushed my thumb over her soft, warm skin. Her shoulder twitched as I leaned in, followed the movement of my thumb with my mouth until I was at the hinge of her jaw near her ear.

"Emmersyn. It's Kane. Wake up, honey."

"Mmm. Hi," she whispered, her voice thick with sleep and her body shivered again as I pressed another kiss to her jaw. "What are you... oh?"

Her eyes opened and I pulled back, staying close and keeping my hand at the side of her throat, running my thumb underneath her jaw.

"You're home."

"I am. We should get you to bed."

She closed her eyes and covered her mouth as she yawned. "What time is it? I tried to stay awake—"

"It's after two. And don't ever think you have to do that for me."

"I wanted to tell you good game in person."

So that was why she didn't text me after the game.

As sweet as that was, and as much as I would have loved to have come to her, wide awake and ready for me, she yawned again and closed her eyes like she could fall back asleep in a second. "Come on. Let me help you up to your room."

She blinked, and a quick frown appeared before she sighed. "Oh. Okay."

"The next time I kiss you or do all the other things I want to do to you, I want to make sure you're awake enough to enjoy them." To prove it, I slid my arm beneath her, and my other beneath her knees, bent down to her side on the couch and picked her up.

"You don't have to carry me."

"I know."

"Kane, come on, I'm not some thin thing you can just throw around like this."

She clung to me like she was afraid I'd drop her, but instead, I readjusted my hold and shushed her. "Does it look like I'm having problems?"

"Well... no."

I took the stairs carefully. It was dark and I couldn't see where I was going, so we slowly made our way up the stairs, Emmersyn clinging to me in fear and uncertainty until I reached the top of the stairs and gently lowered her to her feet.

"Get to bed and sleep well." I leaned in and kissed her cheek, another one at the corner of her mouth. She turned, caught my lips with hers, and I took her offering as gently as she gave it.

Kissing Emmersyn was a sweet experience, where she used her entire body in a simple, soft kiss. Her hands went to my arms, slid down to my hands, and I took her hands in mine and brought them up, settled them at my chest so she could feel the rhythmic pump of my heart. I held one to my chest and cupped the side of her neck with the other. A full body shiver rolled through her, eliciting a slight gasp from her, and before I could lose all control with a woman who was still half asleep, I pulled back, ended the kiss, and squeezed her hand at my chest.

"Go to sleep, Em. We'll pick this up when we're both ready."

She sighed and opened her mouth but I didn't give her a chance to argue.

The first time I took things further with her, did everything I wanted to do, I needed to make sure we were on the same page. And awake. Coherent enough to enjoy everything.

I reached around her and opened her door, guided her inside as she grinned up at me, shaking her head. "Such a gentleman," she muttered.

"Always. Good night."

"Night, Kane."

I left her room before I could show her exactly how un-gentleman-like I could really be.

TWENTY-THREE
EMMERSYN

I closed the door after Kane walked away and settled my back against the door. Breathing out a sigh, I scrubbed my hands through my hair and blew out a breath.

It'd been a long time since I felt that heated pulse at the tops of my thighs from a simple kiss. Even longer since I'd been woken from a deep sleep and been turned on by a whisper in my ear.

Lincoln would have never woken me up on the couch to carry me to my room. He would have given me a blanket, tucked me in, and kissed my cheeks, sure. And it would have been sweet. Made me smile.

Carrying me to my room, up a flight of stairs with the ease of lifting a simple bag of flour? There was no way in hell he would have done that for me.

Kane wasn't Lincoln, though. There was truly no comparison, not with the man Lincoln had revealed himself to truly be. And as I rested against the door, my heart still racing from that kiss, my lips still warm from Kane's and that pulse only growing in arousal instead of lessening, I made my choice.

I knew exactly what I could have from Kane, exactly what he

was willing to give me. So maybe it would never be love or last forever.

Did that mean we had to torture ourselves for the next year? Besides, after Lincoln, a *real* long-term relationship wasn't exactly something I was considering diving into. Not when there was still so much drama left to endure before I would be truly free of him.

Decision made, I pushed off the door and went to the closet where I'd hung the clothes Kane and Heather had bought for me, and a few more items I'd ordered last week. My nightgown was a soft, creamy cotton with a lace trim that fell right over the upper curves of my breasts. The bottom lace hem hit me right above mid-thigh, barely covering my backside. It wasn't the prettiest nightgown or lingerie I'd ever bought, but it was simple, light-weight, and practical. Regardless, it was better than showing up in his room in my boxers and tank tops I'd been wearing. I slipped it on and shivered as the cotton brushed over my hardened nipples and skimmed down my sides. My tan gave me a darkened olive skin tone and made the cream appear even brighter.

In the bathroom, I did a quick wash of my face, moisturized and brushed my teeth. Done, I took in my pink cheeks, my swollen lips and the way my nipples pebbled through the thin cotton.

Oh dear sweet Jesus—I *really* hoped he liked what he saw.

Before I could grow too insecure with my faults, the rolls above my hip bones or the cellulite that appeared on my ass and upper thighs when I looked at my profile's reflection in the mirror, I flipped off the bathroom light, inhaled a deep, settling breath and opened the door to my room.

Kane's bedroom door was closed, but a light shone beneath.

I stepped that way with my knees wobbling, my pulse racing, excitement and fear tripping over themselves in my veins.

It was possible when he said we'd pick this up when we were both ready he meant *him* and not me, or how tired I was.

My hand shook as I grabbed the French handle and pressed

down. The door opened with a click that echoed in his room and as I stepped in, I gasped.

His bedroom was enormous. The same dark, gleaming gray wood floors that were downstairs were laid in a herringbone pattern across his floor. A dark gray rug took up much of the space, and several feet around his bed. A black, four-poster bed took up the center space in his room and outside his room, I caught sight of the pale, twinkling lights on the golf course and the glow of the moon.

I'd done his laundry while he was gone, tried to help out and clean his house, but I'd resisted the urge to enter his bedroom, his private space, and I was feeling no more confident now as I surveyed the room.

There was rich, dark grays and blue artwork on the walls above the bed but before I could inspect them too closely, a door to my right clicked, a bright flash of light lit the room before Kane stepped out in nothing but white boxer briefs that hugged his ass and showed off his own tan before he flipped the switch, bathing us both in a pale light from a bulb fixture above his bed and the light from the hallway.

His head jerked, surprised, and he turned toward me.

Dark eyes flared and widened and he blew out a breath. "What are you doing here?"

"I'm not tired anymore."

"Emmersyn." He spoke my name like a wish and a curse.

And oh shit. Maybe he really wasn't ready for this. For me.

He moved toward me, sleek as a panther and all muscle with languid steps. His chest rose and fell with heavy breaths, high-lighting his bricks for abs and the muscles at his sides. As he did, he grew harder, longer, until an undeniable bulge was pushing against his boxer briefs, outlining *all* of him.

"I don't want to hurt you," he admitted, a softly spoken promise held tight by the tension in his tone.

"I know the score, Kane. I know you won't love me."

I'd have to be okay with that. Wrap my heart in stone and steel so I didn't fall in love with him.

He moved closer. His chest heaved.

His air conditioner kicked on, the hum startling me right before cool air skated across my skin. I shivered from the chill in the air and my nipples tightened into painful points.

Kane's gaze fell straight to them and his jaw ticked as he took another lethal step toward me.

"The things I want to do to you…" He shook his head, as if he needed the moment to clear it, and our eyes met. "Tell me to stop if you change your mind."

"I promise—"

His hands cupped my jaw, silencing me.

"Good."

He lunged.

Maybe it was me.

The next thing I knew, his strong, warm arms were wrapped around me and I was plastered to his body. My breasts pushed against his, nipples scraping lace and his chest. A mewl escaped me as he plunged his tongue inside my mouth, held me hostage with his hands and turned me, walking forward while he forced me backward.

"Fuck," he groaned. "Your mouth is heaven. I can't wait to taste the rest of you."

He was hard as steel, his entire body including his erection that pressed against my stomach, and yet he held me with a tenderness that made my head spin.

This man could do *anything* to me, and I would probably enjoy every moment of bliss.

"Kane," I rasped against his mouth, my hips rolling with need when I finally pressed the backs of my legs to his bed.

"Ready to stop?" There was a hint of humor in his tone, but deeper than that, *desire.*

I shook my head and climbed up backward onto the bed until I was on my knees in front of him. "Not a chance in hell."

"Good." He chuckled and kissed my throat, sending goose bumps skating down my limbs.

My stomach tightened as his hands went to the sides of my nightgown, but he didn't lift it. His hands learned my body through the thin cotton fabric, cupping my breasts and running a thumb over my nipples until I gasped with need.

"Feel good?"

"So good," I moaned into his throat, inhaled the fresh spicy scent of him and kissed my way up to his ear while he played my barely clothed body like he'd already memorized every part of me.

When his hands drifted down to the hem of my nightgown, my thighs tightened. Nerves and that stupid fear made me gasp and look down the length of my body.

"You're beautiful," he murmured against my throat, dipping down to suck a nipple and lace in between his teeth until I bucked with pleasure. "So fucking gorgeous. I've been wanting you ever since that first breakfast."

It was his words that made me relax, and as I did, he lifted my nightgown with one hand, tucked his knuckle of his other hand beneath my chin and lifted my face until our eyes met. "So beautiful, Em. You shouldn't ever doubt that."

My lips parted in surprise and then were met with his mouth, his tongue, only separating until my nightgown was torn off me. Breeze from the fabric and the air conditioner cooled my skin, but that was only flesh deep. Inside I was boiling.

And once I was bare for him, he gently guided me backward, climbing on the bed with me, until I was on my back and he hovered above.

His eyes roamed my body, a look of fierce need in his eyes, and a tightness of his jaw as he finally bent down. He played with my nipples and fondled my breasts and I spread my thighs for him as his hand brushed up my inner thigh, my lower stomach. He used hands and teeth and mouth and tongue to discover every inch of me until his fingers were at my center.

He spread me open for him like a man who wanted to enjoy the pleasure, and then he glanced up at me while he slipped a finger inside.

"Fuck," we both rasped at the same time. My hips arched into him, seeking more, but he continued his discovery with a slow, controlled pace driving me crazy.

"I want to taste you. Can I?"

I nodded, tongue swiping my bottom lip, and I rolled my lips together as he spread me farther open.

At the first lap of his tongue against my sex, I reached out, clung to tight and large and muscled biceps, tried to stay still but I was already so close, so needy that it took moments of him, swirling his tongue around my clit, dipping his tongue deep inside and when he added two fingers, twisted and crooked them and slowly pressed them to my perfect spot, I exploded, chanting his name and digging nails into his arm.

My entire body exploded in a burst of white-hot pleasure as he ate me through my orgasm, continuing it far longer than I ever thought possible. My abs were tight, my inner thighs burned before he slowly brought me down and when he moved up my body, my own desire glistened on his mouth.

I pulled him down to me, kissed the taste of me off his mouth and tongue, and shivered as his erection, still clothed, ran over my sensitive skin. My fingers slid into his briefs and I pushed them down, but he shook his head and looked up.

"Not tonight," he whispered. "Tonight was for you."

"But." I glanced down. He was hard and thick and oh dear god he would feel *glorious* once he was inside of me. "I want to see then."

"You want me to jerk off?"

"I want to watch."

Surprise widened his eyes, replacing his desire and then a grin split his face. He slammed his mouth to mine and kicked off his briefs before crawling up my body, straddling my stomach. "You are fucking perfection."

He gripped his shaft, thicker than I'd thought possible one could be. Long, with a vein that ran the length of him, his hand tightened as he pulled and tugged. Every move made me grow wetter, want him more, until he shoved up his chin, veins popped on his throat and he came, coating my breasts, my nipples, and my stomach.

"Fucking hell, Emmersyn." Kane rolled off me and pressed the length of his body to my side, and still trembling from his own climax, he kissed me in languid, slow moves, slowing us both down until our bodies calmed.

"*You're* perfection," I whispered against his mouth.

He chuckled against mine. "Let me get you a cloth and clean you up. I wasn't expecting that."

I wasn't expecting any of it, but boy, had he blown my mind.

And we hadn't even had sex.

How in the world would I survive *that?*

TWENTY-FOUR
KANE

I woke to Emmersyn's hand at my stomach while I was on my back. She was on her side, facing me, and her hair was a halo of thick chocolate, covering her chest, draping over her shoulder. It was still dark outside, not a peek of sunshine coming through my blinds.

Last night, or rather this morning, had been incredible. Surprising, absolutely. I hadn't expected her to show up in my room, dressed in seduction and wrapped in nerves that I'd turn her away. Only an idiot would do that, and as much as I was trying to be careful with her heart, the moment she promised she knew the score between us, I snapped.

She probably thought I didn't have sex with her last night out of some gentleman need to take things slow, but she couldn't be more wrong. There was no chivalry involved in my decision not to have her the way I wanted, but pure panic. I hadn't had sex in over three years. No way was I embarrassing myself last night. Had I taken time to get myself off to make sure I'd last for her, made it good for her, nothing could have stopped me.

Now, it was morning, my morning erection created a tent in my sheets below my waist, urgent to escape the confines of my briefs I'd pulled back on.

Emmersyn hadn't re-dressed in her nightgown when I told her I wanted her next to me, sleeping with me. No way was I sending her to the guest room after that glorious moment with her. Which made this morning easier, because with how hard I came last night, I was pretty certain this morning wouldn't be nearly as embarrassing.

Her lips were parted as she slept, dark, thick lashes two moons on her upper cheeks. I reached out, smoothed a finger over her eyebrow to see how deep she slept and when she didn't flinch, I rolled to my side, slid my hand beneath the sheet and found the curve of her hip.

She projected confidence in almost everything I'd seen her do, had a competitive streak on the golf course I imagined would stretch to other areas of her life. She had passion to want to help the less fortunate and she had absolutely no damn need to ever hide her body, any part of her, from me. Hell, if Lincoln ever felt like she didn't have the shape of a goddess, it was just one more reason to hate the asshole.

As my hand slid up her side, my thumb caressed the softness of her breast, the side, beneath. I cupped her generous weight in my hand and scraped a nail over her nipple. She flinched at that, and I smiled as she pressed closer. Her hips shifted, the rustle of my white sheets the only sound as she moved her legs and with another scrape and gentle pinch at her nipple, it hardened into the gorgeous bud that made my mouth water.

Her eyes fluttered and her breath increased, but I kept my touch on her light, exploratory. After last night, I wanted to learn more. Everywhere that made her make those little pleased noises. I wanted to find the areas where she was self-conscious so I could worship those until she never hesitated to show her body to me again.

My hand slipped down her stomach, past her belly button and as I came close to the apex of her thighs, she rolled to her back and spread her legs to give me access and let out a gentle hum of pleasure.

"Beautiful," I whispered. And leaned closer, arching over her so I could kiss her cheek, her jaw. "Wake up, beautiful. I need more of you."

Emmersyn's lids fluttered again and slowly opened. Surprise made her green pools widen and clear and as she recognized me, she smiled.

"Hey." She grinned and leaned in for a kiss. As I bent down to answer her silent plea, I brushed two fingers over her clit.

"Fuck, you're already wet," I moaned, and kissed away her shocked gasp, pushed my tongue into her mouth and shoved my fingers deeper. "Shit. Tell me this is okay." I meant to ask first, make sure she wanted more, but her answer was a nod, and her arm flung over my shoulder, pulling me to her.

"Always. Whenever... oh God, you are *good* at that."

I laughed against her mouth and worked her slowly, bending to pay attention to the nipple and breast I'd neglected earlier. She tasted sweet, a light sheen of sweaty salt from sleep, but it only made me more feral, made me want her more.

I didn't need Emmersyn dressed up and cleaned and moisturized and perfumed to perfection—she was perfect the way she came. I worked my fingers inside of her, reveled in every hitched breath and gasp when I bit her nipple. She was sensitive but seemed to like it when I was a bit harder and her other hand came to my neck, slid up my scalp and held me in place as I lapped at her nipple and added my thumb to my hand working her sex.

"Fuck, Kane. I'm going to come."

"Do it. Shatter for me, and then you'll go again with me deep inside of you, crying out my name so damn loud Alix hears you."

His bedroom was on the opposite end of mine. I'd have my work cut out for me, but I was a competitor. And I was hard as rock, desperate to slip inside her wet heat.

I rubbed harder with my thumb, slowed my fingers to put pressure in the spot deep inside of her and when she came, I bit down on her nipple so she cried out in ecstasy. Before her orgasm was done, I'd shucked off my briefs, yanked the sheets off her body, and in the pale glow of the now rising sun, had my first, complete unhindered look over every inch of her magnificent body.

My hands went to her shoulders, and I ran them down her body, the length of her, her stomach. I squeezed her hips and skimmed my hands down the tops of her thighs, widening her legs so I could slide in between, and then I shoved them back, opened her for me. She was shaved, completely bare, and her sex was still wet, pussy still throbbing from her orgasm.

I moved closer, leaned over her while I wrapped my hand around my shaft and right as I brushed the tip of my dick over her clit, I stopped.

"Fuck." I squeezed my eyes closed and the head of my cock so I didn't come.

"What?" She reached up and slid her hand along the side of my throat, over my shoulder.

"I don't have any condoms." Hadn't needed them. Hadn't used them in a decade. Goddamn, I was a fucking moron. "I could go ask Alix, but he'd never let me live that down."

She laughed and leaned up, bracing herself on her elbows. The movement made her breasts jiggle and sway and caused my mouth to water. "I'm on the pill. Take it religiously. Never missed a dose, and I was tested... after I found out..."

Shit. I should have thought about that, at the very least.

"All clean?" I asked. "There hasn't been a woman for me..."

"In years." She swallowed heavily and looked over my shoulder. "I know. You mentioned."

Right, because discussing *Ava* right now would be a great idea for either of us.

Green, worried eyes came back to mine. "I trust you, but if you want to be careful, because of Lincoln and everything..."

I pressed my mouth to hers to shut her up. Of course I trusted her. And he deserved less time in this bed than Ava did. "I trust you, but I can say the same to you. If you want to wait—"

"No. I want you." She whispered it against my lips. And it was beautiful.

It'd been a long time since I was wanted. A long time since someone wrapped their legs around the backs of my thighs. And fuck.

"I might totally embarrass myself here," I warned her, as I reached down, wrapped my hand around my dick and rubbed it through her slickness. I bit back a groan as soon as my head met wet, soft flesh.

"I doubt it, but I'm sure you'd make it up to me."

I laughed at that and then kissed her again. I slid my tongue into her mouth and lined up at her entrance. At that first, true feel of her, my jaw tightened and I had to stop myself from cursing.

"Oh..." she sighed as I pushed in.

I counted my stats to keep from shooting off like a rocket, and then once I was deep inside of her, I held her hips to keep them from rolling and seeking more.

"Give me a second." And fuck, this was embarrassing. I was a thirty-year-old man. I couldn't make this bad for her. Not our first time.

She pushed her head back into the pillow, arched her back. "Take all the time in the world. You feel incredible."

"Same." I looked down. At her full breasts, her tight nipples, the softness of her stomach that just *did* something to me and then where we joined. I slid out, watched my dick come away wet with sweetness and then slid in, rocking as I did, and pulled a groan from deep in her throat.

"Yes," she moaned, arching again, unable to keep those hips still, but fuck this.

I was a fucking athlete. I wouldn't embarrass myself, and even if I was at risk, hard and fast was always good too.

I moved then, slowly, gritting my teeth, and every time I rocked into her, she expelled a breath like I was her fantasy come true. We came together in tongue and teeth clashing, hands roaming and exploring. I grabbed her breasts, pinched her nipples and her hands dug into the flesh of my ass until I braced myself with a knee and rolled to my back, bringing her with me.

"Oh." She mewled as she felt me deep inside and then glanced down her body and slowly up to me.

"Ride me, Emmersyn. Let me see everything."

My hands went to the soft area above her hips, and I yanked her against me. Her breasts bounced, so close to my face that I leaned up and sucked one into my mouth, swirling my tongue over her nipple.

"Kane." There was uncertainty in her tone, and I shook my head.

"Fucking gorgeous. Ride me, Emmersyn, and get me off."

I thrust up, bent my knees behind her, and planted my feet, and even while she still looked uncertain, I plunged into her again, slamming her down onto me. "Let me see you. Every fucking inch of beauty."

"You're insane," she gasped, but as I continued moving beneath her, she eventually set the rhythm, and soon we were working together. I held one of her breasts, played with her nipple, and used my other hand to brace her against me. Every time her breasts swung close to my face, I almost came.

Every hitch of her voice, every noise that escaped her throat made me feel ten feet tall, and then she put a hand on my chest, straightened her back and pushed off, head thrown back, she rode me like she hadn't had an ounce of self-consciousness wash over her and she used my body like her own personal toy.

"Fuck. Yes, Em. Squeeze my dick. Work it. Just like that."

She came on a cry, her core pulsing around me so damn hot, so damn tight. She squeezed my dick from the inside of her, her palm against my chest, and I was pretty damn sure, that was the moment she made my heart start beating again.

"Shit. Yes. Keep coming. Almost..."

I grabbed her hips, thrust her down onto my dick while she screamed my name and *yes* and *shit* and called out to God and then I came, matching her cries with my guttural groans.

She collapsed onto me, hair in my face and her breath at my neck, and I wrapped my arms around her, cupped the back of her head with one hand, and ran my other up and down her back. "Never... never feel like you have to hide an inch of your body from me. Ever again. I like everything I see."

And that was the first lie I might have said to her.

Because *like* wasn't the word I'd wanted to say at all.

"WHAT'S UP, OLD MAN?"

Max laughed through the phone, hearty and happy, like always. "Fuck off. We've had this talk. Nice to see you're still an asshole, but I'm pissed off at you."

"Me?"

"Yeah. You went and got fucking *married* and didn't invite me? I'm hurt, brother."

There was Max's general teasing in his tone, but beneath it, sadness.

"Shit. Fuck, Max, I'm so sorry. It happened so fast, and it's not what you're thinking. It's not..." I cleared my throat, because after last night and this morning, saying my marriage wasn't real felt like another lie. "It's a long story. I swear I'll tell you, but—"

"You finally over Ava then?"

God. No. It wasn't that, but I was pulling into the practice arena and running late. After we calmed down, I dragged Emmersyn into the shower with me, where she shook her head, told me no way in hell we were having shower sex—it wasn't her thing—and we cleaned up. By the time I fed us breakfast, omelets for both of us, and my protein shake, I was behind schedule.

And yet, as Max's question registered, I didn't have the general punch of rage I usually had when she was brought up, when I was asked about her. Max was one of the few guys who would ever bring her up to me before. The only one with enough guts to risk a right hook to his jaw.

"It's complicated," I told him. "But getting there. I think?"

"Well fuck, if you're married, you better be over her."

Shit. I pulled into my spot in the team's parking garage and climbed out of my car. I'd left the Range Rover for Emmersyn, even though she didn't need to go anywhere, and closed the door to my Aston Martin.

"I can't talk about it right now, Max. I'm late for practice, but we'll get caught up. I can call you later."

"Sure, sure. I retire, and now I'm just that old guy..."

"Max. That's not it and fuck you for not being at our game the other night, too, by the way."

"Not ready." He cleared his throat, and now I was the asshole. "Sorry, man. Kimmy asked if we could go, but I'm just... I need more time."

"God, yeah, of course. I can't... I can't imagine. And I'm giving you shit, being an ass because you're kind of putting me on the spot about Emmersyn and..." I yanked open the door to the arena, showed my badge to security. "She's my sister's friend and needed some help. Like I said, it's a long, complicated story, but I can fill you in when I can. Okay?"

"Yeah. Yeah. Okay. I gotta get to my next class, just wanted to reach out when I figured you'd be home. Things are okay, though? The team?"

"We miss you. Every practice and every game."

"Hell yeah, you do. I'm awesome." He laughed, but there was still that sadness.

Max had *lived* for hockey. Hadn't wanted to retire or even dream of it, but one too many concussions and he had no choice. He was good with his decision, but that didn't make it easier. I figured if I was forced to retire before I was mentally ready, I'd feel the same way.

"I mean it, man. I'm not sure I'm the guy for your job, you know? But we're doing good. Playing hard, and next time we're in California, Anaheim or LA, you know we'd love to see you. Even if not at the game, at the hotel for drinks."

"Damn straight. Who's making sure you guys are partying now and not taking yourselves too seriously if I'm not there? You need me."

We did. That was a given.

"Alix—" we both said at the same time.

"All right. I'll let you go, but next time you know you're going to end up in the papers, give me a heads up first, yeah?"

"Promise. Kick ass at school today, sweetheart."

He laughed again, but that was Max. Always laughing. "Fuck you, too."

He hung up, and I hit the locker room. Since I was behind, most of the guys were dressed, kicking around a soccer ball or tossing up a football. I grabbed a pass from Easton to Dom in the air and then threw it to Joey on my way to my locker.

"Not like you to be late." Dom saddled up next to me, settling his shoulder at the locker. "Late night? Early morning?"

How in the hell could he read me?

"Shut up." I shoved him so hard, he tripped over his skates, fell over Garrett's knee and ended up in our goalie's lap. "Aww... quick. Who's got their phone?"

Dom struggled to get out of Garrett's lap, but he just held him tight and pushed his lips out. "Oh, come on, Dominick. It's okay to show your love for me."

He leaned in, pretending to kiss him on the cheek while Dom struggled, beet red in the face, and Joey shouted, "Got it!" He grinned at his phone. "Nice. Definitely going on my Instagram."

"You assholes. All of you," Dom muttered, but where at one

point we might have actually been afraid of that look on his face, now there was no heat behind it.

"You started it," I reminded him.

"And I'm not wrong." He swirled his finger in a circle in front of my face. "You got that *I'm so happy because that was seriously great sex* stamped all over that goofy grin of yours. Deny it."

I opened my mouth, but nothing came out.

Dom laughed his ass off and walked away. "That's what I thought, Kane. Looks like you might be having a honeymoon after all."

Heads swiveled in my direction. Brows rose in question.

I ignored them all and started stripping out of my street clothes into practice gear.

I'd already lied to Emmersyn once today. I didn't need to start doing it to my brothers or myself.

I grasped my phone in my hand, my entire body sore from this morning and wound tight with nerves as the receptionist answered the phone. "Yes, this is Emmersyn Houghton. I had a message to return Megan Barton's call from yesterday?"

It was time I bit the bullet. Yesterday, I'd spent a day avoiding my reality, but with both Kane's lawyer calling me and this Megan woman from my grandma's old firm, I couldn't keep denying what was happening.

"Of course, Miss Houghton. I have a note to send you straight back to Megan as soon as you call. Hold on one moment."

"Thank you." My throat, dry as the Sahara, croaked as I thanked her, but if the woman noticed, she was gone before she could say anything.

Elevator music played quietly through the phone, and I grabbed a bottled water from the fridge to help settle my nerves. I was mid-chug when the phone clicked over from gentle, pseudo-soothing tunes and a woman's voice came through the phone, crisp and clear, it was immediate this woman meant business.

"Miss Emmersyn Houghton? This is Megan Barton."

"Hi." I choked on my water and cleared my throat. Great first impression. "Yes, hi Miss Barton. Thank you for taking my call. I apologize for missing yours yesterday."

"No apologies necessary." Rapid clicking of computer keys or fingernails on a desktop came through the line. "I have to say, when I received a call from a Mr. Banks? Is it?"

"Yes. John Banks, he's—"

"Your husband's attorney. Contracts. Very well known in the sports world, and well, everywhere else. Yes, I know him. You probably don't know me, but we actually met when you were younger."

"We did?"

"Yes. I was in law school at the time and your grandmother brought you to the office to meet with Bob—good man, we all miss him—anyway, I was doing a summer internship with my father, Patrick Barton that summer. We went to lunch together, all of the partners and your grandmother. Some new hip-hop star they had signed."

I had no idea how old this woman was, when she would have been in law school, but I only had a vague recollection of the times I went to the firm with my grandparents. Usually it was my grandma going, so it'd make sense, but, "I'm sorry... I don't recall."

"No worries." She laughed, a tight, businesslike laugh like manners demanded it but she didn't quite want to be wasting the time. "I think you were ten. Maybe younger, but when Mr. Banks called and requested a partner to look over your trust, I jumped at the opportunity."

"Thank you." A rush of breath fell from me. "I really appreciate—"

"No appreciation necessary, and no apologies. Truly, I was shocked when Mr. Banks told me what he found when he looked over your copy and I jumped at it. We all loved Bob, and we miss him, like I said. He's a good man, an even better attorney, but between you and me, he made some questionable decisions in his last couple of years. One of which was the lawyer he wanted to assign your trust to. That man has since been imprisoned for embezzlement, so we're all a little ashamed of that. Regardless, I've called Bob and left a message with him. He and his wife Suzie are traveling through Italy this month and with the time change, getting a hold of him has been difficult. Regardless, I'm curious as to the decisions he made since he helped draft the trust."

My heart beat erratically. Her no-nonsense approach only had me further on edge instead of calming me. Every time I reached out, it felt like I was only getting more questions, fewer answers— and that didn't even touch on the whole embezzlement thing.

"So." She tapped something else. She had to have long gel nails or acrylics or something for them to make such a harsh sound. "What I've determined is one, Mr. Banks is correct. The trust drafted by Mr. Dickerson never should have left our office. I understand you moved it to Fowler, Hayes, and Miller, correct?"

"Yes. Glen Hayes. I haven't been able to get a hold of him."

"I'm not surprised. My assumption is he knows he's not supposed to have it. Taking work like this, knowingly violating a contract doesn't speak highly of him, so to be honest, I'm quite pissed any of this has happened and it should be us offering our apologies as well as our solutions."

Solutions. *Finally.* My pulse slowed as she took a breath, and a few more taps on the keys.

"Now, Mr. Banks mentioned why you transferred the trust over to Hayes, but just to ensure we're on the same page, can you please tell me what happened?"

"Of course." I told her about getting engaged to Lincoln, dating him the two years prior. After we got engaged, I'd asked him to come with me to Dickerson's office to talk with Bob about the trust agreement once we were married. I went over Bob introducing me to the lawyer at the time and didn't get a good feeling. Lincoln didn't either because that was when he suggested I move everything over to the firm his family used.

"So, your fiancé at the time was set to become a very wealthy man."

"Ex-fiancé, but yes. I mean, he's wealthy in his own right, but he knew of my wealth and knew my inheritance was in a trust. We'd been dating over a year before I told him about the marriage condition though."

"And just how soon after you told him that, were you engaged?"

I shook my head, tried to remember, but couldn't. "I don't know. It was several months later, though. At least six, I think. It wasn't like he proposed the next day or anything."

Until Lincoln went on a rage these last couple of weeks, I wouldn't have considered our engagement had anything to do with my trust anyway. Now?

I didn't want to think about it.

"Okay. I have a call in to Mr. Hayes, who has yet to return my call, which I understand you've had the same issues with. I'll try again this afternoon, and if I can't get through to him, might just have to head there and wait for him."

The balls on this woman was encouraging. Unlike me, who might wait weeks for Hayes to return to the office after his vacation, Megan was clearly not that patient.

Thank goodness she'd spoken to John.

"Thank you. I really appreciate this."

"Like I said, it's us who owes you the apology. Hopefully, I can get back to you by the end of the week with better news and a resolution. You'll be hearing from me soon. Do you have any questions for me?"

"No. Not at this time. Just thank you."

"Take care. We'll speak soon."

She hung up without a goodbye, and I imagined Megan, probably jet-black hair, pulled back abrasively into a tight knot. She probably wore black suits that were molded to a lean, fit frame, and her take-no-shit attitude most likely permeated from her pores. Most likely, she was on her next phone call, and I couldn't help but smile.

She'd help get everything figured out. I knew it.

Which meant getting access to my trust would be sooner rather than later.

"THAT'S GREAT NEWS," Kane said and twisted spaghetti noodles around his fork. "I hope it works out this time. This Megan...?"

He looked up from his plate of food for confirmation he had the name right.

"Megan Barton."

"Yeah, she sounds like a real ball-buster." He winked and went back to eating. "In a good way."

"I know what you meant." I slid my plate of food to the side and took a sip of water.

After I'd gotten off the phone with Megan earlier, I'd reached for the wine, then realized how much I'd been drinking ever since I showed up in Vegas. When I took out Kane's recycling earlier, the whole thing sounded like one glass bottle hitting another and shattering.

Time for me to slow down and put a pause on my wino-ism for a day or two at least.

I drank my water while Kane ate his dinner. Simple spaghetti from a jar, but that didn't seem to be stopping him from piling a helping as large as his plate on to it. I was glad I'd used two pounds of beef. And bonus—I didn't burn the meat or the sauce, and the noodles weren't stuck together. Lucky me.

"This is good. Thanks again for cooking." He smiled at me, a smile that could just about make me drop to my knees and give him anything he'd want from me. "It's nice to come home to company."

He wiped his mouth with his napkin and crumpled it into his fist. "Besides this meeting with Megan, did you do much else today?"

"Not really. I ordered a Kindle so I can do more reading. I added it to the tally of what I owe you and Heather, though."

"Shut up." He rolled his eyes and grabbed both of our plates. "You cooked, I'll clean. What kind of books do you like to read?"

"Anything. Everything. Crime thrillers. Paranormal type stuff, vampires, and werewolves—that kind of thing."

"Like *Twilight?*"

"Yeah." Racier, though. *Way* racier. "Do you read much?"

I had yet to find a book in his home. The women's fiction I'd been reading last night I borrowed from Sophie, along with a small stack of other books I had in my room. Women's fiction wasn't really my thing, though. I either liked to fall into a spicy romance book of all kinds, no limits for me, or I enjoyed getting the crap scared out of me with thrillers. Plus, when you added in vampires or werewolves, I could have the benefit of both happening.

"Nah." Kane closed the dishwasher and grabbed a washcloth, wetting it so he could wipe down the counters. I'd been right that first day. The man was *clean.* Always wiping down a counter or putting a random cup in the dishwasher. "I used to read. Read a lot of self-help-type books when I was in college and after I was drafted early in my career. Those kinds that were like *how to be the best* type books?"

"I know what you're talking about."

"Then I read some investing books. That kind of stuff about how to handle money, invest, save, etc. Figured once I went from being a broke college kid to a millionaire like that"—he snapped his fingers—"I wanted to make sure I was smart enough not to waste my money."

I let my gaze roam around his modest home, definitely modest, based on the public salary I saw he was making, at least based on a Google search that night when I was looking for a game of his to watch. "Seems you've been pretty careful with it."

"Ah. Well, yeah..." He scratched his jaw, a light scruff of dark hair I knew would be gone tomorrow before he left for his game. "I moved in here after Ava left. Alix knew the previous owner was moving, so I got it for a steal."

Right. Of course, he hadn't lived in this house with his wife. This wasn't a family home, it screamed bachelor pad. I was beginning to think there were two parts to Kane.

Before Ava and after Ava.

He must have read my thoughts because his voice softened, a rough scrape to it I felt in the tips of my fingers and toes. "I have to be able to talk about her, Em. We were together for a long time."

"I know. Of course." It didn't mean I needed to hear about it.

"Then why do you look like I just punched you in the gut?"

TWENTY-SIX

KANE

It's a crazy thing—life with women or love or lust and regret and guilt. All of it screws you up, until I wasn't so sure what I was feeling anymore when I thought about Ava. I didn't know how much it had to do with Emmersyn, this sudden shift and lack of pain when I talked about Ava in the last couple of weeks. Maybe it was my constant state of attraction to the woman standing in front of me, looking exactly how I just accused her.

Maybe it was the passage of time and a shift in perspective I hadn't considered, but when I thought about Ava, ever since I kissed Emmersyn, it didn't *hurt* so much anymore. It was more of a weighted stone, low in my gut. That heavy feeling reminding me I'd done something wrong, hadn't given my relationship all I could.

I rubbed my chest, feeling that familiar pinch of pain which I think I was starting to learn wasn't a broken heart, just an old guilt for hurting a good woman.

And damn. What a time to realize it.

"Come on." I held out my hand to Emmersyn. We didn't need to talk about Ava anymore. "I had a hell of a day and need to relax and would like to do it with you."

I wiggled my fingers. With a hesitation to her step, Emmersyn came around the kitchen bar and slipped her hand into mine. "What did you have in mind?"

"Time in my sauna?"

Her green eyes sparkled. That playful spirit of hers I was so drawn to these days emerged as she shrugged. "I mean. What else do I have to do?"

I could think of a dozen things I could do with Emmersyn, including many in the sauna.

"That's the spirit."

I held her hand until we were to the top of the stairs and brought our interlocked hands to my mouth. "Change into a swimsuit and meet me in there?"

"All right." Her lips parted in surprise as I kissed her.

Ever since I kissed her, I'd been unable to stop thinking about her, and thank God I finally knew how good she tasted. "I'll be waiting."

It was five minutes later when she opened the door. I'd slipped into a pair of swim trunks and was sitting on a towel. Usually, I didn't bother with the swim trunks, but I didn't actually want to scare her by being naked when she walked in.

My head was resting against the back wall, eyes closed. The heat was atrocious and perfect, sweat was already making my skin shine, but damn, I loved this thing. Twenty minutes a few times a week in here, and I was a new man.

The door creaked as she opened it. She inhaled a quick, harsh breath as the heat slammed into her. I peeked open my eyes, caught sight of her cobalt blue string bikini—not something I had bought for her which meant she'd gone shopping and promptly closed my eyes again.

No sex. Not now, at least. And I'd do better with remembering that if I wasn't staring at her breasts and ample cleavage.

"Come on in." I pointed to the bench where I'd folded and laid out a towel for her.

"This feels like the Seventh Circle of Hell."

"Nice, right?"

"It's incredible. I've wanted to sneak in here and use this so many times."

"You could have. Why didn't you?"

"Because it's your space and I hadn't been invited."

I opened my arms wide. "Consider this your invitation, and some pics of you in here, preferably without the swimsuit on while I'm on the road wouldn't upset me either."

That earned me a snort, and she tucked wisps of hair behind her ear. She was still getting adjusted to the heat, and by the way she fidgeted, trying to get comfortable not wrapping her arms around her stomach to hide herself from me.

I bit my tongue. I'd told her enough for a day that she didn't need to hide herself from me. The rest would come with time.

"Tell me something."

"What?" she asked.

"You told me you went to school for education, right?"

"Yeah."

"So why didn't you go into teaching?"

Her hands curled around the edge of the wood bench, flexed. "Who said I didn't?"

That had me sitting up straighter. All she'd told me was that she did volunteer work. "You did?"

"Yeah." She huffed a laugh and rolled her lips between her teeth. "It always feels like I'm such a rich bitch when I explain, but I quit after my first year."

"Why?"

"Because teachers needing the work needed the money more than I did. The schools did. So I quit after my first year and started subbing."

"So when you said you did volunteer work, what did you do?"

"I meant substitute teaching, at least partly. Whatever money I make I put back into the schools where I spent time. I did other volunteer work, though. At homeless shelters and food pantries. I'd serve meals, help package sandwiches that would be delivered to people on the street who wouldn't come to the shelters. I stocked shelves, I don't know. Whatever needed to be done, I guess. I also spent time on some local campaigns, going door-to-door, that kind of thing."

She shrugged like it was no big deal, but it was. She would someday be so damn fucking rich she'd never have to lift a finger and could pay or hire anyone she wanted for anything. Hell, she could have personal shoppers delivering food to her home, a private chef, a housekeeper, and yet I hadn't missed the fact that when I came home, my house was cleaned. She was trying to cook. She would do my laundry and leave it in a basket outside my bedroom.

She might have been given the gift of privilege, but she didn't take it for granted like so many others.

"What do you like the most?"

Her eyes lit, green pools of excitement. "You really want to know?"

"I wouldn't have asked if I didn't."

"The kids. I worked mostly with the youngest ones, those who didn't realize how little they had and I tried to always sub in schools that were most high need. Sometimes it'd be for months at a time until they could hire permanent teachers. But I loved the kids' innocence. So many of them came from situations, emotionally anyway, as a family, so much worse than mine, and yet I could relate to that feeling of being unloved... unwanted—"

She pressed her lips closed. Shut down. It happened in an instant, and where she'd arched her back and sat up straight and tall while she talked about what she loved, when it got to how she'd been hurt, her shoulders slumped and she curled in on herself.

And I sat there—having no idea how to fix it, because I'd never felt that or been subjected to it.

"Anyway, yeah... it was the kids."

At least I could relate to that. "My parents used to do a day camp for kids at their farm."

"I know." She smiled slowly, bringing herself out of her thoughts. "Heather used to tell me about it. How you two would be forced to work, but you got out of it because of hockey."

I barked out a laugh. "That shit. She lies so bad. The poor girl who had to do the work because I wasn't around."

"That's not true?"

"Fuck no." I was still laughing. The audacity of my sister. "I was up at four in the fucking morning with my dad, cleaning stalls, feeding cows and horses and goats or hogs or whatever animals we were raising for FFA kids that summer. My ass was in the damn tractor before sunrise, moving hay for the cattle to eat before Heather's ass was ever out of bed. Yeah, she had to play with the kids at camp and teach them how to ride or feed and care for the animals, but I had practice most mornings at six or seven, and my parents always had my ass up before then to help."

She chuckled and brushed her hands down her jawline before settling them at her sides. She didn't bother covering herself, and I noticed.

Fuck yeah, I did.

"You know. We may not be all that different. I don't know if I ever said that to Heather."

There were a shit ton of ways we were, but she was smart. Thoughtful. "How so?"

"We both had good lives, good upbringings. My grandparents were there when my own parents failed me and made sure even though we had all the money in the world, I used it for the right purpose. They kept me grounded. You were raised with being grounded, didn't have a lot, but once you earned it, you kept that same grounding."

There was something in that compliment, something I couldn't pinpoint, but it sounded like the best fucking compliment I'd ever been given. And that was when it hit me. She'd said I'd *earned* it.

And yeah, I fucking had. But to most people, even fans, they looked at us like we were rich assholes who played games for a living and got rich off them.

Yet here was Emmersyn, recognizing in some way the work, the sacrifice, the dedication involved in all of it to get to that part.

"I think if you stripped away our moneys, you'd find we're even more alike."

"Yeah?" She smiled as sweat beaded at her temples, dots of it slid down her cleavage.

"Yeah. Like you said, we were raised right. To respect and leave the world a better place than when you found it and take care of everyone you meet, regardless of what that looks like. You come from good stock, Emmersyn. And your grandparents would be proud of you."

It might have been sweat. Might have been tears. She wiped her eyes and sniffed and smiled at me, a smile so blinding with her bright white teeth and pillowy lips I was lost in it.

"Thanks, Kane. That means a lot."

"Right. Now, how about we shower off this sweat and nastiness and get to bed?"

COME **and eat lunch with us. We're headed to Carbone's at noon.**

Our team started a tradition years ago. On game days, after our morning skate, media meetings, and then team meetings, we went to lunch at Carbone's within Aria's Resort and Casino. We have a team chef who prepares meals for our dinners, but those are always high protein and lighter so we're not weighed down. We'd been going there so often now, the restaurant had our schedule, knew when to expect us, and would have our favorite meals prepared so we didn't need to wait long.

It was only a couple minutes before Emmersyn texted back. **Are you sure?**

Far as I knew, wives had never been invited. I was breaking protocol. Who gave a shit. I'd woken up with my arms around Emmersyn this morning and had to slink out of there without waking her. We hadn't even done anything last night. I was so tired after the sauna and shower that I simply pulled her into my bed, tucked her in close, and turned on the television, where she forced me to watch *Dirty Dancing*.

Hell yeah, I'm sure. I'll send you the menu. Text me your order. Grab an Uber ride and I'll drive us back home after.

This time, her reply was instant. **Okay. Since I have nothing better to do ;-)**

I'd give her something better to do. Me. After lunch. I'd make sure she wore me out nice and slow so I could take a nap before I had to come back to the arena for the game.

See you soon.

"Ready, slowpoke?"

I pretended to chuck my phone at Ryder's face and laughed when he flinched. "Yeah. Come on." I threw my arm around his shoulder, slapping him once, and we followed the rest of the team from the media area to the team's meeting room. We fell into leather chairs, and like we were automated, all of us grabbed the tablets in front of us, unlocked them, and waited for Coach Vik to get done with the media briefings so we could run through last-minute videos.

After, I forewent the team bus that took us to Carbone's—and followed them in my Range Rover. Emmersyn was outside the restaurant, and my mouth watered at the sight of her.

She was wearing another dress, this one longer. It brushed along the ground as she nervously chewed on the side of her thumb. Her hair was curled, one side pulled back with a clip, and strappy flat sandals tapped to the beat of the trendy pop music filtering through the casino's speakers.

I walked in with Garrett on my left, and he noticed Emmersyn as soon as I did. "You invited your wife for lunch?"

He sounded surprised, but not upset.

"Couldn't help it. I wanted her here."

"I sure hope you know what in the hell you're doing, Kane."

Me and him both.

Emmersyn finally noticed us, caught me in the swarm of hockey players, and her smile was bright enough to lighten the entire casino.

"You look incredible," I said, leaning down to whisper it only for her. "Thanks for coming."

"I talked to Lizzie. She said wives or girlfriends are never invited to this lunch."

Ah, so that was what the nerves were for.

Funny, how it had been Lizzie's husband who said the same thing to me. "What can I say? I missed you."

"Will they be mad? The guys?"

"Only the superstitious ones." I was kidding. No one would give a shit.

"How many is that?"

I shrugged and took her hand in mine, my fingers finding the spaces between hers like it was the most natural thing to do. "All of them?"

"What?" she shrieked, and several customers in the restaurant turned to stare at her. "You're kidding."

"Of course I am. Come on, we have a back room."

We walked through the casino to the restaurant, and I wasn't the least bit surprised when phones came out from diners and pictures were taken. Most of them were tourists, and I never quite knew if they knew who we were or just figured a group of men, built like us, who had a private room had to be *somebody* important, and they didn't want to miss the shot in case someone they knew recognized us.

Whatever. Didn't make much difference to me.

"Does this happen a lot?" Emmersyn asked, noticing the phones out and pointing in our direction.

"Not all the time. A couple years back, Joey gave an interview to a sports blog asking him what his game day routine is like. We'd already been coming here for lunches before our night games for a year or so, and he mentioned the restaurant. After that, there were tons of fans, but our biggest ones seemed to have the most respect for our time and need to focus." I escorted her to our table, where the restaurant was so fantastic, they left us name cards, always mixed up, so we sat next to different team members, and found Emmersyn's card next to Dominick, three seats down from me.

I switched her card with Alix so she could sit next to me instead.

"Hey. No moving the cards," Braxton said as he took his own seat across the table from me. "It's the rule. One you and Max made, isn't it?"

"Move a card and we lose a game," Arlo chimed in, finding it hard to hide his grin. "Every damn time."

"Fuck off," I told them all, laughing as the team tried to stare me down.

"I can sit where my card—" Emmersyn started, and her face had paled with fear.

These fuckers.

"The fuck you will. They're giving you shit. And me. Welcome to the team, babe."

I switched the cards and pulled her into her chair. Across the table, it was Braxton who laughed first. "We're kidding. I mean, it is a rule we don't move the cards, but just giving you shit. Sorry if we scared you."

"Mean." She scowled at all of them and shook her head. "That's mean."

"Don't listen to them," Dom said from her other side once everyone else found their seats. "They're all assholes."

"Says the largest asshole of them all." Arlo raised his glass in Dom's direction.

Dom shook his head.

Soon, lunch was served. Salads first for everyone who'd requested one. None for Emmersyn, but she dug into the breadsticks like she was the one prepping for a game that night.

We ate. We talked. We laughed. She was mostly quiet through it, happy to sit back and laugh with us, and when I settled my hand at her thigh, eating my spicy rigatoni with vodka sauce and chicken while she devoured her lobster ravioli, her hand came down on top of mine and squeezed.

"Thank you for inviting me. For including me."

Her smile was soft, and I had to fight against leaning in and kissing her in front of my entire team. I didn't care, but I didn't want to embarrass her either. So I let my own look say everything I was thinking and hoped she understood how much I liked having her with me.

After lunch, we headed out to the valet parking area. We were waiting for my SUV to be brought around when a teenage boy with a forest green hat flipped around backward and tufts of hair sticking out every which way beneath it, hesitantly walked closer to us. He stopped, looked back to a man and woman with smiles on their faces, parents, I figured, and came another step closer.

"Hey, man. What's going on?" I grinned at him.

This kid was nervous, but I knew what he wanted. He had his phone in one hand and a card in another.

"Hey. Mr. Andrews, right?"

"That's me. But you can call me Kane, yeah?"

"Yeah." He nodded frantically. "Yeah. I mean, cool. It's awesome to meet you. I'm a big fan of your team. I was wondering if I could get your autograph?"

He held out a menu card he must have grabbed from somewhere in the casino.

"I have a pen," Emmersyn said. She dug through her purse and handed it to me. She was smiling at the boy as she did, and he looked to her and back to me.

"Thanks. I mean, this is really cool. We're here for the game tonight."

"Yeah? You live close?"

"No. We... uh... we live in Texas, but I really wanted to see you, so yeah..." He trailed off, red rising high on his cheeks and his hands would not stop trembling as I slipped the card from his hand. "What's your name?"

"Kaden. Kaden Stanford."

I scribbled out my autograph, personalized for him, and then looked up to where his mom and dad were still standing and waved them closer. "How about we get a picture, yeah? With your family?"

I glanced back toward the casino. The team bus was just pulling up which meant any minute, there'd be thirty guys coming out, and wouldn't that just blow Kaden's fucking mind.

"Mind if we get a picture together, Kaden?"

"No. I mean, yeah, that'd be awesome!"

"You mind?" I asked Emmersyn, but she was already holding out her hand toward Kaden.

"Absolutely not."

We grabbed a couple pictures with just me and him, and then I invited his parents in for a picture. Right as we were getting done, the guys came out, boisterous and loud like always.

"Yo," I called out to them. "Come here a sec."

"Holy shit," Kaden gasped. "I mean, I heard y'all ate here, but I wasn't sure it was true but holy fuck..."

"Language," his mom snapped. "Come on."

"Sorry ma'am, sorry, it's just... the whole team."

"Picture time?" Joey asked with a grin and strolled up to us like he did this every day, all day long.

"Fan from Texas. Meet Kaden and his parents."

They introduced themselves. Pictures were taken, and by the end of it, Garrett and Joey had shuffled around who was using their tickets for the game tonight—Lizzie would sit with Emmersyn, Gabby would move and sit by Sophie, which left their four tickets unused, and a hell of a lot better than the ones the Stanfords had purchased in the upper rows.

"Wow. This was wonderful. Thank you so much," Kaden's mom, Molly, shook my hand, tears in her eyes. Her love for her son obvious in her overflowing emotion.

"No problem." The guys slapped Kaden on the shoulder. Pretty sure he wasn't ever going to wash the shirt again, and his menu card was now autographed by almost every guy on the team. "See you tonight, all right, Kaden?"

"Yeah. Definitely. Thanks!"

The family started walking away, Kaden continually glancing back. The valet was still at my SUV, pulling up during the pictures and staying near my car.

And after they'd turned the corner, Emmersyn grinned up at me.

"The city loves you. Or at least your fans."

"The city hasn't ever had a decent professional sports team and doesn't know what to do with hockey players in the desert."

"Well, I think I might like my desert playing hockey player."

"Enough to have him for dessert?" I leaned in and brushed my nose down hers until I was at her mouth. Her hand on my chest held me back. Not that I couldn't overtake her, but I wouldn't.

The corners of her lips curled up. "I guess that depends on how well you play tonight."

"Smart ass." I smacked her ass as she climbed into the car, and once I rounded the back of it, Alix was there, smirking at me.

"Still pretend and temporary, huh?"

Of course he had to see that.

"And if it isn't?"

His blond brows tugged together. "Then I am happy for you. What else would I be?"

Who knew.

Who fucking knew.

Because only God knew what I was feeling... but it felt a lot like happiness.

And I'd done and screwed the pooch on that one really well before.

Let's just hope I didn't end up doing the same this time.

TWENTY-SEVEN

EMMERSYN

Kane's garage door sounded through the house and I turned off the post-game show. One thing I'd learned in the last two weeks since the real season started was once he walked in that door after a game, he didn't want anything to do with hockey or sports.

For as much as he said they'd worried about the team this year with new players and the loss of Max, they hadn't yet lost a regular season game.

I stood from the couch once I heard him enter the laundry room. He'd drop his gear, strip out of his suit and change into sweats or swim trunks and soak in the hot tub. His routine post games was as organized and predictable as I was learning the rest of him was.

"Good game," I called out when he came into view. "And that tripping call the ref called was complete and utter bullshit." Thanks to his lessons and some of the wives, I was starting to know what I was talking about.

He smiled as he saw me standing with my ass to the back of his sectional couch, arms wrapped around myself. His smile vanished and something much more feral took its place.

I'd pat myself on the back, but it'd mean losing the way I'd intentionally stood, showing off my brand new, hot pink bikini. A *thong* bikini he hadn't yet seen.

"Turn around," he said, and a shiver rolled down my spine. "Slowly."

I did what he asked—more demanded, and as soon as he saw my ass, his inhale was quick and severe. From the reflection in the glass doors, he tore off his jacket and tossed it to the floor. His tie followed.

"Do you know what I need?"

I turned back and faced him. His brown eyes darkened, and like every other time he got that look in his eyes, my stomach knotted with anticipation.

"What?" I slid to the left, away from him. Not from fear. It thrilled me when he stalked toward me, all that muscled body and intense gleam centered on me. Especially after a game. Any left-over energy or adrenaline turned from focus on the ice to me.

And it was *divine*.

"You. In my hot tub. Now." He lunged for me and he was fast, faster than I could move away. I was swooped up and over his shoulder—another way he showed his strength. It didn't matter my size or my weight, Kane could always put me exactly where he wanted me.

"Kane!" I cried out as his hand slid up the back of my thighs. His hand drifted higher until he found the thin strip of the fabric of my thong and slid his fingers beneath. "Oh God." I groaned as he found my center. Hot. Wet. Always for him.

He slapped the button at the side of the garage door and as it opened, he turned, his teeth scraped across my now bare backside, and I shivered so hard he tightened his grip.

"You're always so wet. Such a fucking turn-on, Em."

Whenever he touched me, I was, definitely.

He stepped outside, and the burning sun and scorching heat hit my ass, making me push up, hands at his backside, and glance around. "It's daytime."

"No one will see us."

He kicked off his shoes as he carried me toward the hot tub, and in another quick squat and swoop of his, I was back on my feet, wobbling from the quick change, and hair was all over my face. I pushed it back and stared up at the man as he was dropping his suit pants to the ground, unbuttoning his dress shirt.

"You going to take off that bikini or make me do it?" He snapped his teeth together, making him look terrifyingly delicious.

"Hmm." I tapped my finger to my lips. Considering. Both had their pros, but as Kane stripped down to his briefs and then was only in his God-given glorious skin, teasing ended.

I'd woken the beast, and he was going to make me pay. *Yes.*

I slipped off my thong, goose bumps pebbling as the cool fabric slid down my legs and reached behind me to untie the top. One quick tug at the back and I pulled the rest of it over my head, throwing it at Kane.

He caught it easily and stepped toward me. His erection was already thick and long, and I reached down and wrapped my hand around it.

"You are the sexiest woman I've ever seen in my whole entire fucking life," he groaned as I applied pressure, and dropped his head to my shoulder, where his teeth met my skin. He bit enough to cause a sharp sting of pain, not enough to leave a mark, and his hands went to my waist where he guided me back into the hot tub until steamy water lapped around my ankles, my knees, and then my waist.

"I want you. All the goddamn time. You're all I think about. On the road, before games. After games. Fuck, Em."

He stared up at me, sunshine at my back shading his face, and his expression stole my breath, and made my legs tremble. There was a seriousness there, a surprise almost like he hadn't known he was going to admit it.

"Well, you have me. Where do you want me?"

He tugged me toward him until I was straddling his legs. His erection pulsed between us as he slammed his mouth to mine and gripped the back of my hair with a tight fist that made me cry out into his mouth.

Rough sex with Kane was the absolute best sex of my life, and he was always rougher, bossier after a game. I submitted to his hold, to the harsh grip on my hips as he rocked me against him, but I didn't need the foreplay. I'd been wet for him ever since the game ended and I decided to surprise him with my newest purchase.

"Ready," I gasped against his mouth and raised up off his thighs.

"Sure?" He stroked himself, the image blurry through the water, but I'd seen him do it enough it was vivid in my mind. The way he took long, slow pulls to get started, quick short strokes when he was close.

"Please."

"Fuck. Begging. Think I like that." He slipped my nipple into his mouth, and bit down harsh enough that I cried out and gripped the sides of his head to push him away, but he kept lapping at my nipples, switching back and forth, tugging and biting them enough that a shock of heat raced to my sex. If we weren't in the tub, I'd be a dripping mess.

Once he lined us up, he pulled back, and with both hands on my waist, slammed me down onto his full length in one forceful pull.

"Shit." My eyes rolled back into my head as he filled me, stretched me, and today, he didn't give me time to get used to the heavy feel of him before he was moving. He bounced me on his dick and held a breast with one hand.

He might have been on the bottom, but he was in full, dominating control, and I loved every punishing thrust, every groan I pulled from him, and every cry he yanked from me.

Kane Andrews was a god on the ice and a beast in bed, and he was mine.

I opened my mouth to cry out, my body trembling and my

orgasm racing through me faster than I could prepare, and as I called out his name, he cupped the back of my neck, and brought my mouth to his. Kane swallowed my screams, and my entire body ignited with an orgasm so fierce, so long while he continued pounding into me from beneath. For a moment, I was worried it'd never end.

Death by amazing hot sex in a hot tub.

There were worse ways to go.

"Fucking hell," he moaned and rolled his hips. His body shuddered as he came, his thick dick pulsing inside of me as he reached his own end and for several long moments, we stayed clasped together. My arms around his shoulders. His around my lower back. Our mouths moved together, slowly and softly until a final shudder rolled through me, and I was pretty certain I could breathe again.

"You almost killed me," I admitted, a smile on my lips as I pulled back. "You keep getting better at this."

He laughed, splashed hot water on his face, and shoved his hair back. "Fucking you might be my new favorite hobby."

I splashed him again and pushed off his lap to the other side of the hot tub. My mouth was dry, but no way was I getting out of there to get something to drink.

Kane rested his head along the back of the hot tub, soaking in the sun and the relaxing heat of the bubbles surrounding us. "You hear anything good from Megan?"

I'd skipped his home game today because Megan's assistant, Shirley, called me last night to schedule an appointment for an update.

It'd been two long weeks since I first talked to Megan, and we weren't any closer to getting a hold of Glen Hayes.

"Nothing good. Not really. She's got a private investigator looking for Hayes now, and no one in the office knows where he went. Since the trust says no one but the trustee can handle it, she's having a hard time getting someone to take a look at the agreement in the first place. They all know it's private."

"But it's not even theirs to have."

"Yeah, but she doesn't want to violate the trust by getting it back behind his back, either. She said it leaves an opening for a countersuit or something. I wish I understood more."

"Fuck."

"I know." Frustration bubbled in me and made my chin tremble with emotion. I bit down so I didn't cry. I just wanted this *over*. The only good news to happen in the last two weeks was Lincoln had stopped trying to call. I turned on my old phone occasionally, and there were never new messages or threats from him.

So he was either planning something or had given up, which was unlikely, seeing as how Hayes was nowhere to be found.

"I'll be in Boston in a week for a game. I could try to make time to go to his office. Or hers? Maybe if one of us shows up in person, it'll get them moving faster."

"Maybe." I shrugged. "It's not even about the money, fully. I want this over, so I know Lincoln's out of my life, for good." He'd stolen enough of it and even in his absence, was still too large of a part.

In the meantime, John Banks finished our post-nuptial agreement. It was everything we'd requested, only assets we brought into our marriage, no trust access for Kane, and I didn't receive any gains on income or endorsement during our marriage. It was completely fair.

Yet a rock had still settled in my stomach when we went to his office earlier this week to sign the papers. It felt so... temporary. The exact opposite of what I was beginning to learn I wanted this to be.

Kane moved in the hot tub until he was at my side, brushing hair behind my ear and kissing my cheek. "Hey. You have me. We'll be okay. So this takes longer, you won't hear me complaining."

Yeah, but I didn't hear him saying he wanted to stay together either.

Earlier confession aside, as I stared into his warm brown eyes, sunshine highlighting his face and making him more Roman god than normal, realization hit.

I'd done it.

I was officially the fool who fell in love with her temporary husband.

TWENTY-EIGHT
KANE

I had no idea what to do to make Emmersyn feel better, so I stayed in the hot tub with her until the heat became more unbearable than comfortable, while she rested her cheek on my shoulder.

"I should go get us towels. And maybe order us some food?"

"That'd be nice." She sounded half asleep. "Chinese would be great."

"Then Chinese it is." I groaned as I shoved to my feet and climbed out of the hot tub without bothering to throw anything on. I'd clean up our clothes later. "Stay here while I get the towels and order food. I'll be back in a minute."

She gave me a half-smile, exhaustion making her moves slow.

I hurried through the house to the laundry room where I kept spare towels, and grabbed a stack of them. I dried off quickly, wrapped the towel around my waist and was dragging another through my hair when my phone started to ring.

Probably the guys, wanting to meet up at Malley's or something, but it was still ringing when I ran back to the kitchen. Except I didn't account for the floor being wet from my trek through to get the towels, and I slid as I reached for my phone. It fell to the floor, clattered, and I grabbed hold of the counter before I landed on my ass.

Towels fell to the floor, and I finally grabbed the phone, and fumbled it before I answered.

"Hello?"

I hadn't bothered to look at the ID.

A sniff came through the line that had me jumping to my feet.

"Hello?" I said again.

And then a voice, all too familiar, I didn't have to wait for her to say anything before I recognized it came through the line.

Ava.

"You're married," she said, and if I wasn't mistaken, her voice shook.

My body jolted in surprise, and my spine went straight. She was *upset* about this?

"Ava..." What else was there to say?

My wife, who I had just fucked so hard I saw stars, was still sitting in the hot tub, bare ass naked, waiting for me to grab her a towel. *Shit.*

"I'm... I didn't expect that. I was surprised."

I grabbed the towel from the floor that I'd lost in my near fall and wrapped it around my waist.

She and I both, really. But why was she calling?

"You wanted me happy."

"I know. I did, but... I guess I thought that'd be with me."

"What?" My head whipped toward Emmersyn, still sitting in the pool, but she was no longer relaxed or sleepy. Her arms had lowered, and I knew without standing by her, she'd wrapped them around her stomach.

I shook my head and refocused on the insane conversation at hand. "You're... you're engaged, Ava. Said you were happy."

"I know." She sniffed, and what in the holy fuck was happening? "I know. And Mark is a great guy. Wonderful. I love him, I do, it was just... I thought, I guess..."

Oh holy shit. She had to be fucking kidding me. "You thought I'd come back?"

"Mark's not you," she admitted with a quiet sob.

My heart squeezed so tightly it took a second to breathe. "I'm sorry." I was sorry for hurting her. All those years ago. When she heard the news.

"Don't apologize. Gosh, I shouldn't have called. I'm sorry. I'm not being fair, and I never gave you a reason to come back for me, but I just kept thinking... we loved each other so much, and..." Her voice drifted off while I stared at my marble counter.

In all the years she'd walked away, there'd never been an inkling that the door was open. Not *ever*. And hell... *she'd* moved on. She got engaged. Part of the goddamn reason I agreed to this marriage so quick was because I thought it'd make her happy for me.

What in the fuck had I been thinking? Goes to show exactly how little I understood women.

"Fuck, Ava." I brushed wet hair off my forehead and shook it out. "I don't know what you want me to say here. You left me, and you called, yeah, but it's been years, and you moved on, and..."

I felt like such a fucking failure as the dots clicked. Was this *why* she always tried to maintain contact? Why she reached out? Why she called to tell me she was getting married?

So I'd wake up, come to my senses and rush back to her?

"I'm sorry. I'm so sorry. I shouldn't have called. I was just so surprised when I saw, and I didn't know what to do, and I guess, I don't know, I thought. I just had to know."

"Know what?"

"Know for sure you've moved on. That you were happy. That you love her."

"Ava... listen... I'm sorry about all of that. But I didn't get married to hurt you."

"So you are in love," she sniffed, and God, I could imagine her pale blue eyes red and swollen, a pile of tissues next to her.

Movement grabbed my attention, and I turned.

Emmersyn was there, standing in my living room, water droplets trailing down her body, arms wrapped across her tits, tits I'd just had my mouth on, and what looked like tears dripping from her eyes.

The fuck?

Emmersyn flinched, and my gaze narrowed. Did she know who I was talking to?

There was no way. I walked to her and handed her the towel. She took it with a trembling hand and quickly wrapped it around her body.

Emmersyn glanced outside, and as she did, she stopped at the rocks next to the hot tub.

And oh fuck....

"I need to go. Bye, Ava."

My phone fell to my side, and the pain in Emmersyn's eyes was vividly clear.

Because those weren't rocks she was staring at. They were speakers.

"My Bluetooth speakers were on," I said.

She nodded, tightened her grip on her towel, and skirted around me. "I need to shower."

I reached for her, but she moved around me. What was there to say? Hell, my head was still spinning trying to figure out what just happened.

She'd heard it all. Heard what I didn't say. Heard me apologize to my ex-wife for marrying another woman.

"Emmersyn..."

"Don't, Kane. Just don't." She had a hand at the railing, tears in her eyes. "I knew what I was getting into. Remember?"

My own words slammed back into me like a sledgehammer. *I will never love you.*

She turned and ran up the stairs, leaving a wet trail of footsteps.

And holy shit.

How had everything I thought was so good turned to utter shit so fast?

And how had I just managed to break two women's hearts in a matter of moments?

———

"YOU WANT TO TALK YET?"

Dom's forearms rested on the booth's table at Malley's. For some damn reason, it was him I'd called when I realized how badly I fucked shit up and needed a drink.

I stood in my living room while the shower in Emmersyn's room turned on and I couldn't bear to see the pain I'd caused her when she got out. After a quick change of clothes, I grabbed my cell and my keys and wallet, and I was gone before she got out.

Did that make me a certified pussy?

Probably.

But it wasn't like she'd want to see me anyway, and it wasn't like I had anything to say. Sure, I could stand in front of her, tell her I'd done nothing wrong. But the only woman I'd ever loved had all but admitted to still wanting me, essentially said I could have her if I wanted... and I'd just been making love to another woman, even if I wasn't ready to admit what it was.

Yeah, I hadn't told her I was in love with Emmersyn. Yeah, I hadn't said much of anything, but that I didn't was bad enough.

It was my job to protect Emmersyn and keep her safe, not hurt her.

I ended up at Malley's bar, calling Dom on the way. He must have called Joey because the man walked in a few minutes behind me, looking entirely unsurprised when he saw me at the table, drink in hand.

He went to the bar, got his own, and took the seat across from me.

Dominick strolled in ten minutes later, grabbed a water because the guy didn't drink much, and joined us.

For ten more minutes, they let me sit in silence, finish a second drink, and the question Dominick asked was delivered with my third.

Warm from the whiskey, and still smelling like saltwater from the hot tub, I tried to roll the tension from my shoulders and realized it was futile. I was one giant ball of stress and regret. "Ava called."

"Shit," Joey whispered. "Why?"

Fuck. I still wasn't even sure. To let me know how I could have had her if I'd just reached for it? To stab my fucking heart with her own pain? What in the hell had her motivation been?

I told them everything, leaving out the part about the hottest sex of my life, and when I got to the part of the Bluetooth speakers somehow turning on—probably in my mad dash to answer the phone while I was skidding across my wet floor, both of them flinched.

Not helpful.

"And you left? Without talking to her?"

"What was I supposed to say? She was hurt, and I did that. She wouldn't have wanted anything to do with me. Trust me—you didn't see the pain in her eyes when she looked at me." I had though, wasn't sure I'd ever forget that look. "Fuckkk. What am I going to do?"

"Do?" Dom asked, and his eyes widened in surprise. "Do about what? You promised Emmersyn you'd be married to her for a year. You're not considering backing out *now*, are you?"

"What? Fuck no." That hadn't even occurred to me. "I meant with making things better."

"God, you're stupid," Joey said. "I mean, you could just tell Emmersyn how you feel. Tell her you don't want Ava, and you want her. That you love *her*."

"I can't lie to her."

"Would it be a lie?" Dominick asked, and I was pretty sure I'd worn a similar smug expression when I'd gotten him to realize how much he cared for Holly and Ben.

"Of course it would." I took a hefty swallow of my drink and winced as the alcohol burned my throat. "I don't... I can't... it's been like a month..."

I trailed off. I couldn't love Emmersyn. Not yet?

Could it?

"Yeah." Joey took a sip of his beer and leaned back in the booth. "Maybe have another drink and think about that one some more."

He grabbed Bonnie's attention, his main manager and the woman who was currently behind the bar.

I took his advice.

Had another drink and since that one didn't help, I had a few more.

***

"COME ON, let's get you inside."

My arm was slung over Dominick's shoulder. My legs weren't working properly and the cement in front of my house kept waving back and forth.

"You don't need to help me like I'm stupid."

"You are stupid and you do need help."

He helped me up the front porch stairs, but I misjudged one—or it jumped out and bit me, and I took a cement edge to my shin. "Fuck." I stumbled and slammed my palm into the air for support.

"Maybe you're right," I muttered.

Dominick laughed and knocked on my door. He'd grabbed my phone before we left the bar, where I was pretty sure I drained the entire place of their whiskey and let Emmersyn know he was bringing me home.

"About what? Being stupid or needing help?"

"Definitely one of those." My throat was thick and my words were slurred. Hell, I probably needed to shove toothpicks into my eyes to keep them open.

Where in the hell had the day gone wrong.

That's right.

Ava.

Or maybe it was me.

The door opened, and Emmersyn stood there, looking almost as messed up as me, with red eyes and her hair a messy pile on her head. She was fully covered, back to the baggy and bulky sweats and sweatshirt.

And *shit*. I'd done that.

"Sorry," I slurred again, and Dom helped me inside. My shoulder banged the doorframe, and the asshole didn't bother apologizing. Couldn't he at least try to help me walk straight? I fell into the wall in front of me and held myself up while the room spun.

"I'll get the idiot to bed," Dominick said and grabbed my shirt with his fist. "Let's go, you drunken moron. Everything will be better tomorrow."

Fat fucking chance of that happening.

Emmersyn thanked him and followed us farther into the house. The stairs swayed and swerved as I walked up them. "I could sleep here."

My knees wobbled, and I started sitting down, but Dom grabbed me and yanked me to my feet.

"Not on the stairs. Keep moving."

He shoved me the rest of the way, maybe carried me. I had no clue except eventually my face landed on white fluffy clouds that smelled like lavender and sunshine, and I closed my eyes and breathed in Emmersyn's scent. "So soft and sweet," I murmured, hugging the clouds beneath me. "I like it here."

"You should, it's your bed."

"Wha?" My eyes peeled open and... "Oh... yeah..."

A shadow came over the doorway, and I rolled to my side,

catching Emmersyn there. Disappointment and sadness on her beautiful face.

"Sorry," I muttered and tried to shake sobriety into my eyes so I could only see one of her.

She ignored me and glanced at Dom. "I can take it from here."

"You sure?"

"Yeah. We'll be fine."

"Except we were fine, and I fucked that up, didn't I?"

She sighed.

Dominick scowled down at me. "Maybe you shouldn't talk right now."

Probably a good idea. I'd had a shit ton of whiskey. Too much. If I spoke again, it might come up.

Hands touched my ankles, too warm and too soft to be Dom's, and Emmersyn went to work slipping off my sandals. "Go to bed, Kane. We'll talk tomorrow."

Great. More talking.

Exactly what I excelled at.

The door to my room creaked open, barely audible, but considering I had the television on a low volume, HGTV in the background while I huddled under my covers, I couldn't miss it.

Plus, I could sense Kane's presence like a bomb-sniffing dog.

"Thanks for the ibuprofen and juice."

Of course he came to thank me for that. I burrowed deeper under the covers, tightening them around me. Stupid of me. I woke up that morning before sunrise, and since I'd tossed and turned most of the night and barely slept, made my way downstairs and made myself coffee. Then, since I didn't want to run into Kane, I hurried back to my room to drink it. But then, because I was a complete idiot and way too damn nice, I'd gone back downstairs and taken him the juice and pills.

"Can you look at me? Please?"

It was the please that did me in. Guttural and torn from his voice. Possibly that was the hangover he had to have, considering it was near noon and this was the first I'd heard of him moving around.

I listened, rolled over, and blinked. Blinked again. "You look like shit."

His hair was in complete disarray. Eyes bloodshot like he'd just finished a seven-day bender. His skin was pale, and even his muscles, displayed because he only had on shorts, looked weak.

"I feel it. My head, my gut. Trust me, in more ways than those, I feel like shit."

He looked it, too. As for me, I pretty much felt the same without the hangover.

I wasn't even upset anymore, just hurt. Worried. Imagine moments after realizing you were falling in love with someone else, that someone else gets a call from the only person they'd ever loved. And is essentially given the open door to take them back. Nothing could take away the pain of hearing Kane apologize to Ava for marrying me.

Nothing.

Not only that, when he'd realized he'd hurt me, he'd vanished. I'd come downstairs, intent on talking to him, letting him know I understood, and hell, I'd give him the out if he wanted it.

I deserved to be someone's first choice. Not their required choice. Not their pity choice. I spent enough years with Lincoln, slowly realizing over the last month he was a slimy little abusive liar who played me in a long con in order to get access to my trust, an amount much more substantial than his own father would probably ever give him. I gave him the ability to live a life of luxury with little responsibility, and now, knowing what I knew of Lincoln now, he would have jumped at that. He didn't want to be working with his dad. He wanted to be out partying, traveling the world.

But Kane *left* me. He bailed before we had a chance to talk, and that might have been a heavier hit to my pride than realizing I'd done the dumbest thing in the world and fallen for a man who wouldn't ever return it.

"Can I come in?" he asked and nodded toward the bed. "I'd like to talk."

I'd prefer to avoid yesterday for the next three hundred and thirty some odd days.

"Fine."

He huffed, a sad sound, a man who knew exactly what *fine* meant from a woman's mouth and came into my room and sat down on the corner of the bed. He faced me, one leg up and bent on the mattress, the other settled to the floor.

"I'm sorry about yesterday. I'm sorry for hurting you and for taking off. That call with Ava." He closed his eyes and rubbed his temples.

I fisted my covers tighter. Her name was quickly becoming a four-letter word.

"It fucked with my head. I can't lie about that. Hearing her, knowing I hurt her. And then seeing how much it'd hurt you. That you'd *heard* it all."

"Would you have told me?"

"What?" He squinted at me, even though the room was dark.

"Would you have told me about the call if I hadn't accidentally overheard?"

His nose wrinkled and his lips pushed to one side. At least he was giving my question consideration. Had to hand it to him for not dismissing me outright.

"I don't know," he finally admitted, and I couldn't hide my flinch.

"Right."

"I know that doesn't sound good. I know you don't like it, but I don't know, Em. It took me by surprise, shocked the hell out of me. Can you blame me for being thrown?"

No. The shitty part was I couldn't. All this time he'd loved her, regretted not being the husband he should have—or could have been for her, and there she was, keeping in touch and telling him about her own engagement in the *hopes* he'd come back. Talk about a mindfuck.

I shook my head. "No. I understand that."

For wanting to talk, he was awfully silent.

He picked at my duvet cover, and the silence ticked on.

"What are you going to do?" The words burned my throat, and I fought back tears.

"Do?"

"Yeah. With Ava. What are you going to do?"

His eyes widened in surprise and he quickly blinked it away. Pressing a hand to the bed, he leaned toward me. "Em. I'm not going to do *anything* about Ava. She left. She played the game she played, and that fucking hurts because I was all cut up about losing her, and she made it seem like she was trying to be friendly, move on. She made it seem like she wanted *me* to move on. And to find out that was all some ridiculous and dangerous and just fucking stupid *game* so I'd put a stop to it? I don't *hurt* knowing things could have been different all those years ago... I'm fucking pissed she didn't *talk* to me."

"Oh." I sat up in my bed and kept the covers tucked tightly around my chest and stomach. "I figured—"

"I know what you figured. It kills me I put that look on your face and those tears in your eyes, too. And I can't sit here and tell you had she called a month ago, or six, with the same thing, things wouldn't be different. I won't lie to you about that, but things are different now. I'm *married*. To you, in case you've forgotten."

As if I needed the reminder. My wedding band was a heavy weight on my finger, and I rolled it with my thumb.

"It's not real," I gulped over the thickness rising in my throat.

"The fuck it isn't."

He shoved off the bed and pushed his hands through his hair, clasping them at the back of his head. "My head feels like I'm at a country bar, and the crowd is doing a line dance on my brain, and I might still throw up, so I know I'm not thinking clearly, but you can't sit there and still say none of what we've shared isn't real, can you?"

He spun in a slow circle and scowled at the ceiling.

Well, no. To me, it'd been real... or became real.

"You married me to help me, Kane. If you want out, all you

have to do is say so." I'd figure the rest out. Hell, I could go back to teaching, or once I got access to my monthly stipend, live off that. That wouldn't be hard and then I could go anywhere.

He turned to me, chest heaving, and since it was bare, it was a glorious sight. "I'm not going back to Ava, Emmersyn."

Well, maybe he wouldn't, but that didn't mean I just had to sit back and "*deal*" with this marriage for a year. I threw off my covers and climbed out of my bed. "And I want to be someone's first choice, not the one they're stuck with."

"You are my fucking choice!"

He cursed and clung to his head, bending over at the waist. Shock whipped around me like a lasso, making me stumble toward the window.

A stinging pain slammed into my chest as he gripped his own head and cursed his hangover from hell.

"Fucking goddamn whiskey," he groaned. With his face still scrunched and the palms of his hands pressed against his temples. He stood to his full height, clearly in pain. "I chose you when I agreed to marry you. I chose you when I kissed you before the ceremony and when we said our vows. I chose you that night I took you to bed and all the nights we've spent watching television and getting to know each other. I chose you yesterday, in that hot tub, Emmersyn, because you're the only woman I've been able to think about at all ever since you showed up on my front porch. I haven't been sitting here, missing Ava, I've been denying that I was so fucking blown away by you, I *wanted* you."

Holy shit. My world spun and tipped and tilted. My entire being swelled with hope as my knees wobbled.

"So what now?" I asked and twisted my hands together in front of me.

He sighed, scrubbed his face, and dropped his hands to his hips. "If you're wanting some kind of declaration, I can't give you that. Not today, especially after everything that happened yesterday, but also because it's too soon. I need to be sure. I need time."

"I'm not demanding forever, Kane."

"Then you need to know I care about you. I respect you. Everything I learn about you only makes me want to dig more. I like that you can kick my ass on the golf course and you don't rub it in my face but stay encouraging. I like knowing you're at my games or home waiting for me when I get home. I like watching you learn to cook and never get mad at yourself or disheartened when it doesn't end up right, and mostly, I just *like* you. I really like you."

He flung his hands into the air and back to his hips.

"That's a lot of liking," I said, my lips fighting a grin. Only Kane could have me close to tears and despair and then feeling like I was walking on clouds. But hell... that was a lot of good things about me.

"I like your body. I like the way you gasp every time I slide inside of you. I like it when you wake up in my arms, and I hated, seriously fucking hated waking up this morning alone, knowing I was the reason you weren't next to me."

I was already moving toward him, my body heating and starting to throb with every wicked word he spoke until I was in front of him, and he reached out, cupped the back of my neck, and slid his hands up into my hair, fisting it gently.

"I do not like that I hurt you or that I made you cry, and I can promise you I'll do everything I can to make sure it doesn't happen again."

I pressed my hand to his chest, where his heart was racing and his skin was burning. "I should have been more understanding. But next time you do get mad at me or hurt me, please don't run out like last night. Stay so we can talk, even if we need space here."

"Deal." He leaned down and rested his forehead against mine. "I need to hydrate, and I need a protein shake, and I need to sweat out this godforsaken alcohol in the sauna, so I'm not a lazy pile of crap all day. But so you're clear, I like you, Emmersyn Houghton. I like you a lot, more than I expected, and it surprises me daily how much I miss you when you're not in the same room as me."

"I like you, too, Kane Andrews. A whole lot. Bunches even."

His grin broke out, slow and sexy, and he brushed his lips over mine.

"How about I make you a shake, bring you some water, and then join you in the sauna?"

"Deal." He kissed me again and stepped back, dragging his hand through my hair and creating a shiver that cascaded down my spine as he bit his lip, examining me with heated eyes.

"And ditch the ugly ass shirt before you join me in the sauna. I like seeing the curves of your body."

He slapped his hand on the doorframe, sauntered off down the hall like he hadn't rocked my world and turned me on and made me speechless in one fell swoop.

Damn Kane Andrews.

He might not have loved me, but he chose me.

We had time for the rest.

THIRTY

KANE

"You're up early." Emmersyn's smoky, sleepy voice drew nearer, and she sidled up to my side, giving me a sideways hug before slipping off toward the coffee. "Big week ahead."

I was at the counter, scrambling eggs for a spinach and mushroom omelet. "How'd you sleep?"

It was only a few days since our fight, and now I had to leave for the airport in a couple of hours for an away game in Los Angeles.

"Good. Someone had a lot of energy last night. Wore me out."

"Hell yeah, I did." We'd been up late after getting home from my game at eleven. It was too bad I couldn't wake her up that way today, too.

She grinned over the rim of her coffee mug, gently blowing on it to cool it down. "Do you have enough eggs for me?"

"Already on it." I pointed to the smaller pan. I'd learned Emmersyn didn't like vegetables, but she'd eat eggs, and the occasional cheese omelet. She only said no that first morning because she didn't want to be a bother. I was working on putting a stop to that.

"Thank you. So..." She pulled a piece of paper toward her on the counter. Didn't know why. We talked about my schedule all the time. "Los Angeles tomorrow, Buffalo on Thursday, and then New York on Friday. Do you often have games back to back like that? Two nights in a row."

"Sometimes, and they suck, but usually only a few times a season and when the cities are that close."

"Will you have time to go see Megan? Or maybe see if Glen is in his office?"

"I absolutely can make the time if you want me to, yeah."

"I want to know what's going on. Why Lincoln stopped bugging the hell out of me, and why Glen won't sign over my trust. But if you don't have the time, I get it. Megan said her PI was going to start looking for him this week, and I haven't heard anything. But yeah, I don't know. At least if one of us meets her face to face, it could keep her interested."

"Then I'll make the time."

I could skip a team lunch on Thursday, grab something to go, and eat in the car and have plenty of time.

"Thanks, Kane."

I slid her eggs in front of her and leaned across the counter. "Anything for you, Em." I kissed her cheek and finished my omelet.

"What are you going to do while I'm gone?"

"I've been looking into getting back into volunteering. I've got a list of homeless shelters and women's abuse shelters I want to look into, see what kind of help they need."

"That'd be great." Bonus for me, if she liked it enough, maybe she'd stay longer.

We hadn't talked about the future since the other day. I couldn't promise her the world or forever, not yet, but I knew one thing.

I was going to miss the fuck out of her when I had to say good-bye, whether it was for my away trips or forever.

THIRTY MINUTES TO GAME TIME. We'd beaten Los Angeles in the preseason, but that was then, and this was now. Both of us were having an excellent start to the season and were both undefeated. One of our teams would lose tonight, and one of us would go on to continue trying to break the record of the longest season-beginning winning streak.

I wanted that record, but more than I wanted that, I wanted to get back to the hotel, call Emmersyn and see how her day was.

God, thank goodness she listened to me the other day. I might not have been able to tell her everything I was feeling, but we had time for that.

We were in the locker room, the arena already going crazy with noise above our heads, echoing down the halls and making the floor tremble. We always had a decent Vipers crowd in Los Angeles. We were close enough that fans would travel, and so it was always a good game.

"All right. Let's get out there. Show LA who they're messing with. Keep your focus, play hard, and kick their asses!" Vik cried out and lifted his arm in the air.

"Let's go!" Together, our sticks pounded the floor, Joey and Alix stomped their skates, and then we were off. Pounding down the halls, focusing.

As soon as I stepped onto the ice, I pushed everything back. The crowd cheered, but most booed. Oh well.

Focus. I grabbed the puck and dribbled it slowly as I skated a circle around the arena. The warm-ups were just that, meant for loosening tight limbs and getting us game ready. Tonight, as I skated past our bench, an asshole fan was hiding his face behind a sign he held. *Vipers Suck.*

Nice work. Had to hand it to the jerk, though. His use of glitter was sufficient. The entire sign sparkled in green and gold. Odd how a LA fan made a sign with our colors.

"Check it out," Joey said and skated up next to me. "You see that shit?"

"I see it."

"He'll be an ass when we're on the bench."

Glass would be pounded. He'd be screaming. Probably drunk off his ass.

"More shit to filter out," I said, and then that sign lowered, and a grin split my face from ear to ear.

"That fucking dick," Joey said but was now bent over laughing.

Because it was *Max*. Max and Kimmy had seats behind our bench, and both of them were smiling, shaking the sign high in the air and laughing right back at us.

If I wasn't on the ice and didn't have to worry about cameras on me, I'd flip him the finger.

Instead, I blew Max a kiss and grabbed Joey as we skated away from him. "He told me a few weeks ago he wasn't ready, that little shit."

"Maybe something changed."

"Or maybe he needed that moment. Eyes on him. A part of us."

"We'll make sure he comes to the hotel after, get a few drinks in him. It'd be good to see him."

We knocked fists, and then we were off. We practiced our plays in slower formation and stretched. I skated up to Garrett and got down on the ice with him, stretching my hamstrings and made sure to put on a show for the fans in the stands—and Emmersyn at home.

"You good?" Garrett asked.

"Never better."

"Joey told Gabby, Gabby told Lizzie..."

"Not doing a game of telephone with you. We got a game to play."

"I know. But from someone who waited too damn long to have the best thing in his life, *in* his life. Don't waste a second."

"I said—"

"That's it." He pushed back to his knees and readjusted his helmet. "That's all, man. You've got this. The game and the girl."

"Damn straight."

"And your stick is broken, brother."

"What the hell?" I glanced down at it, and sure enough, a hairline crack right above the tape. "How in the fuck did that happen?" That would have snapped off at face-off.

We went through over a hundred sticks a season. A broken one wasn't a big deal, but it was the first time I could remember breaking one after I taped it up and before a game. "Shit."

I pushed to my feet and skated toward the bench. As I stepped off, Alix called for me. "Yeah?"

"What's up?"

"Nothing. Broken stick." I scanned the sticks lined up in case something like this happened during the game and frowned.

"Problem?" I turned to Jay Lamonde, our defensive coach. His thinning head of shimmering white hair shined in the arena's lights. Bets were being placed on when he'd finally retire, but he'd be a loss when the time came. A big one.

"My sticks aren't out here."

"Shit. That's weird. I'll head to the locker room and see what's going on."

"No. It's cool. I got it." There was usually another supply of all the sticks outside the locker room. Mine were probably there, and with the strange crack in this one, I wanted to check them myself. "That okay?"

"You know what you're doing." He shrugged it off and went back to the bench. Alix yanked me over to where Max and Kimmy were at the gate. Fans crowded around, calling our names, but it was Max who held my attention.

"Not ready yet?" I slapped his shoulder.

"Worth it to see the look on your face. Weird as hell though, seeing your ugly faces from this side of the glass."

"I bet." I climbed up and gave him a hug. "Good to see you.

You're coming to the hotel tonight?"

"Wouldn't miss it. What's going on with you?"

"Nothing. Missing sticks, whatever. I'm headed to the locker room."

"Want me to come with?" Alix frowned as he scanned the sticks lined up. He knew how weird this was. "Help you look?"

"Nah." I knocked my glove into Alix's. "Be right back."

I hurried down the hall, where arena workers were dressed in black pants and gray polos with the LA team's logo on their chest. The sticks weren't outside where they normally were, so I shoved open the door to the locker room to find someone from our team's crew.

What in the fuck was going on? Not that I knew where they hung out during games, but there was usually someone here, or in the visitor's team's lounge and dining room.

"Missing something?"

The hell?

I spun on my skates and holy shit.

It was *Lincoln*. I'd looked up pictures of him. Dark brown longer hair that gave him a surfer boy look. In the photos I saw online, he was always dressed in typical rich boy business casual attire or to the nines in suits. Hair perfectly gelled and slicked back, even if it was longer.

"What the fuck are you doing here?"

"You fucked everything up," he said, and his body trembled like he was on day five of detox after a lifetime of hard drugs and alcohol. My eyes searched the room.

Why wasn't anyone here?

"I didn't fuck anything up. You did. What the hell are you doing here, Lincoln?"

His hands trembled at his sides, and he lifted one and scrubbed it through his hair. His usual perfect clothes were a mess. Wrinkled light blue polo, denim jeans that looked like they'd been in a ball and not shaken out before he pulled them on.

"What am I doing here?" He shoved another hand through his hair, eyes dancing all over the place. And this was bad. Because no one was here. "Well, I can't be in fucking Boston anymore. Dad fired me. But it's not like that matters. He was never going to give me the company or anything from it anyway. No, I was counting on Emmy, but you fucked that up for me, didn't you?"

Well shit. That explained why we couldn't find him, at least somewhat. And why he was so pissed.

I took two quick, shaking steps to the lounge, but he held up his hand.

"Door's locked," he said and pointed to the room. "And they might be tired." He leaned forward and, with a manic tinge to his voice, whispered, "I think someone spiked the drinks."

"You are fucked up." I took two steps back. *This* was the guy who beat the shit out of Em? Who made her feel like trash and cheated on her?

"Where do you think you're going?" he asked and his arm swung behind his back and then back out. Straight at me.

Where he was holding a goddamn gun.

A fierce roar rushed through me as reality hit.

Jesus. I stumbled away from him, stick in my hand I held down at my side. If I could keep him far enough away, I could hit the gun out of his hand.

No one but Coach Lamonde and Alix knew I was here. No one was coming.

And this fucked up, drugged mess of an asshole was waving a gun.

"You ruined everything," he shouted. "Everything! I had her. I had her right where I wanted her, and she would have given me everything, and now, it's all fucking gone."

Shit. What did I do with this? I might have been bigger than him, stronger and definitely more sober, but I wasn't used to being on this end of a handgun. And fuck, I was in my skates. Not like I could out run the guy.

"Hey. Lincoln, just calm down, okay?" I lifted my gloves. "If you need something, I'm sure Emmersyn can help as long as you get Hayes to call her back. You need some money?"

He roared out a laugh, as maniacal and disturbed as the rest of him. "Hayes? That fucking piece of shit Hayes is halfway to Fiji or the Caribbean or goddamn Argentina. And you think he left that motherload of billions behind? Fuck no. It's *gone*, you dumbass. And none of it would have happened if it wasn't for you."

The hell?

"Her money is *gone*?"

"Have you not been listening to a damn thing I've said? Yes, it's gone. Fucking Hayes had access, I had Hayes, and I had Emmy until she got too smart for her own good."

Everything was going so fast. His words were clipped and rushed and occasionally slurred, but I got the gist of it.

Fuck. Emmersyn was going to be devastated.

"What do you want then? Emmersyn? Because I gotta tell you, pretty sure you're not getting that birthday wish handed to you."

"No, you stupid fucking jock. I definitely won't get Emmersyn back. Won't be able to fix what you and her broke, at least, not while she's still married. Will I?"

Oh shit.

He lifted the gun again, but he wasn't smart enough to hold it with both hands. Typical rich kid who'd never shot a gun in real life. It wasn't steady, so I moved quick, dodged his aim and pulled back my hockey stick. I lunged toward him, raising my stick, but that was when he fired.

A hot, searing pain tore through my arm. I stumbled on my skates, but Lincoln was moving again, raising his gun. I swung. This time, I made contact. I slammed my stick into his forearm. He cried out and gripped his forearm with his other hand. While he was howling in pain, I lifted my stick again and swung it like a baseball bat to his kidneys.

He collapsed onto his knees and screamed up at me. Sweat

beaded at his forehead and dripped off his cheeks and his pit stains on his shirt were the size of grapefruit. He lifted the gun he'd managed to hold on to, and I raised my stick, and then out of nowhere, another stick slammed into the side of his head.

His eyes rolled back, a skate kicked away the gun, and he slumped to the floor, blood dripping from a gash in his temple.

"What the hell happened in here?"

"Alix." A rush of breath left me, and I collapsed to my knees. Then my ass. "Fucking hell."

"Who is this?" He stared down at the collapsed heap of man.

"Lincoln. Emmersyn's ex." A hot burning pulse tightened my pipe like a vise. "And I think he fucking shot me."

"What?"

I grabbed at my jersey and tugged it off. Blood was already showing through the jersey, though, which left it obvious.

"Shit. What do you need me to do?"

"Check the lounge. He said it was locked, that they were knocked out, but there has to be a trainer here somewhere. Or fuck, I don't know. Get Coach? Any staff out there? Just get me a goddamn doctor."

Alix took off while I tugged the strap of my helmet off and threw it to the floor.

Jesus. My head was spinning. With my gaze on Lincoln, making sure the asshole didn't move, I tore off my jersey and pads, and shoved my jersey over the blood gushing from my bicep. Fuck. It hurt like someone shoved a cattle brand into my skin.

It was seconds. Minutes. Hours as I kneeled on the floor before Alix returned, followed by a half-dozen people, and then all hell broke loose.

"I'M OKAY. I'M OKAY."

On the screen, Emmersyn cried, hair a mess and cheeks

streaked with tears. "I was so scared. They said there was a shooting, and I couldn't get a hold of you, and the women didn't know what was going on."

Strands of dark hair were plastered to her cheeks. Emmersyn paced my kitchen, and in the background was an opened bottle of wine on the counter.

I was taken via ambulance to the hospital. A deep graze to my bicep and ten stitches later, and I was now in a hospital emergency room, waiting to be released after talking to a handful of police officers who followed the ambulance.

The arena was shut down and the game was canceled. I had no idea what they did with the crowds, but shortly after I was brought in, our team's crew followed. I'd heard Rohypnol mentioned and almost used my good arm to punch a hole through the wall.

Fucking Lincoln. How in the hell had he gotten inside? Not only not being noticed with as strung out as he'd been, but with a gun, for fuck's sake. Even players had to go through security.

"Hey. Emmersyn. Take a deep breath and look at me, okay?"

Her phone shook as she shoved wet hair off her cheeks and sniffed. "You were hurt. I got you hurt."

"Fuck that. None of that's on you. It's on Lincoln, and he's currently enjoying a nice overnight stay in the county jail and hopefully longer." Not actually true, but hopefully would be soon. He was brought to the hospital to have his head wound treated, courtesy of Alix's stick, but I'd heard there were police guarding whatever room he was in. He'd already been arrested. They were waiting for transport, but knowing he wasn't in jail would only make Emmersyn worry more. "And I'm fine. A few stitches. Give me a week, and I'll be good as new."

"Your games..." She sniffed and grabbed a tissue and wiped her face.

"I'll miss a couple. No big deal." The curtain was shoved back and a police officer, followed by our coach, Vik Boucher, walked in. I looked at Emmersyn. "I need to go. Coach is here, but I'll be home soon." I arched a brow at Vik. "I assume I'll be flying home?"

"Private charter with security, just in case."

"See?" I grinned at Em. "I'll be home in a few hours."

"Okay." She smiled, a tear-filled but relieved smile. "I... I'll be here."

She bit her lip, but I'd caught that look on her face. That wasn't at all what she was about to say.

And fuck it, I didn't want to do it over the phone, but she had to know.

"Same, Em. I feel the same." I winked, ended the call, and turned to Vik. "What's going on?"

"Police are doing their job, still investigating the arena. There were a couple other injured guards they found. Our crew should be all right by the morning, probably massive headaches. But shit. What a clusterfuck, and I gotta say, I'm not liking the news swarm that's going on right now, both outside the arena and inside, and around the hospital."

He was scowling at me like it was my fault. Instead of reminding him I was the victim in all of this, I bit my tongue. "When can I go?"

"We'll get you home soon like I promised. Take care of your arm and the rest of your body, okay? Rest up and heal. We'll need you back on the ice."

Of course he'd be most primarily concerned about my ice time. Vik Boucher was a damn good coach, but personable he was not.

"Will do."

"Good." He clasped my good shoulder and gave me a firm shake. "I need to go check on everyone else. Team has been moved to the hotel, locked down for their safety, although from what you've said, the police think the threat is over."

"Pretty sure that was a personal attack on me, so yeah."

After he left, the police officer stepped forward. "We just have a few more questions for you, and then we'll get you out of here."

Gabby and I stared at the television screen. I hadn't been able to take my eyes off it, and as soon as we learned what happened, that Kane had been taken to the hospital after a shooting at the arena, Gabby rushed over to make sure I was okay.

We'd now gone through two bottles of wine, and neither her company nor the alcohol was helping me calm down.

Lincoln showed up in LA with the sole intention of shooting, or worse—something I refused to consider—Kane. To get me back?

To punish me?

"I have no idea when my life turned into a soap opera."

Gabby chuckled. It wasn't the first time I'd compared the last month of my life to a daytime television drama. "Yeah, but the news is making it seem exciting."

"Shut up." We both chuckled. It was laugh or cry, and I'd done enough of the latter while waiting to hear from Kane.

She wasn't wrong. There was a constant ticker on the bottom of the television screen. *Hospitality mogul's heir shoots ex's husband.* The sports news station that was supposed to show the game had been talking about the shooting and the ensuing mayhem all night long, forgoing showing Carolina playing in Chicago. I was surprised all games weren't stopped until they determined this was an isolated event, but Kane said he identified Lincoln as soon as security guards and LA's team doctor swarmed the locker room. Apparently his assurance this was a one-off attack was enough.

It was late, almost two in the morning, and Gabby had to be exhausted, but she was refusing to leave until Kane got home.

She curled up next to me on the couch and we pulled a blanket over our laps. Her head rested on my shoulder, and I was so damn thankful she'd rushed over to keep me company. I would have lost it without her here.

"You can stay here, you know."

"I might." She yawned, and I rested my head on hers. "I need to text Joey. He'll worry if I don't reset the alarm."

She leaned forward, sent Joey a text and when she came back, we snuggled up next to each other again.

Warm breath skated across my cheek, followed by soft, full lips and a spicy scent I knew so well. My eyes opened slowly, and I jumped as I took in Kane, hovering over me.

"You're home," I whispered, eyes widening with surprise.

He glanced to my side.

Gabby was still resting on my shoulder, lips parted as she slept.

"I'm home. Should we wake her?"

I nudged my shoulder, but she didn't make a sound. "Let her sleep." I stood from the couch slowly, grabbing a pillow and settling it on the cushion as Gabby fell to her side. She grabbed the blanket we'd covered ourselves with, muttered something in her sleep, and went quiet.

"That was easy," Kane whispered and took my hand. "I missed you."

I flung myself at him. I might have been half asleep, half terri-fied out of my mind all night, but he was here.

He grunted like I hurt him, and I pulled back. "I'm sorry. So sorry. Did I hurt you?"

"Only a bit. It's fine. Come on." He took my hand and tugged me toward the stairs. "I didn't sleep a second on the damn plane, worried about you."

"Me? I was worried about you. You were the one who was shot."

"Ten stitches in my bicep, I'll be fine." He had a T-shirt on and lifted the sleeve so I could see the wrapping and tears filled my eyes all over again.

"I'm so sorry I dragged you into this mess. I'm so sorry I got you hurt, and you had to deal with all this." Tears burned my eyes again. They felt like sandpaper for as much as I'd cried that night.

"Come here." Kane palmed the back of my head and brought me to him until my forehead collapsed against his chest. Gently and more carefully this time, I wrapped my arms around his lower back. He walked us slowly toward his room, guiding me carefully. "I told you on the phone this wasn't your fault. All the blame lays with Lincoln and whatever problems he's into."

From the little Kane said on the phone, that was *a lot* of problems.

He finally loosened his hold on me when we reached his bedroom but kept a hold of my hand, pulling me toward the bathroom. "It's late. I'm exhausted, and I need to sleep. We'll talk about the rest in the morning, okay?"

"There's more?"

I *knew* he'd been holding back in the hospital.

Kane smirked, looking ravishingly sexy with the glow of his room shading his features in the pale bathroom light. A delightful shiver coursed through me at the sight of him.

I took him in, the tired slope of his shoulders and the circles under his eye. I avoided the white patch of bandage around his bicep and blew out a breath.

Kane was home. Healthy. *Alive.*

That was all that mattered.

I WOKE to a start and flung myself to sitting. Heart racing, I settled my palm at my chest and blinked to clear my mind, the dream—nightmare—from my mind. The room was dark, and it took me a second to recognize Kane's bedroom. A pale glow from outside peeked through the curtains, and other than a dim light coming from the hallway beneath his door, the only sound in the house was the quiet sounds Kane made while he slept. He was on his back, injured arm draped over his stomach like he was protecting it, and fear laced through me.

Lincoln had done that. *Hurt* him. So much worse than he'd hurt me.

I shook my head and tried to erase the nightmare that had woken me up. Monsters and gnashing of teeth and blood and then a body was slumped in front of me, ripped open and....

"Shit." My heart was still racing, and I couldn't get the images out of my head. Blood and gore and bombs going off and devastation. A rocket scientist wasn't necessary to decode the dream, but my entire body was still trembling as I tried to breathe in slowly, and exhale to calm myself back down.

"Hey. You okay?" Kane's warm hand settled at my lower back and rubbed in a large circle. "Lay with me, Em. It's all right."

"I can't. If I close my eyes, I'll see it."

He pushed himself to sitting and slid his hand from my back to my side, bringing me to him until I was straddling his lap.

"Your arm."

"It's fine." He peppered me with slow, gentle kisses along my jaw, to my cheek, down the column of my throat. "I knew you wouldn't sleep well tonight. Talk to me."

"I don't want to talk."

I draped my hands over his shoulders and pressed my body against him. Kane's flesh was warm, but it was his strength and gentleness that was my security blanket. I melted into him, and matched my breathing to the rhythmic, slow beat of his, until images from my nightmare didn't appear. I blinked. "I'm sorry for waking you."

"Stop apologizing. I have a week to sleep."

He whispered the words against my jaw, and the heat of his breath sent a shiver of warmth to the tips of my fingers. My toes curled, and on instinct, my hips rolled against him.

"Fuck," he groaned. "Again."

His hands drifted down my lower back until each of his palms cupped my ass. He pressed me against him and his length hardened beneath me. Both of us moaned softly and then his mouth found mine. He slipped his tongue inside, continued working my body against his own, and soon we were panting, breathless. A needy pulse thrummed in my core, and I leaned back enough to tear off the T-shirt he'd given me to sleep in.

On my knees, in front of him, his eyes skimmed every inch of my body, and every moment that passed, his touch grew firmer, more desperate until his fingers slipped through my sex, and he hissed as he felt the wetness there. "You'll have to be quiet," he whispered, pulling me back to his mouth. "Don't want to wake up Gabby."

I dropped my hand, squeezed his length protruding from his boxer briefs, and shook my head. "You're going to have to be quiet," I whispered right back and slid down his body. My fingers dipped into his waistband and he lifted his ass long enough for me to tug down his underwear.

He was bare before me, all muscle and manly body and tanned olive skin I wanted my mouth on every inch of, and I'd get to that... after I took care of him.

"Em," he whispered my name like a prayer or a blessing, his hand skating into my hair, holding the back of my head. "You don't—"

"I want to."

His head fell back to his pillows, and I settled onto my elbows, ass in the air. I realized it was the first time I'd bent over like this to take care of a man without worrying about how much shaking he'd see, if my stomach would drop too low or my ass be too big.

Kane helped give me that true confidence, and I took him into my mouth, kissed his wide tip with the sudden urge to show him exactly how thankful I was to him for it.

"Yes," he hissed in a breath as my lips brushed over him, as I sucked him into my mouth and hollowed out my cheeks. He was wide. Thick and hard and soft and silky at the same time, and I ran my tongue down the length of a vein, cupping his heavy, full balls with my hand while I sucked him back into my mouth.

I worked him slowly but firmly with long, slow moves down his shaft and quick, firmer sucks at the tip like I'd seen him do with this hand. Every swipe of my tongue earned another pleasured hiss, and when he hit the back of my throat, making me gag, he cursed and groaned at the same time. I added a hand to his length, unable to take him all, and the slickness of my spit and the salty taste of his precum made my hand wet. But nothing could make me wetter than knowing that it was *me* driving this god among men to the absolute brink of pleasure.

I glanced up at Kane, chin dipped down, and our eyes met as I pulled up and sank back down on him. His abs constricted. His free hand fisted the sheets next to him and his other hand dug into my scalp. "Fuck, you're so good at this. That's it. Deep as you can go. So sexy, sucking my dick like you love it, Em. I could never get enough of you."

He praised me while I worked him. He grit out words I didn't quite understand while he grew close, and then his hand at my head was pulling me back. "Going to come, Em. You feel so damn good. I can't wait to be inside of you again, feeling your pussy clench around me."

I shook my head and swallowed him deeper until his head was at my throat. I breathed in through my nose, opened my throat, and he cursed the heavens and my skills, and as I swallowed, he came, shooting his climax down my throat.

"Yes..." he bit out. "Fuck. That was good. Get your ass up here."

I pulled off him slowly, cleaning him with my tongue as I did, and then his hands were at my hips, dragging me up his body. "Sit on my face."

"Your—"

"So help me God, if you worry about my arm one more damn time right now, I'm going to spank your ass."

My body tightened in surprise. He wouldn't. And yet... I was pretty sure the needy pulse in my sex grew thicker.

"Get your ass up here."

He threw a pillow to the side, grabbed my hips and he yanked me up his body until I was hovering over him, my hands braced on the dark headboard wall behind him.

"Kane." I glanced down and caught his gaze.

"Sit," he growled. His hands shoved me down and then his tongue was right there, scruff from not shaving all day scraping my thighs in delicious friction. He added a finger and pressed his tongue over my clit and my thighs were already trembling, from nerves, from getting turned on while I took care of him and everything he was doing to me.

My hips rolled, seeking that perfect spot, and Kane took over. He didn't taste me. He didn't flick his tongue over my clit in tiny perfect circles. He *ate* me. Devoured me like the taste of me was his favorite dessert and when he added a second finger, crooked them, twisted and used his fingers and tongue, I bit down on my bottom lip to keep from screaming, and I came, all over his face, all over him. I rode out my climax on Kane's face like he was my new favorite ride and he didn't miss a beat.

He continued his frenetic pace until one orgasm became two, and sweat covered my entire body, and when I was a wrung out, a quivering mess and my limbs were jelly, he guided me off him, rolled me to my side, and he wrapped his body around me. The scrape of the covering on his arm made me flinch, but he reached down, took my hand in his, and kissed the nape of my neck. "Go back to sleep, Em. Things will look better when the sun rises."

I blinked, tried to steady my racing heart for an entirely different purpose, and as my breathing evened out, his followed.

He kissed my neck again, lingered there, and right before sleep pulled me back under, I heard him say, "When I said *same* earlier. I meant I love you too, you know."

THE NEXT TIME I woke up, Kane's bedroom was bright, the curtains pulled back, and the sun was shining. Next to me, the bed was cool and empty, but lights were on beneath the bathroom door. I sat up and stretched, groaning at the ache in my thighs from the mid-night workout.

The bathroom door opened and Kane stepped out, wearing only athletic shorts like usual and a fresh white bandage on his bicep. Guilt curdled in my stomach and I sat up as he walked toward me, smiling softly.

"How'd you sleep?"

"Better the second time," I admitted. "Is Gabby still here?"

"She woke up when I went downstairs. Sent her home about a half hour ago."

"I should call her. Thank her for staying with me last night."

"She knows. Said she had to get to work."

"Okay. What are you doing up? Shouldn't you be sleeping? Resting?"

I pointed at his arm. His other hand brushed over it, and he shrugged. "It's a bit bruised, but it's fine. Stop worrying about it."

The last words I heard last night returned like a whisper in my mind, and I blinked and gripped the covers of the bed. He couldn't have meant it. Could he? Now wasn't the time to bring it up, so I slipped out of bed and grabbed the T-shirt I'd flung to the floor.

Kane gave me a kiss as he walked by toward the doorway.

"Take some time and get ready. I have a feeling today isn't going to be as relaxing as you thought it would be. I'll go get breakfast started."

Right. Reality slammed back into me. That didn't stop me from enjoying the view while he walked away.

"SO, WHAT HAPPENS NOW?"

Kane filled me in on all the things Lincoln said to him and the way he behaved. He told me about the team's crew being roofied and how he most likely paid workers at the LA arena to mess with his sticks. It was a good thing he forced me to eat my avocado toast first because had I waited, I would have lost my appetite and avocados were too expensive to go to waste.

"I don't know. I'm going to call John's brother, Jordan, today to see if he can give me any insight. He's a defense attorney, but he'll know more than I will."

"Jordan?"

"Jordan Banks," he confirmed with a nod. "He represented Dominick when his shit went down last winter, so he'd be a good starting resource. I could call Kimmy, Max's girlfriend too, which I should do anyway since they were at the game last night."

"Was he the one holding that Vipers Sucks sign you and Alix laughed with?" I saw it on TV while announcers were prepping the pre-game warm-up right before everything went to shit.

"Yeah. Who knows what time they were let out of the arena. But Kimmy's a lawyer in California. Family law, but maybe she knows someone. I mean, fuck. The dude's from Boston. We're in Nevada, but he commits a crime in California. This has massive mess all over it."

"Not to mention what he said about Hayes—"

"Which is why we'll call Megan as soon as we can."

His jaw shoved out, and he cursed. Lowering his voice, ice slid down the back of my neck. Kane braced his hands on the counter across from me, prepping me for whatever bad news he was about to spill. "There's another phone call I should make after I call my parents."

There was worry in his eyes, a hint of sadness. I wasn't a genius, but didn't need to be to know what brought that look on. "Ava."

He nodded. "Ava. And I know. I know maybe I don't have to, but I at least feel like I need to call her to end things with her on a different note than we did last time. I think I might need that closure too."

I fucking chose you. His words bounced around my brain, easing the knot of fear knitting itself together around my avocado toast. "Okay."

"You're okay with that?"

I smiled, feigned a braveness I didn't quite feel, but he needed it. "You chose me, right?"

"Every day. For as long as you'll have me."

Which, hopefully, would be forever? "Then why would I worry?"

He prowled around the counter, grabbed my hands, and tugged me to my feet. He slipped his hands up my arms, creating a river of delicious friction following in their wake until his palms cupped the sides of my neck, thumbs brushing my jawline.

"You almost said something to me last night on the phone. And stopped yourself."

Oh dear. He was bringing this up. "Yeah." Nerves dried out my lips, and I licked them. "But—"

"No buts. You were sleeping last night—"

"I wasn't. I heard," I admitted, and if I didn't have a fierce grip on his hips to stay standing, I'd be gnawing on the side of my thumb.

"Good." His dark eyes danced back and forth between mine, and crinkles dug into the outer corners of his eyes as he smiled.

"Then let me apologize that the first time I told you I was falling in love with you, it wasn't to your face where you could see how much I mean it."

"Yeah?"

"Yeah, Em." He chuckled and brushed his lips over mine. "I wasn't prepared. Wasn't ready. Everything happened so fast, and I know there's going to be a lot to dig through in the next few months, but I meant it when I said I love you, and I meant it when I said I'm here for you as long as you want me."

"Then be prepared to be saddled with me for a very long time, Kane Andrews, because I'm falling in love with you too."

"Good." He kissed me then, swept me off my feet, and even though I protested due to his arm, it didn't stop him from tossing me onto the couch, shoving up my shirt before he ditched his boxer briefs and claiming me in his living room, whispering all the parts of me he loved, and ending it with our hands entwined, pressed to his beating chest while he took us both over the edge.

Together.

EPILOGUE

Emmersyn

GLEN HAYES WAS FOUND EXACTLY where Lincoln said he'd be.

In the Caribbean.

Turned out, he'd been stealing from my trust fund ever since I transferred it over to their company with Lincoln's approval. Also turned out he'd siphoned seventy percent of it into offshore accounts. All of those accounts were now frozen, and I wouldn't be seeing them for quite some time.

Glen Hayes was working his way through the penal system while currently residing in his new home in a white-collar, maximum-security prison in Massachusetts.

The money didn't matter anymore, though. I could end up with nothing in my trust account, and I'd still be fine—monetarily, emotionally, and physically.

"Thanks, Megan. I appreciate all the help."

"No worries. Trust me, this has been fun."

If by fun meant you had to rescue the trust fund back to the rightful trustees from psychopath attempted murderers, embezzlers, and all-around criminals, I guess it was fun. She'd call to tell me she was depositing my monthly stipend and the lump sum from my marriage. Apparently, Glen didn't steal *all* my money. He left enough for me to receive the amount I would have had I stayed married to Lincoln.

Thoughtful of him.

As for me, I was planning on donating the remainder. The first lump sum was plenty, and outside fun money, my monthly stipend was being set aside to someday help fund my first charter school.

I went back to substitute teaching in November. It allowed me to get to know the needs of Las Vegas while keeping a flexible schedule to work around Kane's schedule.

He missed four games after the incident in October we rarely ever talked about unless we were forced to with our attorneys.

Lincoln had been held in custody in Los Angeles's county jail and would remain there until his trial began after the first of the year. We'd have to fly out, give depositions, and be called as witnesses for the prosecution, but unless we were talking to our attorney who Kimmy had set us up with, Lincoln never entered our conversations.

In all, my life had taken a drastic turn back at the end of September. October was no different, but by Thanksgiving, things were finally starting to calm down as pieces fell into place.

And by Christmas? Well, I was hoping tomorrow, after Heather and Tracy and Chuck flew in, we'd end up having the best Christmas of my life.

As it was, my current view of Kane hanging ornaments from the sixteen-foot tall and *real* tree he'd insisted on cutting down himself, hauling inside, and setting up—with the help of Alix—was already ensuring my holiday was off to one of the best possible starts.

Did I mention he was shirtless?

And that immediately after Alix left, Kane had thrown me to the floor and made me cry out his name beneath the tree?

Yeah.

Life couldn't get much better.

"Hey. Come here a second, would you? I need some help."

He was standing on a twelve-foot ladder, arms stretched out to the top of the tree while he finished stringing the lights.

I kicked my feet off the coffee table where I was enjoying the view of his muscled back, his perfect ass, and a glass of red wine. "But the view was so pretty from where I was sitting."

He popped his muscles and made his pecs do a little dance.

"You're a dork."

"I'm *your* dork."

He climbed down from the ladder and pushed it off to the side.

"What do you need help with?"

He took my hand in his and led me toward the tree. His hands went to my shoulders, and he angled me *just so.*

My brows puckered in as he turned away from me and dug through a plastic bin we'd purchased and then proceeded to fill with a gazillion and two ornaments. "What are you doing?"

"Just hold on. I need to find something. The cord to turn the lights on and something else. Ah." He stood, a long cord twisted and curled in his grip. "Stay there one more second."

How I was helping him by standing still was anyone's guess, but he hurried around me. He crouched down, took the string of lights and pushed it into the extension cord, ran it to the corner of the living room, and shoved it into the socket.

The tree lit up in shining white lights, millions of them. Totally overboard, but there was a blank area in the middle of the tree.

"What the..."

Marry me... for real?

Was stretched in dancing, glistening lights, two rows at odd angles, but the fact they weren't perfect didn't stop me from gasping and rocking back to my heels.

"Kane…"

"Marry me. Again." He fell to his knee in front of me, box open.

"I already have a ring." And a wedding and a marriage certificate.

"I know. This one's better because I bought it after I fell in love with you, after I knew what you'd love. Marry me, again, Emmersyn Houghton, and this time, take my name. Make a family with me, and most importantly, *dance* with me at our wedding."

"You're insane." I laughed, and tears ran down my cheeks. "Of course I'll marry you again."

He stood to his feet, and kissed me before I could fully see the glimmering diamond. My original wedding band was removed, and in its place sat a rock the size of the Bellagio on my ring finger. "Holy shit, it's huge."

"I know. Just like my love for you."

"Dork." I laughed against his mouth and threw my arms around him.

He bent and grabbed the backs of my thighs. He took two steps when the alarm system blared, followed quickly by, "*Intruder! Intruder! Intruder alert!*"

"I'm going to kill him," Kane groaned. His erection was thick and hard between us, and I knew my cheeks would be burned pink with lust and desire. But Kane still set me on my feet, pointing a finger at me. "As soon as we get rid of him, we're redoing that moment."

Alix stepped around the corner then, shoes already kicked off, a bottle of beer in one hand, the rest of a six-pack in the other.

"Am I interrupting something?"

"No," I said.

"Yes," Kane growled.

I slapped his chest and laughed.

Alix had quickly become the irritating, playful, European brother I never knew I wanted but somehow always needed in my life. He was a staple in our home, and since he and Kane had been friends for so much longer, he was always welcome.

"Good." He nodded once and plopped his ass onto the couch. "I came to watch Kane work—" His eyes squinted. Head tilted to one side. The other. He glanced back at us with furrowed brows. "You two are already married, no?"

"What do you think? We were just getting ready to go celebrate."

"Ah." Alix sipped his beer and turned back to the tree. "Looks nice. Go ahead and celebrate. I will be here. Alone like always."

"Give up your search for the blonde?"

I'd heard the story so many times now I could recite it in my sleep. The night Alix found a blonde girl at the bar, the same night I showed up at Kane's. He had the night of his life with her, an incredible morning the next day. She kicked him out and disappeared, and Alix has not been able to stop thinking of her since.

"I need to give up. But no one compares. I have not been with a woman—"

"Okay, that's enough of that." There were lots of things I listened to Alix talk about. His sex life was absolutely off-limits.

I plopped back down on the couch next to him as Kane scowled at us both.

"It's Christmas," I reminded him. "Love? Joy? Family?"

"Yeah, well, I wanted to *love joy* and practice putting a *family* in you for the next twenty hours, but now I can't, can I?"

It wasn't the first time he'd mentioned kids. I wanted time together alone with him. There were some days it felt like we barely knew each other. Other days where it felt like we'd been together since our childhood. Either way, he made me feel like he'd always been destined to be mine.

I waved toward the tree and grinned at Alix. "Come on, honey. Finish decorating the tree. You'll make Alix so happy. And then you can *love joy* and *practice* after all you want."

He hmphed but complied.

Alix and I sat on the couch two days before Christmas, watching my man—my once temporary and now permanent husband—decorate the tree to Christmas carols and wine and beer and laughter. A lot of laughter.

It was perfect.

I was officially living my best life.

With the best possible man partnering with me in it every step of the way.

THANK **YOU** for reading Goal Chaser! I hope you enjoyed it. If you're still loving the Vipers as much as I am, stay tuned this December for Alix's book. It's a wild adventure you won't want to miss! You can pre-order Secret Keeper here:

https://amzn.to/3mu5vaP

DON'T MISS a single sale or new release announcement. Join my newsletter and you'll be the first to know whenever something exciting is happening!

THANK YOU

HUGE thank you to Nina and all the incredible women at Valentine PR for throwing your full enthusiasm and support behind me and these books. I've loved working with you and can't wait to see what the future brings us.

Ellie and Virginia, as always, thanks for putting up with my mess and spit-shining each manuscript until it sparkles. Thank you especially during this crazy time in our world for your flexibility and your extra hard work.

Shannon, you're the best. Always. Forever. Your talent is astounding and I'm thankful I can call you a friend.

To my Sweeties! I love you ladies and your excitement for my books!

To all the bloggers who devote their time and passion into reading books, book tours, release events, leaving reviews, promoting and pimping – you are all rockstars! Thank you for all the love over the years.

My family— I love you all to the moon and back. I don't know what I would do without you in my corner, cheering me on every step of the way. Your support is everything to me and I love you all with all of my heart.

To my girl crew— Tamara, Lauren, Niccole, Cassy, and Bree. What would I do without you ladies? Thank you for blessing me with your friendships. My life is a hundred times better with y'all in it, and a gazillion times more entertaining! To the SteelP! May we forever reign.

And last but definitely not least – to you the reader. I'm blown away with every release how much you adore my books. You have made my dream a reality and I hope I can cheer you on with yours. Please don't forget to leave reviews on Goodreads or whichever retailer you've purchased this copy from. It helps us so much!

ABOUT THE AUTHOR

Stacey Lynn likes her coffee with a dash of sugar, her heroes with a side of bossy, and her wine a deep shade of red.

The author of over forty romance novels, many of which have been best-selling titles, she loves being able to turn her vivid imagination into a career that brings entertainment and joy to her readers. Focused on sports romance and emotional, small-town romance, she also loves stretching herself in different genres.

Born in Texas and raised in the Midwest, she now makes her home in North Carolina and loves all things Southern. Together with her ultimate tall, dark, and handsome hero, she has four children. Her life is a chaotic mess that fights with her Type-A, list-making, neurotically organized preferences and she wouldn't have it any other way.

Subscribe to her newsletter so you can stay up to date on all her new releases. www.staceylynnbooks.com

OTHER BOOKS BY STACEY LYNN

<u>Las Vegas Vipers ~hockey romance</u>

Final Shot (free on all retailers)

Game Changer

Dream Maker

Rule Breaker

Shot Taker

Goal Chaser

Secret Keeper – December 2022

<u>Ice Kings Series ~hockey romance</u>

Playing With Fire (free on all retailers)

Playing To Win

Scoring Off The Ice

Hooked One Her

Hard Checked

Fighting Dirty

<u>The Rough Riders Series ~football romance</u>

Dirty Player

Filthy Player

Wicked Player

Cocky Player

<u>Love and Lies Duet ~angsty slow burn, romance</u>

The Luminous Series ~BDSM romance

Dominate Me

Crave Me

Long For Me

Just One Series ~rockstar romance

Just One Song

Just One Week

Just One Regret

Just One Moment

The Nordic Lords Series ~MC romance

Point of Return

Point of Redemption

Point of Freedom

Point of Surrender

Standalones

Remembering Us

Don't Lie To Me – billionaire romance

Try Me – A Don't Lie To Me Novella